THE

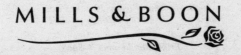

MILLS & BOON

*First published in Great Britain 1999
Harlequin Mills & Boon Limited,
Eton House, 18-24 Paradise Road, Richmond, Surrey TW9 1SR*

© Juliet Landon 1999

ISBN 0 263 81920 5

*Set in Times Roman 10½ on 12 pt.
04-0001-76528*

*Printed and bound in Spain
by Litografia Rosés S.A., Barcelona*

Chapter One

Springtime 1359

If Mistress Merielle St Martin had had her own way, she would have been soaking in a warm bath scented with lovage and lavender. Instead, she had felt obliged to accept a wreath of pennyroyal for her aching temples and then to listen with convincingly appreciative smiles to the love poem read to her by the faithfully adoring Bonard of Lincoln. It was not because it was in Latin that her mind wandered but because the day had been an especially long one with so much to be done before Sir Adam's arrival.

She stretched her legs along the bench in the sunny courtyard and arranged the fine woollen folds to droop gracefully towards the stone-flagged floor, rotating her aching feet and watching how the evening light caught on the stones and pearls of the silver filigree nutmeg-case. Its pungent scent had been useful in the steaming dye-house that morning and then later in the messy pilgrim-packed streets of Canterbury where the odour of sweat and filth was inescapable.

Bonard's voice was conspiratorial, which went to show, she thought, how little he knew about her, for he had assured her that the poem was his own composition, written for her alone. He read in Latin ostensibly because he said it sounded better, but more truthfully because he derived a secret pleasure from saying to his employer out loud things he dared not say in English. Now he was almost whispering.

Poor Bonard. He had been her late husband's employee and good friend and, for the life of her, Merielle had not been able to dismiss one who believed himself to be one of the family. Even though his position as assistant manager had now been taken over by a younger man, Merielle found him to be a useful chaperon, escorting her with chivalry but leaving her the freedom to make her own decisions without interference. She could never have borne that, for it was now almost three years since Philippe of Canterbury's death and interference had not been one of his weaknesses. Far from it; her grieving had been more for the unborn child she had lost than for her husband.

The whirring of the great wheel caught her eye and she watched from beneath thick black lashes how the bonny honey-coloured Bess flicked it on by one spoke and eased her other hand away, attached to the bobbin by a fine strand of madly twisting yarn. The maid caught her mistress's eye and shot a quick look heavenwards, which she knew Master Bonard would not see for he wore a red scarf tied across one eye.

'Oh, do take it off, Bonard,' Merielle said, gently. 'How can you possibly read with one eye in this light?'

He swivelled his head in an exaggerated arc to see her, the words *Vultum Dioneum* dying on his lips.

'And what's this *goddess's reward*, then, for heaven's sake?' As if she didn't know.

His mouth dropped open as his papers sank to his lap. 'You...you understand it, mistress?'

Merielle sighed, smoothing the soft green fabric over her thighs. She had not meant to let that out. Preventing a further explanation, a diversion of sounds turned their heads towards the covered walkway that bordered the courtyard and Merielle swung her legs down, ready to stand at Sir Adam's entrance, her hands already welcoming. The gesture was not wasted, but it was not the expected brother-in-law.

'Gervase. You're back already?'

'I came immediately. Scarce had time to brush the dust off.'

Two lies at once, but she smiled her sweetest. 'I'm flattered, sir. Welcome. Have you eaten?'

Gervase of Caen was one of those responsible for the supplies of food that passed through the king's household each day. Such a man never went unfed for long, not in any sense of the word. He took her hands in his and kissed them individually. Slowly. Then her two cheeks. Then her mouth. His smile was intimate. 'Enough to keep me upright, that's all. What delicacies do you have to offer me, Mistress Merielle St Martin of Canterbury?'

An obvious answer sprang to her lips, but Bonard of Lincoln's red scarf and baleful eye were rising over Gervase's right shoulder like an angry sunrise and she would not ignore him. She swung their hands in his direction, prompting the handsome young man to remember his courtesies.

Gervase bowed. 'Master Bonard, forgive my interruption, if you please. Another of your creations, is it?

Ah, such talent. Will you continue?' Gallantly, he waved a hand, inviting the poet to resume his recital despite the discouraging retention of Merielle's hand in his own. At twenty-six years old, his seniority over Merielle could have been taken for more than five years. His sleek fair hair curled obediently over the blue velvet silk-lined hood of his short tunic, a pleated and scalloped creation that did not, nor was meant to, cover his neatly muscled buttocks, or the bulge at the front. The pink and blue part-coloured hose clung to his legs and showed no sign of contact either with saddle or with dusty road, but his own fair skin was creased, and professed a world of experience in its folds which allowed him to ignore the attention-seeking red scarf and to quench his invitation with a subdued chatter against which the Latin stood no chance.

Merielle withdrew her hand, hoisting up the silver nutmeg by its chain, caressing its jewelled surface as they sat, pleased that the one who had given it should see it being worn. 'You know that I'm expecting my brother-in-law, don't you, Gervase?' she whispered.

'He's not arrived yet?'

'No, I've been expecting him all this week. The second week after Easter, he said, and here we are, a week after Low Sunday and he's still not appeared. I've been preparing and packing and tying up ends all day, but still no word.'

'Well, you won't be travelling this side of Monday, will you? He'll not want to set off back to Winchester again as soon as he's arrived.'

'No, indeed. He's not a young man, you know.'

He poked a finger at the silver ball in her hand, chuckling. 'No, he's not, is he? So there'll still be a place for me, will there, even if you decide to marry him?'

'Shh.' She smiled and looked away, nodding to Bess to remove the wheel and the basket of fleece. The answer should have been a firm no, of course, but even after eight months of pondering the question, she was still undecided whether to accept Sir Adam's informal proposal or whether to continue her pleasant life with her own flourishing business and a flattering supply of male admirers.

That Sir Adam Bedesbury was amongst these was in no doubt, but Merielle was not so oblivious that she could not see the advantages to him of marrying his late wife's elder sister and thereby obtaining an instant step-mother-cum-aunt for his nine-month-old daughter. His grief had been genuine, but had not prevented him, only a month after his wife's death from milk-fever in July last year, from suggesting to Merielle that she might consider taking her place.

Emotionally sapped by her sister's birthing and death in quick succession, Merielle had almost given in to the potent urge to take care of the little creature who had shown such dependence upon her mothering, especially since her own recent losses. But she had not been able to overcome her doubts then, and had allowed Sir Adam to escort her home to Canterbury with only an assurance that she would give the matter some thought—how could she not?—and that she would return this year to see her niece, with an answer. His message had arrived before Easter to say that he would shortly be in Canterbury on some business for the king, whose Master of Works at Winchester he was, and that he would be happy to take her back with him as soon as it was concluded.

'I've never bumped into him,' Gervase of Caen said probingly.

'I don't suppose you would.' Merielle removed the coiled end of her heavy black plait from his fingers, then the silk ribbon that bound it. 'He spends most of his time at Winchester on the renovations to the royal apartments after that fire.'

'Which is why the king stays at Wolvesey Palace, I suppose.'

'Yes, I believe so. I expect the archbishop's palace is as well appointed as any of the king's are. But Sir Adam's manor is outside the West Gate in the suburbs, with a large garden and orchards and green fields beyond.' Her eyes roamed the shadowed courtyard, seeing the greenness superimposed upon the stone. Here, it was solid, comfortable and convenient, and she had converted it to her own taste during her widowhood. But it had not been her choice. The lure of a country estate and clean air was strong, but there were those here who relied on her for their employment.

'You'd like that, wouldn't you? But what of him?'

Her sigh told him that the doubts of last year were still firmly in place, and the construction he placed upon it were typically masculine. 'I can guess. The thought of having an older man in your bed instead of…'

Merielle's eyes flashed wide open in alarm, showing him the startling blue-whites around the velvet-brown irises. 'Shh!' She darted a quick look towards Bonard's one searching eye. She knew his teasing. He would not have embarrassed her before her household.

Even during puberty she had never been the shy maiden but had suddenly blossomed like a luscious bloom and, at fifteen, had been eager for marriage, though she had wished that the man her father had chosen for her, a middle-aged but wealthy Lincoln merchant, had looked more like Gervase of Caen. In 1353, the same year as her January wedding, another outbreak of the terrible pestilence had swept across the country. Merielle's father and husband had been amongst the first to go, leaving her rudderless but extremely wealthy and healthy with properties in both York and Lincoln and jointures she had not expected to have the use of for at least twenty years.

One who had come seeking Merielle's glowing voluptuousness and statuesque beauty was Philippe St Martin of Canterbury who, although totally inexperienced in the ways of women, offered her youth, security, wealth and a comfortable escape from an unknown city of so many bad memories. Even now, Merielle could scarcely recall how the fumbling and inept young man had managed to father a child on her, though she could well recall his embarrassed jubilation at the news, and if that one act had been a disappointment to her, the thought of bearing a child made up for it.

Sadly, the future had come to a bleak halt when the overcome father-to-be left his newly pregnant wife to give thanks for the event on a pilgrimage to Jerusalem, as if it had more to do with fate than the physical performance. That had been the last she had seen of him, receiving the news during the summer that he had died from a snake bite in Sicily. It was then that she had lost the child, here in this great house, alone and very angry that she had made such a stupid mistake so soon in her life. Eighteen years old, and already twice widowed. She could still feel the loss, though these days it was being chanelled in more positive directions, given power by her wealth and business abilities. Her age and beauty were interesting additions, she knew, but a northern level-headedness inherited from her father warned that these attributes alone were not enough to guarantee the interest of true and honest men. Indeed, she was quite sure that they were not.

Merielle had no wish to be seen as cynical or manipulative, but nor could she ignore the delights of being sought and courted, which had been lacking until now, to savour the freedom to choose without pressure from one's family; even to sample, if she were discreet about it. Gervase was experienced, but she did not fancy herself to be in love, nor had she felt more than a warm excitement from being the recipient of his attentions, and though there were others in Canterbury who showed an interest in her, both for their sons and for themselves, she had not allowed them to come too close.

But Sir Adam's suggestion carried weight, if only because his ready-made family was also her niece to whom she felt she owed some responsibility. Yet she was bound to admit, somewhat guiltily, that the lure of a motherless babe to call her own seemed to be a grossly unsporting bait to dangle above Sir Adam's middle-aged and chaste bed. It had been chaste during his marriage to her sister, too, by all accounts, though Merielle had never been made aware of the details except that somehow, presumably by the usual methods, Laurel had become pregnant.

The suspicion which had leapt to the forefront of Merielle's mind since then had sadly been allowed to fester unhindered by charitable thoughts, and although she had put past differences aside to be with Laurel at the birth, no confidences had been exchanged. Consequently, the grain of information that had been dropped about Sir Adam's failure to perform had taken root at Canterbury during a visit in the year of Laurel's marriage, and the delicious art of putting two and two together had been Merielle's delight, even then. Now, she was unsure whether she could expect to bear a family with Sir Adam, should she accept him, or be treated to yet another inadequate partnership for the sake of her conscience. Understandably, her anger smouldered at the less-than-perfect choices before her, despite her attractions, and at that particular moment she would have given all she owned to turn time backwards to when her sister was still a convent-bred child of fifteen in York, unaware of the king's wife-hunting Master of Works in Winchester. The rest of the story she pushed aside.

Her face must have been registering signs of interest, for Gervase, blissfully unaware of her musings, was giving way to an overspill of daily accounting that still impressed him by its size. 'Fifty marks for nine thousand red herrings during Lent,' he was saying. 'And I've brought you a lamprey pie, to bribe you with, of course. It's with the cook.' He smiled.

In the moment's silence that followed, they became aware that the flow of Latin had ceased and that Bonard of Lincoln was waiting for a chance to continue, a hope that seemed to be dashed still further when Bess returned with a tray of goblets, wine, and a dish of warm macaroons sprinkled with nuts and cinnamon.

'Please continue, Master Bonard,' Merielle said, pouring the wine. 'This will keep our guest quiet for a moment. Where were we? Goddess's reward, was it? Or had we moved on?'

Bonard shifted uncomfortably, scanning the page

with second thoughts. 'It's difficult in this light, as you say, mistress.'

'Try,' Gervase told him. 'You cannot stop in mid-verse, man. And why in Latin? Let's have it in English, shall we?'

The red scarf jerked up in alarm but sank again under the level gaze of his audience. He cleared his throat, shuffled the papers and put them behind him. 'The rest is not quite complete, as yet,' he said.

A deep voice called from the shadow of the thatched overhang. 'You mistake, my friend. The rest you must have forgot. There are six more verses, all highly un-suitable for a lady's ears. Shall I tell them, instead?' The tall man with thick dark hair stepped down into the courtyard, the low sun highlighting his strong cheekbones and nose, almost closing his laughing eyes.

Gervase of Caen rose, indignantly. 'No, sir. Indeed you shall not. What do you here, Sir Rhyan? Do you have an invitation to this lady's house?'

The man walked down into the courtyard and stood before them with feet apart and head back, his white teeth gleaming. 'I thought I'd find you with a woman, lad. Saw you emerge from the ale-house a while back. Must get our priorities straight, eh?' He gave Master Gervase no time to respond. 'As for having an invita-tion, well, that was for my uncle Bedesbury, but I've come in his stead. Will you be able to contain your disappointment for a few days, lady?'

Merielle was rarely at a loss for words. As owner of a tapestry workshop she had her need of wits at every moment, yet this was so totally unexpected that her usual civility eluded her, her only thought being that his uncle could hardly be blamed for tactlessness when presumably he knew nothing of her acrimonious communications with his nephew three years ago. Since then, she had met the obnoxious man only once when he had come down from his estates in Yorkshire to be at his uncle's wedding to her sister and then they had kept well clear of each other. Nevertheless, she could criticise the man's lack of diplomacy in taking his uncle's invitation for his own.

'You mean to tell me that you assumed the invitation to Sir Adam to apply to you equally? I am astonished, sir. Is your uncle indisposed?'

'Busy, mistress.' Sir Rhyan's laughter faded at her reproof. 'I had business here in Canterbury and offered to do his for him also, which includes escorting you to Winchester. If you find my company too difficult to stomach...' He made a movement as if to turn away, then added, 'But I could hardly discover your mind on the matter without speaking to you, could I? Was I expected to send a carrier pigeon, perhaps?'

His manner was everything she would have expected from one such as he, the man with whom cold and blighting letters had been exchanged through lawyers, which she had countered at a cost he would never know. She had tried to put it behind her, once she had won, but the bitter taste lingered with the foreboding that one day they would have to meet again and that the nearer she came to accepting Sir Adam, the sooner this would be. Sir Rhyan was his uncle's heir and his visits to Winchester not infrequent. It crossed her mind for the second time that here was yet another excuse not to go to Winchester, but she ached to see the tiny moist bundle, and the negative thoughts dissipated while the haunting scent of babes lingered in her nostrils.

Merielle was tall, Gervase of Caen even taller, but

this man was both broad and tall, topping them both with ease. She had been well aware of his strength: his uncle boasted of his nephew's prowess at tournaments and her sister Laurel at his companionship during the first homesick months of her marriage, telling of his skill with falcons until Merielle had closed her ears, sick to death of their glorifications. They had not experienced his other aspect, nor would she enlighten them.

Gervase ignored the man's rhetorical question and asked, for Merielle's sake, 'Did you arrive in Canterbury today, sir?'

'Good Lord, no. Days ago. Before Easter.'

Merielle found this unacceptable, too. 'And you have only just seen fit to come and—?'

'Would it have made any difference? My uncle sent you word to say to be ready after Easter, so surely you've had time to prepare. Have you—' he looked around '—prepared?'

'As it happens, sir, I have. But would it not have been more courteous to—?'

'No, it wouldn't. It would have spoilt your Easter and, in spite of what you believe, I had no wish to do that. I leave on Monday. Do you come, or stay? The choice is yours. I can tell my uncle...'

Merielle knew precisely what he would tell his uncle. That she was with her lover and doting servant and that she had no inclination to see her sister's brat (of whose sire she was in doubt), or worse. Whatever he chose to tell his uncle would not be to her credit, she was convinced of that. 'You will not tell Sir Adam anything,' she said. 'I shall tell him myself. I shall be ready to set out early on Monday. There'll be dozens of other travellers on their way home after Easter, I'm sure, so I shall not depend on your escort, sir. I have servants of my own.' The speech sounded brave enough, but the man was unmoved by it.

'Hah!' He turned to look at Master Bonard's red scarf with contempt. 'Your one-eyed shepherd? He had two last time I saw him. What happened?'

'Nothing happened.' Merielle came to his defence. 'Tell him, Master Bonard. Chivalry will be a novelty to Sir Rhyan, I believe.'

Taking courage from her support, Bonard took a step forward, still clutching the twists of paper in one hand. 'I have made a vow,' he said, 'to use only one eye until I have saved my mistress's life. There, sir, now you can scoff.'

The looks that passed across the faces of Sir Rhyan Lombard and Master Gervase of Caen were pictures of incredulity and pity, their reactions the only thing about which they were likely to agree on this occasion.

Sir Rhyan discarded ridicule in favour of reason. 'On the contrary, no man should scoff at true chivalry, but have some sense. How much use d'ye think you'll be to your mistress on a hundred-and-thirty-mile journey when you've only got half your vision to see what danger she's in? Eh? What kind of protection d'ye call that? You'd be more of a liability wearing that thing. Take it off, man, and think again.'

Gervase agreed. 'He's right. Use your sense, or you'd be better staying behind.'

'Others do it,' Bonard said, lamely, looking at Merielle.

'Maybe,' she said, kindly, 'but they don't recite Latin poetry to me, Master Bonard, and I find that more acceptable.' She felt Sir Rhyan's scrutiny upon her cheek and wondered if he knew he had exposed Bonard's deceit and then protected him from scorn.

Master Bonard lifted a hand to the back of his head and removed the blindfold, revealing a compression of sandy hair and an eye that blinked with relief. He bowed. 'Another time, perhaps. You two are acquainted, I believe?' Meaning Gervase.

'Only slightly,' Gervase replied. 'My work at the exchequer brings me into contact with those who owe the king rents and dues for their land. Your lamprey pie, mistress, is part of Gloucester's rent. They also give him eels three times a year. Sir Rhyan sends him…'

The conversation was leading them towards shaky ground. Merielle put a stop to it. 'Gervase, there must be much that awaits your attention after your absence. Shall you leave us now and return to say farewell on Sunday?' She knew that Sir Rhyan would make of that what he liked.

'Are you sure?' Gervase whispered.

'Yes. Please go now. There are matters…' She offered him her hands and, to her relief, he kissed them, bowed, and left quietly, leaving the courtyard to darken with hostility.

'I think we should continue our conversation indoors,' she said, leading her guest along the walkway and through studded oak doors into the hall where tables were being prepared for supper. On one, pewter candelabra stood with candles already lit, and she indicated a bench, placing Sir Rhyan within the circle of light while she sat opposite, affirming as she did so that her late sister's adulation was typical of her shallow insight. He was indeed exceptionally handsome, but looks could be deceptive. He had done his best to injure her, once. He would not be allowed to forget it.

The hall servants kept a discreet distance, but Master Bonard was closer at hand in an obvious display of protectiveness, and although Merielle spoke in a low voice, she knew that he would hear. 'Let us understand one another, Sir Rhyan, if you please. I had far rather Sir Adam himself had come to escort me to Winchester for then I would have been in pleasant company. I go with you on sufferance because we happen to be going the same way at the same time. Is that clear? I do not intend to make polite conversation with you for appearances' sake and I would rather you respect my wishes to be left alone. A safe conduct to Winchester is all I require.'

'Still smarting, I see. You got the land back, for all the good it's done you. For all the good it's done the tenants, rather. Sheath your talons, lady.' He held his head high on great shoulders and sturdy neck, his unusually blue eyes showing not the slightest flicker of consternation at her blatant antagonism.

'It can be nothing to you, sir, whether I smart or not. It was an agreement between my father and yours, presumably based on some whim…'

'No whim, lady, and you know it as well as I, so cut out the sham, for that's something I cannot abide.' His glance bounced off Master Bonard and back to her again.

'Then you must be having a hard time of it in this world, sir, for life is borne along on such minor deceits made out of our care for others' feelings.'

'And you must be well practiced, judging by the company you keep. Does Sir Adam know of the competition, or shall you sign yon pretty lad off on Sunday?'

'Mind your tongue, sir! Until your appearance, the company I keep is of my own choosing, and my choice of husband will never be a concern of yours, whatever your late father chose to believe.'

'Yours, too, don't forget. And you are mistaken, lady, if you think that their agreement is now at an end by reason of their deaths. The pestilence that took them both from us in the same year does not alter one whit of what was written and signed while your mother was alive, and that agreement you are bound to, now and for ever. I shall enforce it. You obtained the king's pardon once, lady, but you'll not do it again.'

'I *paid* for it, damn you!' Merielle snarled.

'Yes, a fine. That was not in the contract,' he said, coldly.

'I paid, wasn't that enough for you?'

'No. Nor was it enough for those poor sods whose living is made on the land you refuse to administer.'

'I do. The bailiffs. The steward. They…'

'No, they don't! The pestilence took them, too.'

Merielle breathed out, slowly, controlling the flow. 'It returned? When?'

'Last month. And never once since then have you enquired what was going on.'

'I thought…' No, she had not thought.

He watched her eyes search the table-top, then he leaned forward on thick leather-clad arms, his long fingers splayed. 'The land your father leased from mine, the manor house, the villages, the fields and mills were taken for a term of three lives, remember. Three lives, not two. His own, his wife's and yours, as the eldest daughter. And as security, because they both wanted to be sure that the property would remain in responsible hands even after their deaths, your father agreed to allow my father and his heirs the right to approve husbands for his widow and daughter. You, mistress. Your mother died, but you are still written into the contract which I took over when my father and eldest brother were taken in the sickness. And there you will remain for the rest of your life. But you chose to forget that, did you not? And after your first husband died, a man of your father's choosing and approved by mine, you went ahead and chose a fool who acquired your property and then careered off to Jerusalem, for God's sake, having no more care for the land that supports his tenants than he did for his breeding wife, it seems.'

Merielle leapt to her feet, trembling with fury. How dared he speak to her like that in her own home? Her late husband's home. 'That's enough!'

But Sir Rhyan's hand darted across the table and clamped around her wrist, holding her back. 'Sit down, lady!'

Master Bonard leapt to his feet, also. 'Sir! You are a guest here. I beg you, release the lady at once!'

He did not, but kept his eyes on her face, waiting for her compliance.

Merielle sat, frowning at her protector. 'It's all right. I told you that chivalry was not in his book. Sit down, Master Bonard.' She felt her hand being released but would not rub her wrist where his fingers had hurt her. 'I have always believed, Sir Rhyan, that no woman should be obliged to accept a man's say in her private affairs. A husband, of course, but not a complete stranger who cannot possibly know what is best for her.'

'Your feelings do not concern me—we are speaking

here of families, mistress, not of one person only. Families who have a right to be protected by law. What did your late Canterbury husband know or care of Yorkshire estates hundreds of miles away to the north except for the rents that poured in each year? What do *you* know of them? He couldn't even look after you properly, could he?'

'You will leave my late husband out of this discussion, if you please. Had things gone differently, we would not now be having this conversation. You vented your malice by confiscating my property—'

'My property! My late father's. And I had every right to reclaim it. Who else would look after those families if I didn't? Eh?'

'I've told you. But you timed your vindictiveness well, didn't you, Sir Rhyan? You waited until I was a widow—'

'Nine months, I waited.'

'—and had lost the child I so desperately wanted,' she panted, willing the tears to stay away, 'and then you—'

'I didn't know of that, then. It would have waited.'

'—sent lawyers to me. I suppose you thought I'd inherited so much from my father and husbands that I could afford to lose a little. Is that what you thought, sir? Did you care about my distress?'

'Do you care about the distress suffered by those families at the hands of your so-called stewards, who knew damn well there's no one to come and see what they got up to? The frauds? The thefts? The unjust punishments? The abuses? The taking of daughters?'

'What?'

'Yes, all of that, and more. It's next to my land, woman, so I know what's been going on. Is it surprising I wanted to get it back, to give those people some normality in their miserable lives? It's good land going to waste with poor management, not enough oxen, ploughs, hardly a roof on the church. And you here, sitting around with your lovers—'

His quick reaction caused Merielle's arm to swing blindly through space, missing his head entirely and slewing her round with the effort. To steady herself, she braced her arms on the table and glared at him through narrowed eyes ready to kill with one piercing stare. 'Hypocrite!' she spat. 'It's all right for men, then, is it? I'll have you know, sir, that I can administer all my property in York, Lincoln and Canterbury, run a household and a tapestry-weaving business and still have energy left over for lovers whenever I feel like it. And if you choose to tell that to Sir Adam to see if you can put him off the idea of taking me to wife, well, don't trouble yourself: I can do it much more effectively. With embellishments. If anyone is going to deter my late sister's husband, sir, it need not be you, I thank you.'

'Even so, lady, that is what I shall do.'

She gasped and stood upright. 'Ah, yes, of course. Just to make sure. You are his heir, are you not? And it wouldn't do for me to get in the way of your inheritance, would it? Think of the dower he might tie up which you'd not be able to reach until my death. I see you've thought of that.'

Unmoved, he stood and let his eyes rove slowly from the wreath of pennyroyal still on her abundant black hair, over her full breasts and narrow waist, the swell of her hips under the green woollen kirtle, then back to her eyes, blazing with anger. 'I've remembered everything, lady, as you say. But let me remind you again, lest *you* forget. You will not marry anyone without my permission. Not even my uncle.'

'And what could you do about it if I did, pray? Apart from reclaiming my property once more, what could you do? Unwed us?'

'Tch, tch!' He shook his head, slowly. 'Do you mean to tell me, Mistress Merielle St Martin, that you would leap into your brother-in-law's bed, another middle-aged and wealthy admirer, just to spite me? I'm flattered that anyone should go to so much trouble, but I'm sure you must have a good reason.'

'Then you are even more arrogant than I thought, sir. The only reason I could have for spending the rest of my life with Sir Adam Bedesbury would be to fulfil my responsibilities to my baby niece, my sister's child. Is that a good enough reason, do you think? If the child were related to you, Sir Rhyan, would you think of doing the same?'

'Alas, lady, the degree of kinship is too close. I would not be allowed to marry my uncle. But in any case, I've always found it too extreme for my taste to suppose that one must needs *marry* the parent of every motherless child, related or otherwise. Responsibility is one thing, but your plan is as irrational as Master Bonard's one eye. I suggest you examine your reason more closely.'

Reluctantly, Merielle saw his argument and was annoyed that he had been the one to advance it. 'I have no plan that you speak of,' she snapped. 'My point is that I have a good enough reason and that, if I choose, there is nothing you could do to prevent me, Sir Rhyan.'

He looked surprised at that. 'Ah, forgive me. I had thought you were quite determined, with your talk of dower and such. In that case, Sir Adam will have the pleasure of trying to persuade you while you will have to exercise great restraint not to accept him. It should be most entertaining. And I *can* stop you, lady. Don't doubt it.'

'Leave my house, sir, before I have you thrown out!'

But even that was too late, for he had already made his bow as he spoke and was turning to go.

Her own exit was meant to show him how he deserved no courtesy, but his hearty bellow of laughter followed her out of the hall and beyond, where she snatched the crown of green leaves off her head and hurled it at poor Bonard who had appeared with condolences at the ready.

'A fat lot of good *that* thing did!' she yelped, massaging her bruised wrist at last. 'And why is Allene not here when I need her?'

Knowing that for her mistress to run through her vocabulary of insults would not improve her temper, the ever- practical Allene placed a beaker of hippocras between Merielle's shaking hands and nudged it upwards, hoping thereby to bring the flow of invective to a halt. She was tempted to revert to the gentle clucking noises of the nursery to calm Merielle's anger, but Allene's experience as her nurse told her that this was neither the time nor the place to attempt pacification.

To Merielle's accusing enquiry about where she'd been, Allene retorted with commendable composure, 'Upstairs, packing. Where else would I be? If I'd known your guest was going to march in and out as if he owned the place, I'd have made it a mite more difficult for him, believe me.'

'Guest? That rat-faced piece of manure?'

'Ugly, was he? Now, my memory's not all that bad, but I seem to remember—'

'Revolting! Should have been smothered at birth. And I'll be damned if I'll ride all the way to Winchester in that monster's company.'

Allene's expression registered no shock; her double chins did not quiver, her kindly blue eyes did not widen. But the outrageous assertion that the unwelcome guest was ill featured made her look sharply at the beautiful woman whose slender fingers clenched tightly around the vessel, tipping its contents this way and that to catch the reflections on its surface. Allene had been Merielle's complete family during the last few years and knew better than anyone every mood, every inflection of the voice, every look and every thought behind it. She had been present at Merielle's birth and at every moment since, and the memory she spoke of was indeed not as bad as all that. So intact was it that she could pinpoint exactly the last occasion when Merielle had reacted so harshly to anyone. Then, at her sister's wedding here in Canterbury when Merielle had been inescapably faced with the same man, her private response had been just as extravagantly savage and out of all proportion, Allene believed, to a man's right to do the best he could with his own land.

With all the property from Merielle's father and two husbands to bring in revenues enough to satisfy an army, Allene had never been able to understand why the thought of allowing some of it to return to its Yorkshire owner should be so very unthinkable. Some women might have been glad to shed the responsibility, especially since officials had to be paid to administer the properties even during the leanest years after the pestilence. Since that dreadful time, it was now becoming more and more difficult to find men to do the work efficiently, so why all the fuss about surrendering it?

Allene would have asked about the man's particular offence this time, but Merielle's next observation forestalled her, astounding the placid nurse by its immoderation. 'He's that child's father. You know that, don't you?'

Allene could not allow this to pass. Her voice sharpened in rebuke. 'For pity's sake, child! You cannot say so!'

Taking the beaker from Merielle's hands, she drew her towards a stool whose top was padded with a tapestry carpet of flowers. 'You *cannot* say that! You have no proof and you are speaking ill of your late sister, also. Now put the foolish thought from your head and replace it with something more charitable. Did Archbishop Islip's Easter message have no meaning for you? You may not like your brother-in-law's nephew, but you cannot lay a crime like that at his door.'

'Yes, I can, Allene. Do you remember the child's hair?'

'Of course I do.'

'Well?'

'It's dark. Look, plenty of infants start off dark and go lighter. Some do the opposite. Your hair was more the colour of new copper when you were born. Imagine what your poor papa would have made of that, if he'd had a mind to. You can't pin Laurel's child on the man by that alone, Merielle.'

'Her eyes are blue.'

'So are all new-born infants; you know that, surely? And why are you so keen to make him the father? Did Laurel ever say as much?'

'Hah!' Merielle stood, turning away from Allene's

good counsel. 'You know how keen she was on him. I could have warned her off him, told her how he retaliated after I married Philippe, wanting to take the land back into his keeping. But she'd not have listened to a word against him, would she? Come, this talk is pointless. I have to find a way out of this situation.'

'You don't *have* to go to Winchester, pet. Send a message instead to say that you've decided against it.'

Admit defeat and hear his laughter ringing in her ears? That was the last thing Merielle would do. 'I do have to go, Allene. I need to hold that child again.'

'There are two whole days between now and Monday.'

'So, are we packed?'

'Of course.'

'Then we go tomorrow instead of waiting.'

'Alone?' The nurse pretended a soupçon of dismay.

'Hardly. There'll be plenty of others going in the same direction.'

'Then why not find out from the guestmaster at St Augustine's if any of his guests will be departing tomorrow and at what time? Then we'll be sure of travelling in decent company. They'll probably call here on the way to the Westgate. D'ye want me to see to it?'

'Aye, send one of the lads in livery so he doesn't get ignored.'

'It's not the ignoring that'll be a problem, but how to get back through the city gate after sunset. Could you write a note?'

'Yes. Where's that…that *creature* staying, I wonder?'

If Merielle had asked where that creature and his uncle had stayed last time they were in Canterbury for her sister's wedding, Allene might have resorted to a diplomatic lie. But she had not, and when the messenger returned some time later to say that the guestmaster would be happy to direct a small escort of returning guests towards Mistress St Martin's house on Palace Street early next morning, Allene felt that her suggestion had been an inspired one.

Chapter Two

It was one thing, Merielle muttered, to be allowed to make one's own decisions, but to be pushed into a plan of action by another did not conform to the portrait of independence she had striven so hard to present to the world since her latest widowhood. Concealing her annoyance in a ferment of activity, she managed to make it appear as if the only factor to influence her unplanned haste was that, by travelling on a Saturday, she would be sure of a day's rest at the abbey guesthouse on the Sabbath before the rush of Monday-morning pilgrims from Canterbury. And in trying to convince herself that all was in her favour, she managed to cloud the image of the ogre—her words—who had in fact precipitated the change.

Bonard of Lincoln was not so easy to convince of the rightness of the plan. He turned the red scarf over and over in his hands. 'I would not have removed it had it not been for their insistence on my being able to protect you better, mistress,' he said. 'Now I see that my gesture was all in vain. I may as well have ignored them.'

The illogicality of this did not escape Merielle, but

she handed him one of the goblets of wine and prepared her mollifying words. 'Dear Bonard, you are
sadly mistaken. You are the only one of the household
with enough authority to leave at such short notice and
the only one I can trust to keep things going. There's
the new consignment of wools to be checked; I would
have done that tomorrow morning. Then there are two
more Flemings to interview first thing, and I can leave
that to no one but you.'

'The tapestry-master can see them.'

'He's a Fleming himself, isn't he? He'd take them
on even if they were one-eyed and fingerless.' She regretted the comparison, but it was too late to withdraw
it. 'I need an independent master who knows the business. You must be here. And besides that...' she took
his arm and drew him down beside her on the wooden
bench, '...I need you to explain to Master Gervase
what's happened. Go round to his lodgings tomorrow,
Bonard. Will you do that for me?' She saw the shadow
of pain that passed across his eyes, but ignored it. She
had seen it before.

'I'd rather wait till he appears on Sunday, mistress.
He must take the inconvenience like the rest of us.
D'ye want me to tell him about your dispute with Sir
Rhyan, too?' The tone of petulance lingered into his
question, making Merielle wonder whether she was
hearing sarcasm or mere pique.

She frowned. 'He knows, doesn't he? He's the one
who got me an audience with the king, remember.'

'I meant this evening's dispute.'

'No, better not.'

His cloud lifted. 'So you'll send word when you're
ready to return?'

Relieved, she prodded him into a lighter mood. 'You're sure I'll return, Bonard?'

He smoothed the red scarf over his bony knees. 'I'm more sure of that than of anything, Mistress Merielle,' he said. 'Your unwelcome guest was flippant about not being able to marry his uncle, but I wondered if he was not also trying to tell you that your own degree of kinship is outside the canon law, too.'

'What?'

Without looking at her, Bonard continued, 'A man may not marry his wife's sister, nor may a woman marry her sister's husband. Was Sir Adam aware of that when he suggested that you might consider taking your late sister's place? *Is* that what he was suggesting, mistress?' Slowly, he turned his head, watching his words register in her eyes. He might have known she would challenge them.

'But people do. Men marry their brother's widows, don't they?'

'To keep property in the family, they do, with permission. You'd hardly qualify for that, would you?'

'So you're saying that I've misunderstood the situation?'

'I don't know exactly what was said, but such things are easy enough to misunderstand. Think. What *did* he say, exactly? He must know the law as well as anyone.'

'Then why didn't I?'

'Presumably because you interpreted it the way you wanted to at the time. Men don't always make themselves plain, do they, when it's in their interests to be misunderstood?'

'Don't they?'

'No, mistress, they don't.'

'So you believe Sir Adam deliberately misled me?'

'To lure you to Winchester? Of course I do. You'd not go so readily if he'd asked you openly to be his mistress, would you? He must know full well that you'd not be allowed to marry, but men like that have to explore every possibility. How d'ye think he's risen so fast in the king's favour? By seeking every opportunity and grabbing at it, that's how. He's an ambitious man.'

'And how exactly is having a mistress going to advance him?'

Bonard sighed gently and plucked the red scarf away out of sight. 'I may be a romantic,' he said, 'but I'm not so blind that I cannot see the way men look at you.' He watched her large eyes withdraw beneath deep crescent lids and a thick fringe of black lashes, then waited until they reappeared, veiled with unease. 'He can see your interest in the child, but if all he wanted was a mother for it, he'd have married again long before now.'

'It was less than a year ago, Bonard.'

'That's nothing when a man needs a wife. But it's you he wants, and he's hoping that you'll believe it's marriage he's offering. Once you're there, he'll try to persuade you. Forewarned is forearmed, mistress.'

'Oh, Bonard. Is that what you believe, truly?'

'Yes, it is. A mother for his infant and you in his bed.'

She flinched at his plain speaking. This was a Bonard she had not encountered before. Even so, there was something he did not know. 'But my sister implied that Sir Adam was not...not like that.'

Master Bonard straightened, recognising the gist. 'Yes, well, you know what Mistress Laurel was like when she wanted to make a point, don't you? Unrestrained, could we say?'

'A family trait, I fear.'

He did not contradict her. 'Sir Adam was not the man for her, was he? Too set in his ways and too interested in her sister. Hardly likely to qualify him for much praise, was it? Could she have said that to put you off, d'ye think? She certainly did her best to make him jealous, didn't she?'

'Flirting with that man!' Her voice chilled at the memory.

'It takes two,' he said, quietly. 'He's severe, mistress, but at least he's honest. Unlike some others we could name.' The quiet comment slipped through the net, and his reference to Gervase of Caen was lost in the previous one, which he extended. 'And from the sound of things he may well understand what his uncle's intentions are, and is trying to protect you.'

'Oh, Bonard!' Merielle looked away with impatience. 'That's inconceivable. The only reason he has for preventing a liaison between me and his uncle is because it would put his inheritance in jeopardy. My personal protection is the last thing on his mind.'

'Perhaps your opinion of him is too harsh, mistress. He was not responsible for what happened afterwards, remember.' His voice dropped, although the servants had long since ceased their arm-laden excursions across the hall and were now seeking dim corners in which to lay their heads for the night. 'And however much you dislike him, he must never know that there was more to it than a straightforward fine. If you had not gone to seek the king's aid in the matter...'

'If that man had kept his nose out of my affairs, Bonard, I would not have needed the king's aid in the first place. And if I'd known what the price would be, I'd never have gone there that day. Even you could not protect me from that, could you?' She had not meant it to sound like censure, but the tired and angry words had a way of emerging point first. 'I'm sorry, my dear friend. You deserve no reprimand. There was nothing you could have done, I know. Nor could I have done without you, that day.'

He had done his best, such as it was, but even the faithful Bonard could not insist on being present at her interview with the king at Canterbury, if the king did not wish it. What had happened then behind the closed doors in the archbishop's palace where the king was staying had had a direct bearing on the fine which was paid to Sir Rhyan Lombard for Merielle's defiance of the contract between their late fathers. Afterwards, Merielle had explained nothing, nor had she needed to. The king's reputation was well known and Master Bonard, romantic idealist, was no innocent in the ways of great men.

'I can make up for it a little,' he whispered, 'if you allow me to accompany you to Winchester. No more Latin verses?'

Again, his words were lost on her, brushed aside in her quick, irritable dismissal of the incident. She stood, and Bonard recognised the futility of repeating his offer.

Long past midnight, the relaxation which the longed-for bath was meant to induce was effectively displaced by new problems that could be shared only in part by those she trusted most. In a cloud of steam, she wondered whether it was marriage or widowhood that made problems worse and decided that, but for men, life would have been simple. Regrets crowded after the dilemma of Sir Adam and his intentions; she should never have agreed to go, even to see her infant niece, to hold her, to nuzzle her peachy cheeks. Beneath the foamy waterline, she passed her hands over her womb, sliding them upwards to comfort the sudden ache in her breasts, remembering with a gasp of longing the tragedies contained there, the last of which she had brought upon herself.

The warm summer days of 1356 had already begun to lengthen by the time the news had reached her of Philippe's sudden death, weeks earlier. From the south, the winds had blown gently, and Sicily was half a world away and what had Philippe been doing in Palermo on his way to Jerusalem? Like many another, it was a question never to be answered in the blank and sickening days that followed. She had not seen the need for him to leave her, nor had she known that the preparations they had made for his temporary absence would now become permanent. Nor had she had time to learn to love him.

'Determined' had been the best way to describe his wooing, for every time she thought she had seen the last of him in Lincoln, he came back for another try until, finally, she came to look forward to his return; the novel idea of being sought with such constancy found a niche in her lonely existence. He had made Canterbury sound attractive. Their wedding night had been a non-event for which she had no regrets; it was only after supping with friends one evening and drinking rather too much of their fine newly imported Rhenish wine that the two newlyweds came to know each other better than during the previous weeks of celibacy.

Philippe had been good at his work, knew everyone

in Canterbury and was well known also by them, and, if he lacked personal authority, his workshop's reputation made up for that. His business partner, who had died just before their marriage, was not replaced; Philippe's new wife appeared to be enough for him. And when, after only a few months of marriage, Merielle discovered that she was pregnant, Philippe's astonishment catapulted him into a pilgrimage, as if thanks offered in the nearby cathedral would not suffice. It was as if they had both been taken unawares by something they had not quite remembered.

Whether from shock or from some other reason, the pregnancy had lasted barely three months, less than a week after the news of Philippe's death had reached her. Merielle, who had never been truly ill before, thought that her world had collapsed with her beneath it, and, at eighteen, howled for all her dear departed ones and for the infant she had hoped would give her life some purpose. Believing no more in expectancies, only in losses, she was both horrified and frightened by the miscarriage, for the painful contractions were every bit as bad as girlhood scaremongers had said.

Then, during her recovery, had come the icily legal document telling her that her Yorkshire lands were to be repossessed by some grasping and merciless landowner who believed he had more claim to them than she did. A typical case, she believed, of stripping the carcass clean. An excusable exaggeration, in the circumstances.

Her worried expression had been commented upon by a pleasant acquaintance of Philippe's, one Gervase of Caen, who had listened readily to her angry tale. He had been sympathetic, and helpful, assuring her that there were ways of dealing with scavengers of his sort.

His advice was perfectly timed. 'The king,' he had said, leaning elegantly against a half-constructed loom that the carpenter was building. 'You must petition the king in cases like this.'

Merielle, who appreciated directness, felt that this was the best advice she had had so far, Philippe's lawyers having offered scant hope and, seeing little further than the end of her nose at that time, she had allowed Master Gervase to elaborate.

'He'll be coming to Canterbury in two weeks' time,' he said, 'staying in the archbishop's palace. You should see the food lists.' He unrolled an imaginary parchment into the air, smiling. 'I can arrange an audience for you. He'll settle the matter.'

In her mind, she had already half-accepted the suggestion, but felt it only polite to protest a little. 'But there'll be dozens of people pestering him, Master Gervase. Isn't it more usual to leave a petition with one of his clerks?'

His smile had broadened at that and he had taken her elbow to lead her to a stool. 'Mistress St Martin,' he said, 'when you have friends in the king's employ, you use them. I can get you a private audience, away from others' ears, where you can explain the problem to his grace. It won't be the first time he's heard of such things happening, you know, to new widows.'

'A fortnight?' She would be fully recovered by then.

'Two weeks. All you have to do is to dress soberly and elegantly, as usual, and I will personally escort you.'

'And Bonard. I must take him.'

'If you will. That will depend on his grace.'

They had taken the letter, too, in Master Bonard's leather scrip, on a day when darkness had fallen too

soon beneath lowered clouds and a heavy drizzle. By
the time they had reached the handsome stone porch
of the archbishop's palace in the cathedral precinct,
they were almost drenched. Step by dark step, Merielle
had followed the curve of the spiral stone staircase
from the corner of the porch up to the small anteroom
where a fire had been lit within a recess in the wall.
She remembered how its stone hood looked like an
upturned funnel.

Master Gervase disappeared through a door on the
far side of the whitewashed room, and then reappeared
some moments later. 'His grace will see you alone,
Mistress St Martin. No—' he put out a hand for em-
phasis '—alone, sir, if you please.'

Bonard had looked deeply uncomfortable, but helpless. 'It is not seemly,' he protested, in a low voice.

Master Gervase raised his eyebrows. 'I cannot argue
with his grace if he insists, Master Bonard, can I?'

Through yet another chamber where clerks at tables
scratched inky quills across parchments, Merielle was
shown into a larger chamber, headily warm after the
cold damp outside and glowing with colour from the
wood-panelled walls. A fire blazed in one corner and
candles made haloes of light that eclipsed whatever
was nearest, their sweet scent of beeswax mingling
strangely with a lingering aroma of linseed oil.

She had met the king only once before when he had
been entertained by the merchants of Lincoln, of whom
her first husband had been one. They had given a mem-
orable feast in his honour and lent him vast amounts
of money for his French campaigns at the same time
and she, as a newly married merchant's wife, had curtsied and been raised to her feet to meet a pair of ad-

miring eyes. As she was doing on this occasion, only three years later.

His hands beneath hers were firm and warm. He was tall and of athletic build, a man renowned for his valour and skills in battle, his love of jousting, of building schemes, a patron of the arts. He was, she believed, everything one expected of a king. He recalled their meeting as he removed her cloak and, unexpectedly, her damp veil, draping them over a stool near the fire. 'There,' he said, 'we'll give them time to dry, shall we?'

He came back to take her hands, rather like an uncle, she thought at the time. 'Now, Mistress St Martin, these are sad times, are they not? But if you will sit with me awhile, I will do what I can to help. Your first husband was a staunch supporter of our French cause, you know.'

'Yes, sire. Sadly, he was lost to me soon after your visit to Lincoln.'

'Indeed. And your father also, I believe. You have had more losses than you deserve at your age. What *is* your age, mistress?'

'I have eighteen years and some four months, sire.'

She did not mention her most recent loss of the infant she had wanted, for she knew that, while she could control tears for Philippe, she could not do the same for the other. She had dressed with care for the occasion, black relieved by edgings of silver inkle-loom braids and silver grey fox fur. With her thick black hair in a nest of plaits around her face, entwined with silver cords and studded discreetly with pearls, the only contrasting colour was the warm apricot skin on her neck, which had now been uncovered. It did not unduly disturb her, for she knew that kings were different from other men in what they were allowed to do. His offer of wine was accepted while he listened attentively to her problem and read the lawyers' letter.

Basking in the sympathy that followed, she saw her troubles receding already and was thankful that he did not ask her why it was so important for a woman as wealthy as she was to keep hold of these far-flung Yorkshire lands. That would have been difficult to answer except that she resented being fleeced like a helpless sheep, especially at a time like this.

He replenished her goblet with more of the sweet wine and held out his own to make a toast. 'To your peace of mind, mistress. Leave it with me, if you will. I'll have the appropriate fine sent to Sir Rhyan Lombard's notary. Sir Rhyan is one of Lord Scrope of Bolton's retainers, you know, both of them the Duke of Lancaster's men. A good man in battle, so my son tells me. He holds fast, as well he should. A lovely woman should not have to cross swords with a man of his calibre.' He smiled at her and leaned his arm along the table behind her. 'Now, tell me of your family. Are they still in York?'

Warmed by the fire and the wine, and more relieved than she could say, Merielle talked to him as a friend might, laughing at the way sisters, who should always agree, did not. She told him of her plans to bring Laurel to live in Canterbury.

The king's eyes, lazily absorbing Merielle's grace and beauty, blinked slowly. 'I may be able to help you there, mistress. I have a well-connected bachelor in mind. Winchester. Would that be convenient, do you think? Near enough for sisters who agree to disagree?'

That had been another of her problems solved in an instant. 'Oh, sire. How can I ever thank you?' She smiled, too radiantly. Looking back, it was probably the stupidest thing she could have said. The age-old response. A child's, not an intelligent woman's. It was the last time she ever said it to anyone.

The king slowly unfolded himself and rose, pulling her to her feet. 'Come,' he said, 'I think I have the answer to that.'

At eighteen, there was no reason for her to distrust him. She had heard, of course, of his reputed lack of scruples, his tendency to withhold repayments of loans, to forget some debts altogether. But he and his friends had, only eight years previously, founded the Most Noble Order of the Garter and that must surely be the ultimate guarantee of his attitude towards women. She thought, believed, that he was about to show her something of interest, and even when he led her across the shadowy room to a small door in the wainscot, she had no idea of what was in his mind.

The tiny chamber was no larger than a closet, built into the wall where the air was stuffy with the smell of candlesmoke and the same unmistakable linseed. Here, Merielle was drawn inside by one hand, still expecting the king, her hero, to light a candle and reveal a book, a relic, a document, perhaps. She found that she could not move backwards for something that pressed against her legs, and the last thing she saw was the king's hand pulling the door closed behind him.

'Sire…I beg you…what?' She strained backwards, but too late to avoid his arm about her waist or the heat of his mouth on her throat, his other hand on her body. 'Please…no, sire!'

His voice was hoarse, his previous manner now totally at odds with his assault. 'You want to know how you can thank me, mistress? Or have you reconsidered?

Am I not to receive some reward for my help…a small token as payment?'

'Payment, sire? I thought—'

'Hah! You thought?' He laughed, softly. 'Don't think. Women like you should not think too much.' While he spoke, his hand was finding its way into the wide neckline of her cote-hardie. 'You'll not deny me a little comfort before I return to France, surely? Something for us both to remember? By God, mistress, you're beautiful.'

In the oppressive blackness, Merielle pushed and twisted, scratching herself on his gold buttons and smelling his heat. 'Sire, I am a widow and recently bereaved. Have you forgot?'

'I've not forgotten that you're free now, mistress, and ready for a man, eh? Come, give yourself to me. You are young and strong.' While he spoke, and without giving her a chance to reply, he leaned on her, forcing her backwards and rendering her helpless either to reach him or to right herself, and she wondered then, in the warning flash behind her eyes, how many other women had been lured into this same trap and held there until payment had been exacted in full, for surely this was not the first time he had done such a thing.

It was the blackest of experiences in which her participation was as unnecessary as her cooperation while he forced himself between her legs, both hands exploring every surface beneath her gown, taking her at last with a suddenness that made her yelp with pain and brought tears to her eyes. Even then, she would not tell him, knowing that if her bereavement could not stop him, then nothing else would. He kissed her only once, when it seemed as if he would never finish and, when he did, she understood why he had felt it nec-

essary to closet them in this small place, for his roar
would surely have brought in his men, if they had heard
it.

The perspiration from his brow dripped on to her.
'By the white swan, mistress, you're good,' he panted.

Dazed and disbelieving that such a thing could have
happened to her, she allowed him to pull her up and
lead her by the hand back to the fire, to be cloaked and
veiled as she had been before, to be offered more wine.
His manner was once more that of the courtier, adding
to her sense of bewilderment.

'No, I thank you, sire. I must go now,' she whispered, pushing a certain dampness off her cheek.
Stiffly, she curtsied. 'I beg you will excuse me.'

Blank-faced, Gervase of Caen answered the king's
summons, revealing nothing to Merielle of whether he
knew or suspected what had taken place. In the clerks'
chamber, no faces looked up but, once in the ante-
chamber, Bonard's expression said it all. He felt her
trembling as she leaned on his arm; he would not let
go of her hand as they negotiated the downward spiral
towards the light; he pulled her arm through his out
there in the slippery courtyard and commanded Master
Gervase, 'Take Mistress St Martin's other arm, if you
please, sir.'

With care, the two men supported her back to Palace
Street, which was not far, and Master Gervase left after
being assured by Merielle that her petition had been
successful. Then, she had clung to the faithful Bonard
in silence, shaking uncontrollably, and had not objected
when he had carried her to her room and given orders
on her behalf to Mistress Allene and Bess.

After that, Merielle had told herself, over and over,
that this was nothing compared to the losses she had

recently sustained and that now she should put it from
her mind. But the one thing she had found impossible
to forget was her own foolish and misplaced trust in
the ways of men, a personal anger that pained her as
much as anything else.

The king had kept his word about her fine, for soon
afterwards the matter was concluded by a tersely
worded and painfully formal letter from Sir Rhyan's
notary to say that a fine had been paid from the king's
treasury office with a command not to pursue the affair.
But for Merielle, that had not been the end of the matter. Far from it. In the weeks that followed, she, Allene
and Bess had had to use all their skills to bring on the
monthly flow that had refused to appear at its appointed
time. An event which, only a few months ago, had been
the cause of such excessive celebration was now the
cause of anguish, for another pregnancy would be well
out of time and a stigma not to be endured by one so
recently widowed. Against all her bodily yearnings and
in another red haze of illness, the tiny spark of life was
intentionally snuffed out, and Merielle's heart almost
broke.

Illogically, she blamed Sir Rhyan, the man who had
appeared from nowhere to prosecute her and then cause
her to hand back the one thing she wanted above everything. Neither he nor the king would ever know, but
she could hold it against them, nevertheless.

She climbed out of the bathtub into the towel that
Allene held. Obviously, she should stay here in Canterbury, after all. Call Sir Adam's bluff. His proposal
was an insult, seen in the light of Bonard's explanations. But the prospect of discovering for herself whilst
ruffling the intolerable smugness of his nephew were
rewards she was loth to concede. Burying her smile

into the bundle of warm linen, she hugged it against her breast, rocking gently and inhaling its garden perfume.

'Come on, lass,' Allene said. 'Into bed. You're dead on your feet.'

Chapter Three

The resumption of her role as mistress of her own destiny was taken up once more in the early morning light that filtered lopsidedly on to the throng in the courtyard, rippling over mountainous panniers and the shoulders of intent grooms who tightened girths with upward-heaving grunts. Merielle sat in silence on her sturdy cob, a chestnut gelding of Suffolk parentage, whose back was broad enough to feast on. Her inner excitement was well contained. Beneath her figure-hugging brown woollen gown she wore soft leather breeches to prevent her legs from chafing on the saddle over the next four or five days, but this was her only concession to practicality. She had no intention of being mistaken for a party of rustics: that was not the best way to secure the best beds at inns and guest-houses or the best hospitality at an abbey.

With this firmly in mind, she wore her hair in an intricate and beguiling coronet of thick plaits coiled around her face and crown, each plait braided and interwoven with golden cords. From the lower edges of this, a pure white linen veil covered her throat and shoulders and this, with her remarkable peach-velvet skin, made a harmony of tones enough to make even the rough stable-lads gasp and nudge each other.

Nor was her retinue likely to be ignored. Two sumpter-mules were loaded with her personal possessions and those of Allene and Bess, and two packhorses carried provisions and food for the journey in wickerwork panniers, their matching harness of green-dyed leather and merrily tinkling bells on their bridles showing them to belong to a person of some standing. The same green and gold livery was worn by the two young grooms, Daniel and Pedro, local lads who would have done anything their mistress asked without blinking an eye.

For Allene, not even the too-few hours of sleep of last night could diminish the heady prospect of herding five adults and nine horses all the way to Winchester and back. She called Bess away from the corner where a young house-servant held her captive. 'Come on, my lass!' Every female was a lass to Allene. 'If your lad wants a job, get him to lift you up into the saddle. It's time we were off.'

'We'll set off without them if they're not here soon,' Merielle called to her. 'You'd better mount as well. Pedro, give Mistress Allene a hand.'

Master Bonard laid a hand on the chestnut's mane, pushing a wiry blond lock over the crest and flicking the green ribbons that cluttered each side of the brow-band. Bells tinkled along the rein-guards. 'Give them a moment more,' he said. 'You requested their company. You can hardly set off before they—' A shout echoed through the archway that led from the courtyard into the street.

'That'll be the market traders coming in,' Merielle said to him.

Bonard stepped forward to peer through. 'It's them,'

he said, leading Merielle on and passing Allene who hit the saddle with an audible squeak, despite Pedro's assistance. Her Irish grey rolled its eyes in alarm.

On the Palace Street side of the archway, a party of almost forty riders had come to an untidy halt, filling every available space until one of Merielle's neighbours opened his door to find a horse in the act of depositing steaming manure on his doorstep. From behind the towering rump, he yelled, 'Get over to one side, will you? Clear the way for Canterbury citizens, dammit!'

Realising that she was the cause of the obstruction, Merielle clasped Bonard's hand in a hurried farewell, took up her reins and moved out into the street, approaching two expressionless nuns, one on either side of a young woman, guarding her closely. Before she could reach them, she was intercepted by a young rider dressed in sober charcoal grey whose pleasant smile and shining tonsure held more of a welcome.

He beamed even more broadly. 'Mistress St Martin? Forgive our delay, if you please. Our prayers took longer than we thought.'

A voice joined in with a lilting Scandinavian accent. 'Longer because you chimed in, lad. Should've left it to the abbot.'

His smile bunched his apple cheeks. 'And who'll be the first person you turn to when there's a problem, eh?' he countered, winking at Merielle.

'The smith, that's who,' another voice called to a chorus of laughter. 'Come on, let's get out of here. Is the lady ready? How many are ye, mistress? Just you and the two gentlewomen, is it? Good God!'

Another roar of laughter went up as the three women were joined by Daniel and Pedro leading two horses each and pouring out through the archway like water from a burst pipe. Shouts of raillery rose above the din. 'Thought you'd got her to yourself did you, chaplain? Out of your depth already, lad.'

Still smiling, the chaplain hauled upon his reins, confusing his mount and backing it rapidly into the others until, by a deluge of slaps on its haunches, it headed in the right direction accompanied by the wail of bagpipes, drums, and the barely heard sound of the St Martin bells.

All along the Saturday streets of early-morning Canterbury, the jests continued, threading their way through the din that cleared a path past heavily laden traders coming into town. It was market day. The Westgate had just opened to the predictable bottleneck of travellers coming in both directions, testing everyone's patience in the jostling to present passes, tokens and excuses.

Merielle's company of nine horses came in for some serious teasing from the men who vied with each other to make the most ridiculous suggestions about what she could possibly be carrying. Running off to meet a lover, was she? No, the lovers would be in the panniers. Merielle smiled and said nothing, not even to Allene's tolerant grumbles, but their wait at the Westgate gave her a chance to study the nearest fellow-travellers and to realise that the two elderly nuns and the young lady did not join in the laughter nor did they communicate with anyone, not even with each other.

The Scandinavian accents belonged to a bluff Icelandic merchant and his brawny son, both of them smothered in boisterous haloes of pale blonde hair through which they kept up an irreverent comradeship with the young chaplain. Their pack-ponies were laden, they said, with furs and amber, but a third pony carried a stack of wicker baskets with square openings through which appeared beaks and furious eyes, striped backs and mottled breasts. Falcons, ready to be tamed; rare and already priceless.

Except for her own party and the silent trio, the rest of the travellers appeared to be men, for the most part respectably dressed, and mounted on strong beasts for which five days travel was nothing remarkable. And though she knew that the one for whom her eyes searched would not be present, the urge to comb the crowd for a certain breadth of shoulder, a certain height and arrogant stare could not be restrained. The most strident of her inner voices protested relief that he was not to be seen, joy at her artifice, pride at her cunning, but a quietly nagging voice sang to a different tune in a minor key.

'A good crowd,' she said to her nurse. 'We made the right choice.'

She recognised the goldsmith and his assistant in the company of two young scholars who would be returning to Winchester after the feast days. Oblivious to the rest of the crowd, their conversation was conducted in a mixture of English and French, and Merielle felt herself fortunate to receive a quick smile and no more. There was a courier, eager to pass with his large leather saddle-bags and air of urgency; he would not be with them for long. There was an unmistakable scattering of palmers, professional pilgrims swathed in coarse wool and lidded with wide-brimmed hats, the front brims of which were turned up to display their collection of pilgrims' badges like a jigsaw of armour-plating. Around and across their bodies was a medley of clanking tools, pouches, flasks and plates, ropes, sticks and spare shoes, ready for the moment their emaciated mounts dropped dead beneath them. Their talk, tooth-gapped and incessant, admitted only those who could boast of their hardships, adventures and achievements.

They were not the only pilgrims; three noisy young Italians moved closer to Merielle's party before she could see them coming, foisting upon her their own brand of English which completely disregarded the usual sentence structure. Finding their questions too fractured to understand and suspecting that they were too personal to be answered anyway, she looked behind to see whether a slight tactical manoeuvre was possible. But a party of part-armoured soldiers had moved in close behind them and, beyond the sumpter-horses led by Daniel, their laughing faces implied that the Italians' antics were not new to them.

The way south-west from Canterbury followed the gentle meander of the Great Stour, though soon the leaders of the cavalcade led them on to the higher ground to the north from where they could appreciate the wetlands and the distant herons reflected in the quiet sunlit waters. Despite all her expectations, the track appeared to be every bit as busy on this day as on any other, and the thought crossed her mind more than once over the next few miles that, if she had waited for Sir Rhyan's escort, she would not now be wondering if she would get a bed to herself for the next two nights. Switching her mind to contemplate the scenery should have helped to postpone the problem, but the panorama filled as they merged first with the tail-end of one group and then another who had set out from the suburbs earlier than they. The groups were engulfed, sometimes overtaken completely like the entire household of one man's family, chickens, pigs and all, but Merielle's party swelled with each mile. With her nine horses, it was impossible for her to race ahead, and by the time they reached the gateway to the Norman castle at Chilham, the village square was teeming with people, many already breaking their fast, and Merielle's hopes of being able to find, or even to reach, the privy at the back of the inn were dashed. The next best thing was a hedge with the outspread skirts of Allene and Bess to screen her.

About the same business was an exceedingly pretty woman whose blonde tresses were bundled untidily at the back of her neck into a black net, with wisps pouring out on all sides like silk in a high wind. She stood and adjusted her travel-stained gown of worn velvet, pulled her mantle across the front of an extremely revealing bodice, smiled and walked away.

Keeping the young chaplain and the two Icelanders in her sights and rescuing Bess from the unwanted attentions of the three Italians, Merielle took her brief meal standing, ready to mount when the leaders did. She found that the blonde young woman had moved nearer, and smiled encouragingly; there were few enough women of her own age with whom she might keep company.

The woman nodded in the direction of two others. Her brother and sister, she told Merielle. 'We started off yesterday,' she said, 'but both our mounts cast shoes and the smith here at Chilham was at his mother's funeral and we couldn't hire a horse for love nor money. Never seen the way so crowded in all my life. My sister's blind, you see, but even so we had to sleep in a room full of men. Nowhere else.' She hunched her shoulders. 'We'd lost so much time having to walk it.'

Merielle liked the sound of her and the look of the other two. Introduced as Emma, her brother as Adrian and the gentle blind sister as Agnes, the three appeared to offer the kind of company Merielle had been hoping for at the outset, good-natured, well-spoken and mannerly. The young man's presence would no doubt deter the Italian infliction, too.

'Pestered you, did they?' Agnes said. 'I heard their shouting.'

Merielle heaved a sigh, but forced a grin to back it up. 'It's young Bess I'm more concerned for. They've practically seduced her already.'

Her new friends snuffled in amusement. 'Well, then, why don't you allow her to ride behind me?' Adrian suggested. 'I'll keep 'em at bay, I promise you. Agnes usually rides pillion with me, but she can go behind you, perhaps? Your chestnut looks as though he could carry a family.'

'Oh, easily,' Merielle said. 'That would solve the problem, thank you. And perhaps if we can move up to the front, we may do better for beds tonight. Shall we try?'

'Where are your party heading for?'

'Probably Wye next. Sometimes they give it a miss, I don't know. Then to Charing, I suppose, and perhaps Harrietsham by suppertime. Look, the chaplain's mounting. Shall we try and keep up with him?'

The sightless Agnes was lifted up on to a pad behind Merielle's saddle, the two arms passing around her waist imparting a comfort uncommonly sweet after the last few troublesome miles. Adrian, the eldest of the trio, took Bess up behind him and the journey from Chilham was lightened accordingly as Merielle described to Agnes everything they encountered along the river valley, through the great King's Wood and along the side of the hill with the river flowing away from them like a ribbon of silver.

They did not, after all, aim for Wye but skirted the hillside to Charing where Merielle would happily have called it a day, but dared not suggest it. Dinner was brief and taken standing by the track, looking, roaming and laughing at Adrian's witty observations of their fellow-travellers whose trail stretched almost out of sight. His sisters obviously adored him and even Allene, usually the last person to be won over, agreed with Merielle that they had been fortunate to find such pleasant companions. Inevitably, Merielle was compelled to fend off gently probing questions about the reason for her journey, resorting to more general conversation at the first opportunity.

But even while she avoided mentioning the escorts she might have had, her mind returned to the implications of her sudden decision, not only the journey itself but the certain explanations she would have to concoct at Winchester. And no sooner had she convinced herself that four days on the road should be enough time to make up a story suitable to smooth Sir Adam's feathers, if not his nephew's, than her more immediate plans for a comfortable night's rest suffered a set-back, for the approach to Harrietsham was obstructed by the slow progress of a nobleman's household. Three four-wheeled leather-covered waggons pulled by six oxen apiece, dozens of sumpter-horses, mules, men-at-arms, retainers and domestic officers, servants and pages, squires and grooms. The small village was jammed solid, all hopes of accommodation dwindling with the light. There was nothing for it but to wait or go on to the next place, wherever that might be.

Merielle turned to consult Agnes but encountered the top of her head as she slipped nimbly to the ground. 'Where are you off to?' she called to her departing friend.

Agnes made no reply, but crossed with surprising confidence to her brother's horse where, astonishingly, she yanked the unsuspecting Bess to the ground by one arm, caught her brother's outstretched hand and vaulted on to the pad behind him, her foot on his. Emma, still mounted, moved quickly after them.

'Hey!' Merielle called after them. 'What's to do?'

Emma called to her, still smiling, 'We'll find rooms and come back for you. Wait there.' Both horses broke ranks, swerved, and leapt away.

Immediately, there was a similar flurry of activity as liveried men sped past, hooves thundering on the grassy verge, and Merielle realised that the rush to get to the guesthouse and the inns, roomy cottage or stable, was now a matter of who could move fastest, and even that held no guarantee of success.

Allene brushed down the bewildered maid. 'What are we going to do?' she said. 'Nay, you're not hurt, lass. Stop yer snivelling and find yer hoss. Should've stayed there in the first place.' She gave Bess a gentle shove and then, with little sympathy, answered her own question. 'Wait a while, that's what. Something'll turn up. Always does.'

That was not the music to her mistress's ears it was intended to be. Merielle was furious and in no mind to wait either for the return of the mysterious family or for Allene's predicted miracle. '*You* wait, Allene,' she snapped, pulling her mount away. 'If they think I've come all this way to sit and watch it get dark, they can think again. I'm going to see what's going on down there.' She kicked at the cob's flanks, but her way was blocked by the group of soldiers who had ridden behind them all afternoon and whose offers of assistance were now of an unmistakably personal nature. It was impossible for her to proceed.

Desperately, she turned again to seek a way through to the other side, berating herself and the circumstances which had brought them to this. Perhaps she should have allowed Bonard to accompany them, after all. Wheeling round, she searched the faces in the crowd, aware of the soldiers' appraisal, their knowing grins, their intentions, sizing up the two lads and the women. Then, as if a command had been given, they scattered and opened up a way for her, dissolving into the crowd completely.

The silhouette of a rider appeared, almost black against the western sky and massively tall on a stallion that made her cob look like a pony by comparison, and it was instantly clear to Merielle that it was his presence that had dispersed the former menace. The breadth of shoulder, the height, the arrogant stare were all in place, but relief at his unexpected presence was quickly swamped by another surge of anger at being seen to be helpless, which she was not, and by being anticipated, which was humiliating.

With as much dignity as she could summon, she kept to her former plan to investigate the sudden departure of her companions, kicking the cob forward again and passing Sir Rhyan without a glance.

Casually, he leaned from his saddle and caught the cob's bridle, pulling it round away from the crowd and so far on to the verge that they had to duck to avoid the low branches of a showy sweet-chestnut tree. 'No, you don't,' he said, 'unless you want our conversation to be heard by half the crowd.' He kept hold, coming round to face her, knee to knee.

'Let go of my horse, sir. I have nothing to say to you.'

'Then that will make life easier for us both.' Facing the last rays of the setting sun, Merielle could see that he was wearing a sleeveless leather gupon over a tunic of dark green with tiny gold buttons from wrist to elbow. His green cloak thrown over one shoulder showed a lining of green plaid mixed with red and black, and his white chainse was open at the neck. There was no trace of tiredness about him; he sat his horse like one who had only just started out, radiating fitness and strength.

With little success, Merielle tried to pull away. 'On the contrary, it will make nothing easier. You were not supposed to be travelling today and I have every intention of avoiding your company, as I set out to do.'

'Which I knew you would do. Why do you think I told you Monday? You were glad of my intervention just now, though. Or did you want to take on six soldiers and three Italians? Eh?'

'I have managed perfectly so far, Sir Rhyan, I thank you. Let me go. I must find my friends. They've gone—'

'Oh, yes, they've gone all right. The whore, her pimp and the cut-purse. What with those three and a crowd of eager bedfellows I'd say you've managed particularly well. A good day's work.'

'Whore? Cut-purse? What on earth are you talking about?' Merielle's senses, already alert, lurched sickeningly. She knew what he was talking about.

His words emerged low-pitched but harsh. 'The blonde woman who calls herself Emma, that's who. She's one of the Winchester geese, woman. And the lad who reckons to be her brother is the other lass's husband.'

'The blind girl? Agnes?' Suddenly her voice was breathless.

'Blind my foot!' he said, sarcastically. 'She's no more blind than I am, but it helps her to say so, as a thief.'

'You're wrong. They're perfectly respectable people.' Her defence of them lacked conviction, nor did it help her own credulity.

He leaned towards her. 'The whore was at the inn where your Master Gervase spent an hour before he came to see you yesterday. I know because my men saw them there together. Affectionately. They're from Southwark, the district owned by the Bishop of Winchester. Hence the name.'

'I know that!' She looked away. Everyone knew that.

'Then you will also know, mistress, that your purse is missing.'

'What?'

Again, he leaned and took hold of the leather strap that hung loosely from her shoulder, half-concealed beneath her cloak, pulling it until the complete length emerged, its ends neatly cut. It dangled from his hand like an eel.

'My purse! She's taken my purse! A thief! I had her up behind me all that way. They shared our food.'

'So now you know what that motley crowd had in mind, seeing you in their company.' His eyes referred to the men he had sent packing. 'But your purse I have here.' He delved a hand inside his leather jerkin and brought it out, its gold clasp still intact, its contents still safe. To her astonished silence, he explained, 'I waited for them to take their leave and then sent my men after them. It was they who retrieved it.'

'Your men. Thank you. You are not alone?' She took the purse, half-dazed by events and fighting to hold back the wave of exhaustion that threatened to engulf her.

'No, I have my men with me, and some others who travel with me to Winchester. It was Sir Adam's wish that you should accept our escort and allow me to find your accommodation. You and the rest of your party.'

She shook her head, her dislike of him surfacing even through her shattering tiredness. 'I thank you, sir, but that's quite out of the question. If you are to be of the same party I cannot stop you, but I cannot travel with you. My mind is made up. You are with friends…'

'They are Sir Adam's friends and colleagues. I told you, I was about his business in Canterbury as well as my own. And I was not asking you, mistress, I was telling you. You will come with me and stay in comfort until Monday morning. Two more miles, that's all we have to travel, then food, a warm clean bed and a long sleep. You'll not get that here.'

Unable to continue her argument with the fierceness it deserved, Merielle turned to look for Allene, Bess and the boys, deliberating as much for their sakes as for her own. Bess's safety over the next two nights would be a nightmare. They were not where she had left them but farther down the track, waiting within a large group of liveried men and others. Sir Rhyan's men. Once more, he had taken charge as if her permission was irrelevant.

'This is intolerable!' She whirled round, reaching out for his wrist to wrench it away from her bridle. 'I will not...'

But her arm was caught and held away in the same iron grip that had left its imprint on her wrist last evening. 'You have a responsibility to your servants, do you not?' he said, showing his anger at last.

'Let me go, damn you!'

'Do you?'

'Yes.'

'Then how can you not allow them safety when it's offered? Are you so choked with resentment that you cannot accept anything from anybody?'

Her fury boiled over, incensed by every word of his well-aimed barb, his presence here, his restraining hand on her arm. He would never know in the slightest degree the cause of her animosity. 'The only thing *you* ever offered me, Sir Rhyan, did me more harm than you could ever imagine. You must forgive me if I am less than enthusiastic about accepting anything else until that wound has healed.' She made one last effort to rid herself of his hand, expecting hers to be the last words. But now heads had turned to watch the undignified tussle.

'Then choose, mistress,' he snarled, releasing her arm but hauling the cob's head closer. 'Either you accompany me in a seemly manner or I leave you here alone with this crowd.' He indicated with his head the sea of faces. 'I have your party, you see. They'll come with me, willing or not.'

Allene and Bess, Daniel and Pedro were now out of sight, enclosed by his men, quite unaware of their impending separation. She could not afford to lose them

and all her baggage any more than she could risk being
left to the predictable attentions of so many strangers.
'Damn you!' she whispered. 'You would not do so.'
'Try me.'
'Then I have little choice, have I? Damn you to hell!'

Chapter Four

The lessons of life had shouldered their way into Merielle's twenty-one years with more urgency than was usual in one so young, but she had had to learn them fast. One of them was that, although it was acceptable to show anger, being a useful manly emotion, tears, tiredness and temperament were womanly and weak and not for the manager of a business. The rules were hard to stick to for one whose emotions lay naturally so close to the surface, and twenty yards was barely enough distance for her to squeeze back the threatening tears of anger that welled up behind her eyes.

As if he understood, Sir Rhyan proceeded slowly along the verge and then, hidden by a rider who crossed their path, handed back her reins. 'Ready?' he said.

She took a deep breath, straightened and nodded, refusing to look at him. The extent of Sir Rhyan's party was far greater than she had imagined from his casual reference to men-at-arms and guests, making anything more than cursory introductions out of the question in that quickly fading light. For which Merielle was much relieved; anything more demanding would have exposed her as inarticulate as well as stunningly beautiful, not a mixture to do her justice. She caught the names of Wykeham and Yeaveley and nodded briefly to each man without the customary smile, and if it seemed strange to them that Mistress St Martin and Sir Rhyan had only just thought to acknowledge each other after a whole day in the same party, they showed no surprise, nor did they comment.

Two miles farther on, he had said, though no more than that, and Merielle would have entered the gates of Hades rather than ask him where they were bound. She would have whispered to Allene—who was looking particularly smug—but for the fact that her own leather purse-strap was now threaded through the cob's bridle, its ends in Sir Rhyan's great fist. Another humiliation. No chance to lag behind.

The dwindling light and her self-absorption joined forces in concealing from her any indication of where she was going or how she reached her destination that evening. Slipping through her bleary senses were acres of wood and parkland, a rising moon, a certain peace after the clamour of the Canterbury crowd, the satin stillness of a lake, drawbridges, greetings and lanterns, welcoming hands and yapping hounds, the smell of roasting meat. Before she could throw off the light rug that covered her legs or protest that she could manage, she was lifted down as orders were given to her grooms.

'They'll be well tended, mistress. Good stables. Warm lodgings and food. We'll have your panniers sent in as soon as they're off. This is Sir Walter Nessey, the castellan. He and his lady will attend to your needs; you have only to ask.'

The castellan bowed, his elegant figure etched sharply in the light of torches that billowed smoke into the blackening sky. 'You are most welcome, lady. Your rooms are prepared.' His manner was efficient.

Through arches and over drawbridges they had clattered, across a large compound within walls with water beyond them, another cluster of buildings ahead. Rooms prepared? To have asked where they were at this point would have sounded ludicrous.

The great stone porch led them into a hall of massive dimensions where trestles had been arranged for supper, those on the dais at the far end covered with blazing white cloths on which silver salt cellars and glass goblets twinkled in the light from wall sconces and from the raftered ceiling. Around the dais, fabric lined the walls with muted colours which Merielle knew would come to life in the daylight. Clearly this was no ordinary guesthouse. A castellan? It was a castle, then?

She came to a halt so suddenly that Allene nearly knocked her over. 'Sir Rhyan! I need to speak to you,' she hissed as he whirled around to face her. 'Now, if you please. Over here.'

He followed her to one side of the mystified group, excusing himself to Sir Walter. 'Look,' he said, 'I know what you're thinking.'

She flared, instantly set alight by his placating manner. 'You do not know what I'm thinking, Sir Rhyan, nor will you ever know. This place is a castle, is it not? The king's. How *dare* you bring me here? Are you entirely devoid of diplomacy, for pity's sake?'

He shook his head, lifting darkly angled brows. 'The king's not here, mistress. I would not have brought you here if he was. You think he would see some form of reconciliation in our being here together, I know, but this is purely a gathering of his craftsmen to see what can be done to renovate the place, that's all. If Sir

Adam had been here in my stead, he would have called here, too, on the way to Winchester.'

'Where are we?'

'Leeds,' he said. 'Leeds Castle. We're still in Kent.'

'Queen Isabella's place?'

'It was. She died last August, remember. It's now the king's. He's sent his men to meet here, and I brought two of them from Canterbury.'

'Those two?'

'Yes. William Wykeham and Henry Yeaveley, John Kenton, too. I'm not involved, mistress, I assure you. I escort them to Sir Adam, that's all, once they're finished here. You'll not be disturbed in any way.'

'You're sure about the king?'

'I swear it. He's at Windsor, I believe. Trust me.'

The sincerity of his plea found no foothold. 'I do, sir. I trust you to find a way of humiliating me at every opportunity.' It was on the tip of her tongue to suggest that she might be accommodated in the queen's own room to complete the affront, but that would have gone over his head, so she held it back.

As it transpired, her cynicism was prophetic, for the room to which the castellan led her beyond a narrow, hollow- sounding passageway had been used by the late Queen Isabella until last year. He apologised for its old-fashioned shabbiness, believing her words to Sir Rhyan in the great hall to have been a complaint, if her demeanour was anything to go by. It was, he told her, awaiting renovation like the rest of the *gloriette*.

'*Gloriette?*' Merielle said, liking the sound of the word.

He knuckled his nose with his fist as if being caught out by the word's newness. 'The keep, mistress. This is the keep, but the Spanish Queen Eleanor used her

own term for it. Sounds prettier, and it's rarely used
for defence nowadays. The old queen loved it. Look
here.'

He walked over to the deep window recess lined by
stone seats cut into the thickness of the wall, and
opened the heavy iron-studded wooden shutters. He
stood to one side, looking out.

A cool spring breeze came across an expanse of water that stretched further than Merielle could see, even
in the moonlight, filling her nostrils with the indistinct
scent of bluebells. Beneath the window, the wall of the
keep dropped sheer into the water.

'That's why she loved it,' Sir Walter said. 'Water all
round and glorious parkland beyond. Good hunting out
there.'

'Water all round the keep?'

'All round the castle, mistress. We're surrounded by
it. Like being on a ship without the rocking; you'll be
able to see it properly tomorrow.' He laughed, closing
the shutters.

The bustle from the doorway made any response unnecessary; here were her two panniers dragged in by
two red-faced lads muttering suggestions as to their
contents. Sir Rhyan and the castellan's wife waited to
enter, watching like eagles and communicating to Merielle an impression that her presence here was an event
of some importance to them, which she immediately
brushed aside as being absurd.

Lady Alicia was as apologetic as her husband about
the threadbare elegance, looking around her at the plain
wall-hangings whose folds had faded to a paler rose.
'It'll all have to be redone,' she said. 'And a new set
for this.' She nodded at the great bed.

Merielle glanced only briefly at the structure that

dominated the room, too tired to donate much interest
or to catch the quick frown that passed from the castellan to his wife.

Redirecting her concern, Lady Alicia pointed out the
fire crackling in a stone fireplace set into the outer wall,
its white plaster hood rising like a conical hat up to the
ceiling. 'To take the chill off,' she said. 'Water and
towels—' she indicated a silver ewer and basins, a pile
of linen folded on the pine chest '—and I'll have food
sent up to you straight away. Or would you rather eat
in the hall?'

'No, I thank you, my lady,' said Merielle. 'It's been
a long day. Please excuse us, if you will. I shall be
asleep within the hour.'

The castellan's wife was round and as plump as a
wren, the top of her white starched wimple reaching
only to her husband's chest, her smile squeaking the
linen against her cheeks. A woman in her position,
Merielle thought, who could dress in the fashions of
thirty years ago would have little idea how to begin
refurbishing a room fit for the king's Flemish wife,
Phillipa. Even through her exhaustion, she could see
that much.

Sir Rhyan began a move to leave Merielle alone.
'So,' he said, 'if there is anything else you need, you
have only to—'

'Ahem!' Sir William nudged his wife.

'Oh, lord, yes.' Lady Alicia opened a small door on
one wall and shot through like a rabbit with a flash of
white. 'Here,' she called. The room was smaller but
every bit as comfortable, with two low beds along the
walls and a log fire in the corner that filled the air with
the scent of burning applewood. 'The old queen used

to bathe in here, but I thought you'd like your ladies close by.'

'You are most kind,' Merielle told her. 'We shall only be here a day—'

'Yes, right then.' Sir William sprang into action, herding his wife out and leaving Merielle to the accompaniment of profuse goodnights.

But Sir Rhyan hovered, holding the door ajar. 'Better than a hayloft at Harrietsham?' he asked with one eyebrow ascending.

'Better?' Merielle said with contempt. 'In what way better? It's the company I've found myself in that concerns me most. What did you have in mind as better, pray?'

He smiled as he made to leave, poking his head round the door to say, 'The security, mistress, what else?'

Lacking the energy to sustain her misgivings, Merielle, Allene and Bess were bound to admit that this was indeed better in every way than having to suffer the discomforts that Harrietsham had offered, particularly over the Sabbath on which no one would travel except those in dire need.

The queen's chamber was large by any standards, high-ceilinged with carved wooden beams and rafters painted once in bright colours, but now faded. The bed which had concerned Lady Alicia was the largest Merielle had ever seen, giving new meaning to the arranged marriages the royals had to suffer in the name of peace. It was raised on a platform high enough to provide a low seat on three sides during the daytime, the whole expanse draped with a heavy figured silk which Merielle recognised as being of Italian origin, probably from Lucca, its padded edges extending well over the floor of polished wood. Like the coverlet, the back-cloth, long curtains and suspended canopy were of the same faded and threadbare gold-coloured fabric, used yet again on the cushions that dimpled the bed and lined the window-seat. Faded pink and gold warmed the room with rosy colours in the light from candles and fire.

Allene folded down the coverlet to expose fur and white linen, more from curiosity than efficiency. 'Sure you want to sleep by yourself, love?' she said, puffing and clambering off backwards.

'Just give me my supper and tuck me in,' said Merielle. 'Bess, go and find the kitchen...er...no, on second thoughts, don't.'

It would have been pointless to make a fuss, but the idea of sleeping in the queen's bed, any queen, past or present, did not appeal to Merielle in the slightest. In the circumstances, she thought, pushing her feet towards the patch where the warming-pan had been, this was just about the most insensitive thing he could have done, not even her usual tolerance exempting him from blame. Her logic also being at a low ebb, she fell asleep well before she had sought a way to give him the slightest credit for this exquisite comfort.

Warmly wrapped in a fur rug pulled from the bed, Merielle sat in the deep window-seat, her eyes feasting upon the scene beyond the shutters. Allene took up one of her bare feet and pushed a fur slipper on to it, fretting at the cool air that had been allowed in so soon.

'Just imagine, no glass! A queen's chamber without glass. You'd think she'd have had it put in by now, wouldn't you? What did she do in winter, d'ye think?'

Sunlight poured into every corner, bouncing off the satin water on to the walls and flooding over the bed-hangings, washing them with a rinse of new gold. Across the lake, birds chased each other in daring swoops, held in the air, then tippling backwards in a celebration of freedom that seemed to emphasise Merielle's enforced security. Slopes of green that the darkness had hidden slid beneath willows at the water's edge, holding a team of ducks that dared each other to take the first plunge. Farther along, swans ruffled their feather-beds and made wedges of white at each graceful launch. As far as she could see, woodland bordered the green, but rock was the castle's pedestal. A breeze sent a dark patch racing towards her and she blinked as it found the window.

Allene was shaking out a sideless surcoat edged with soft grey squirrel fur. 'It may be after Easter,' she said, brushing a hand over the crumpled blue velvet, 'but there's still a chill in the air these mornings. And if we're not going anywhere, you may as well wear your best. Come on, lass. It'll be time for Mass before you're ready, and your hair not done yet.'

The pensive young woman stepped down into the room and let the rug fall away. Allene had seen her mistress's body almost as many times as Merielle herself, yet never did she tire of admiring the faultless skin, the slender waist and hips like ripe pears, the superb breasts, high and full, the long limbs and shoulders now mantled with wave after wave of thick black hair cascading down her back.

Reaching up, Merielle scooped it into her hands and twisted it. 'Here, stick it into a caul. As you say, we're not going anywhere.' Hands on head, she was totally unaware of the picture she created.

'The pink cote-hardie, or the yellow one?'

'Neither. The figured pale grey. It's loose and comfy.'

'I see. And you're not going to give 'em an eyeful with the fitted ones. Is that it?'

'Something like that.'

To become a temporary recluse would have been both discourteous and tedious, and Merielle had already prepared herself for the civilities which would be expected of her while she was in their company. But that would not be for long; there was some exploring to do and the silver-grey semi-fitted cote-hardie with its long bodice and sleeves was infinitely less noticeable than pink or gold.

But the result, whether she willed it or not, was enough to turn every head in the small crowded chapel. The blue-grey ensemble, girdled with a silver and enamelled chain around her hips and covered with a fur-lined mantle of pale-blue velvety fustian may have concealed many of the curves, but not the graceful bearing and long neck, or the mass of glossy hair piled into the silver pearl-studded net and the flimsiest of white veils.

She had not meant to be late, but the priest's intonations relieved her of any muted debate about where she should stand; she sidled into a space at the side of one of the men to whom she had been introduced at Harrietsham. He smiled and made room for Bess and Allene and, at the first opportunity, turned to speak to Merielle in a whisper.

'Rested?' he said. He was tall and large-framed with the leathery skin of one used to all weathers, his eyes sharply observant, his mouth wide and ready to smile.

She nodded, returning his smile with her eyes, aware

that some kind of explanation for her former reticence would eventually emerge. 'Thank you, Master…?'

'Henry Yeaveley.' He smiled again and nodded towards the figure of Sir Rhyan Lombard who stood a short distance away. 'It's all right. Lovers' quarrels never last very long, you know.'

A further exchange of words was impossible, and Merielle's desire to have the remark explained made her participation in the Mass an effort of supreme concentration. Even when the priest's familiar words found a niche in her thoughts, her eyes were busily assessing the texture of a certain head of dark hair, compact ears and breadth of back beneath a mulberry hood. Lovers' quarrel? Had he told them that they were lovers, then? Or was that Master Henry Yeaveley's interpretation of events? She must do her best to correct the mistake.

As though Sir Rhyan had guessed her intentions, he joined her at the altar rail, kneeling by her side and then remaining with her as she struggled to keep her mind about its business. But the Mass, usually so meaningful, was an ordeal. It should not have mattered that the place was so dowdy, that the altar was bare of the usual colourful tryptich or that a chill from the bare walls lent a clammy odour that the incense could not disguise, but she blamed these factors for her preoccupation, then gave in entirely to a similar critical appraisal of the man at her side.

He wore the same tailored tunic as yesterday but, over this, a loose mulberry-coloured cote-hardie which almost reached his knees, loosely belted over narrow hips with wide loose sleeves cut away at the elbows. Yesterday's leather riding-boots were now replaced by pointed leather-soled hose that clung to his long legs, showing the hardened muscles of an expert horseman, and Merielle's quick upward glance showed her that he had had time to shave, for his square jaw was smooth, his mouth unsmiling.

He caught the glance, but to his quick greeting Merielle merely inclined her head. Despite her efforts, she could not fault his appearance.

Taking the most convenient excuse to escape his company after Mass, she responded to a greeting from one who plainly expected her to remember him. He was pleasant-faced and in his early thirties, though already balding, perhaps a few years younger than Master Yeaveley. Master Wykeham's courtesy was impeccable.

'I've been wanting to tell you, mistress, since I heard that you were to be with us, that I own a tapestry made in your late husband's workshop. A St Martin tapestry, no less.' Spreading his hands apart to the width of a platter, he smiled, ruefully. 'Alas, it is only so big. The only one I could afford at the time.'

Judging by his handsome, well-cut tunic, Merielle felt it was safe for her to suggest, 'Then I think it's time you paid us another visit, Master Wykeham, when next you're in Canterbury. You are no doubt ready for a larger piece.'

His ready smile became a laugh. 'Ah, a good salesman, I see. Well, we shall certainly be glad of your contribution to liven this place up a bit. Have you had a chance to look round yet? Of course, a new storey above this one is what this part needs most. More rooms, you know.' His lively commentary on the castle's main requirements, broken by the single file of narrow passages and doorways, was kept up all the way to the hall where the castle's inmates stood waiting to break their fast. His inclusion of herself in the working-party was, she supposed, part of his natural enthusiasm and civility, and so she attended with half an ear, using the other three halves to catch the voice of Sir Rhyan behind her.

The high table, again covered with white linen, glass and silver, was soon filled by those who had been at Mass in the chapel, a development which surprised Merielle for she had believed them to be of the castellan's household.

Master Wykeham stayed by her side, happy to take up her query. 'Ah, no, mistress. Like us, they are craftsmen in the king's employ. Most of them have been here since Friday, but no one was allowed to use the queen's room till you arrived.'

Again, his inclusion of herself amongst them puzzled her and she looked to see who was nearby to give a more balanced view of the business. But Sir Rhyan was edging his way purposefully along the table, past others with similar intentions. 'My privilege, good sirs, as the lady's official escort,' he was saying, good-naturedly wedging his way into the space at her side. And though they grinned and grumbled, they gave way at his persistence.

'There was really no need, Sir Rhyan,' Merielle whispered as the hall shuffled into silence for the chaplain's grace. 'With all these courteous men at hand.'

The ensuing clatter covered his reply. 'Yes, I seem to have heard that before, and look where it got you. From now on, I shall be keeping you by me, whether you like it or not.'

She could not resist baiting him. 'You think Sir Adam would prefer me in one piece, then, do you?' she said, not looking at him.

'I think, lady, that it doesn't matter a damn what Sir Adam would prefer. He's not getting you.'

No doubt he was provoking her for the sheer enjoyment it gave him, but for the life of her she could think of no answer to that, short of losing her composure. Moreover, she found it difficult to understand his meaning. Was he still determined to interfere in her plans, whatever they were?

Master Wykeham was more than happy to divert her attention, pointing along the table at those assembled on the king's matters: William Hurley, John Sponlee, Henry Rutland, John Kenton and young Walton, Master Yeaveley's assistant. 'Yeaveley's the king's mason now, you know. Brilliant architect. He was made a freeman of London five years ago. Nothing he can't tackle.'

'And you, Master Wykeham? Is that your craft, too?'

'Not in his league,' he said, modestly. 'No one is. I have to make myself indispensable in other ways.'

Merielle did not doubt that he would. He had the knack already. 'How?' she said.

'I've been in the king's service, one way or another, since forty-seven. Started with the royal hounds. I'm surveyor of Windsor Castle and parks at the present time, in charge of building works in the Upper Ward. His grace wants me to take a look at this place, now it's come into his hands, before we go on to Winchester.'

'To see my brother-in-law, Sir Adam Bedesbury? Good. I had no idea you were to come, too.' She allowed herself a convenient lapse of memory.

'And Master Kenton, the king's painter. Sir Rhyan is borrowing him, I believe. Did he not tell you that, either?'

Hearing his name, Sir Rhyan leaned forward. 'No, William. Not yet. We have some catching up to do.' The ambiguous words and the conspiratorial half-smiles spoke volumes, removing any doubt in Merielle's mind that both Wykeham and Yeaveley had reached the same conclusion about her relationship with Sir Rhyan.

She would put a stop to it, here and now. 'Master Wykeham, I must tell you…' she began.

A young squire held a basin of water between them; by the time another page had poured water over their fingers and patted them dry on the towel draped over his shoulder, her audience of one had switched his attention to his other side. She turned on Sir Rhyan instead, but he was ready for her.

'Not now,' he said, placing slices of meat on to their shared trencher of bread. 'Too many ears. We'll discuss it later.'

'What have you *told* them?' she insisted, glaring at him.

'That you're a spitfire who needs taming. Here, eat that.'

She gasped. 'And you told them that you would take the responsibility upon yourself, yes?'

'Correct. Go on, eat it. You're being watched; don't choke.'

His advice was appropriate. Merielle was never more close to choking than at that moment. She swallowed, hard. 'Thank you for the early warning. I'm sure they'll understand better when I give them my version of the story next.'

'I've told you, we'll discuss it later, but if you're so desperate for them to know that you run a thriving business with an unfortunate habit of breaking contracts, then go ahead and say it now. They'll understand that all right. More? Look, here's a dainty morsel.' He held a piece of succulent partridge dripping with blackberry sauce on the point of his knife and watched patiently as she overcame her reluctance to take it. 'Thank me and smile. Where are your manners?' he said.

'In a different book from yours, sir,' she replied, snappily, putting the food into her mouth and, with what began as a bold stare, refusing to accept his command. But the resolute expression in his eyes was too much for her, and for all she knew, the food might as well have been bread and water.

Not for a moment did she doubt his word. On the contrary, the picture fitted together perfectly: the complete lack of contact during the journey, the purse-thong through her bridle, the words later on in the hall. Of course they'd believe it. Who would not? Unwilling even to pretend an affability she did not feel towards him, she could at least show the others how biased was his opinion of her. With this pulrpose in mind, she joined in the conducted tour of the castle at the men's insistence, walking with each of them in turn and discovering far more in common than she had expected. They were all craftsmen of one sort or another and enjoyed telling others about their work as much as listening and learning, discussing and estimating. The one possible exception was Master John Kenton, the king's painter, who stayed too close to Sir Rhyan for Merielle's comfort.

The keep was far too small for the present king's needs, the rooms being arranged round an almost central courtyard, the queen's own suite taking up the whole of one side. In the daylight, Merielle discovered that the only link between the main castle and the *gloriette* was a covered wooden bridge across the water, linking two islands together, but so intent were they on their discussions that none of them ventured out beyond the drawbridge into the surrounding parkland.

Sir Rhyan stayed to shadow Merielle, which afforded her the delight of being able to ignore him whilst enjoying the security his presence brought. She did not need it, of course, but it was there to be savoured, and to make a nonsense of his uncomplimentary epithet seemed easy enough in the company of such men as the glazier, Master Rutland. Like herself, he saw a need for more colour in the castle and, standing together in the open space of the castle bailey, he expressed his pleasure that she was to be involved in its renovation.

'Involved? Oh, no, I assure you, Master Rutland, I'm not in the least involved. I'm here under false pretences,' she laughed. 'I leave for Winchester tomorrow. I believe you come, too, Master Kenton?' She turned to where he stood nearby.

The voice of William Hurley, master carpenter, called over to them, his ears pricking like a terrier's. 'Going tomorrow? Who? Mistress St Martin? Kenton? Nonsense, we'll need at least another day. Can't go clambering about on the Sabbath, now, can we?' He was a wiry energetic man whose mind seemed ceaselessly to advance from one ingenious solution to the next. He carried on two entirely different conversations at the same time because one set of thoughts was not enough for him, and here he was, bald and gnarled, solving the problem of time shortage. Make more of it.

William Wykeham strolled across to her. 'Nay, mistress, you'll need more time than this to decide—'

'Decide what, Master Wykeham? I don't have to decide anything. I'm here on en route to Winchester, that's all.' She shook her head, partly in amusement at their assumptions, partly in apology. 'I can offer you my ideas for what they're worth, but what decisions are made are no concern of mine. And I *do* have to leave tomorrow.'

Master Wykeham looked across to Sir Rhyan, who leaned against the battlemented wall. 'You said there was no rush, didn't you, Sir Rhyan? A day or two either way, you said?'

'Of course there's no rush,' the carpenter called again, lifting his head from his wax writing-tablet, his stylus poised like a dart. 'Can't do this kind of thing in a rush. We need you here, Master Wykeham, and the lady, too, and you, Master John. Another day at least. Let's get this business sorted out while we have the chance or it'll look like a pig's ear again and our reputations gone. What do you say to that, Sponlee?'

Master Sponlee, the king's architect at Windsor, agreed quietly. 'It's true. Can *you* persuade the lady, Sir Rhyan? Will she give us another day of her time, d'ye think?'

Sir Rhyan sauntered across to Merielle, reading the resumed hostility in the set line of her mouth, the eyes that darted angrily from one face to the other in search of support. They rested on him accusingly as he drew near, both of them seeing her efforts of the last few hours about to be thrown away.

Using his gentlest manner, but without any hope of success, he held out a hand to take her arm. 'Come, mistress,' he said. 'A word in private, perhaps?'

Whatever he could have said would have been useless. Before his hand made contact, she had whirled away and was marching towards the gatehouse as fast as her legs could carry her. Bemused, the group watched as Sir Rhyan followed without attempting to catch her up, their mouths gently widening.

'Whew!' Wykeham said. 'Anyone know where the water-buckets are kept?'

'I think I may have put my foot in it,' said the master carpenter, picking his teeth with the stylus.

By chance, the two Canterbury grooms met their mistress as she approached the stables. They also saw who followed.

'Pedro. Daniel. Saddle my cob, then find Mistress Allene and see about getting the panniers packed—'

Sir Rhyan overlapped the last words. 'Forget that order!' His head tipped in silent command, dismissing the grooms before Merielle's order was complete. They blinked, hesitated and went.

'*What!* How *dare* you dismiss my servants? Leave me!'

'Keep your voice down, unless you want the whole castle to hear.' He walked towards her, backing her through the stable door where the shining rumps of two horses could be seen beyond empty stalls. The warm stable was scented with sweet hay, the light softly muted, but anger was upsetting the balance of Merielle's senses, leaving only two in working order.

She strode away from his intimidating advance. 'Leave me alone! I do not need you, sir, to persuade me to give them another day of my time,' she mimicked the architect. 'My time is my own to do with as I choose, and I do not choose to stay another day.' She was breathless with indignation. No matter how she had tried to put matters right, they continually went askew. It should have been the pleasantest of journeys. Instead, it was becoming a nightmare.

Framing himself against the light, Sir Rhyan stepped between Merielle and the doorway, his face deep in shadow. 'Go on,' he said. 'I'm listening.'

Her eyes widened in another flash of annoyance. 'Go on, what?' Her shaking arm pointed to the door, seeking a way for the sentence to emerge. 'You've seen them…heard them…out there. What's going on? What is all this? What are these extra days you've agreed for this visit? Tell me! I've a right to know what's being done with my time.'

'I made no arrangements for an extra day. None at all. The day or two either way that Wykeham mentioned was to do with setting off. Either Saturday or Monday. You yourself chose the earlier day. You might still have been at Canterbury, so why all the rush now?'

'I am a businesswoman, Sir Rhyan, and my days go according to my plan, no one else's. And what if I had set off with you tomorrow instead of yesterday? We'd still have been delayed here at Leeds?'

'The arrangements were made by Sir Adam, and those men are the ones he would have met if he'd been here instead of me. Ask *him* why he particularly wanted you to see the place. I don't know. And anyway, is one extra day such a catastrophe?'

'I would not have set off earlier if I'd wanted to arrive later, would I?' she snapped, coldly logical. 'And another thing you might explain, if you can, is why *they* think I'm being employed by the king, for pity's sake. Who gave them that idea? Was that Sir Adam, or was it yet another of your attempts to discipline me?'

'They think *what*?'

Exasperated, she turned away but, finding nowhere to go, turned back again, pointing towards the bailey. 'You must have heard them. They've been talking ever since chapel about me being one of them, involved in the renovations. It's ridiculous. They must know that the last people to be called in are those who decorate the walls while *they're* still pulling them down and putting them up again. Until new walls are built, how can anyone plan how to cover them? And the king's painter, too. What good is it him being here?'

'John Kenton's with me. I've seen what he did for Sir Adam and I asked to borrow him for a few months, that's all. He'll be doing work in this place afterwards; that's why he's involved. Does he believe the king's employing you, too?'

'Apparently.'

'Then perhaps it has something to do with the reputation of your workshop. Perhaps they assumed that your being here must have some significance. Could that be the reason?'

'Well, even if it is, that doesn't explain why the castellan and his lady are making such a fuss of me. Surely they don't go to such lengths for every female guest. I'm not even a noblewoman. Why, she implied that I could have *carte blanche* over the design of the queen's chambers. I'm a tapestry-maker, not a silk-weaver. Why should I care what her bed's covered with?'

'Why, indeed,' Sir Rhyan muttered, another frown fleeting across his brows. 'All the same, mistress, I believe we may have to give them their extra day.'

'Oh, no! An extra day for you to humiliate me more. No, thank you, I'll be no puppet for your game. Play it on your own, sir.' She lifted up the hem of her skirts

from the floor, ready to leave, then thought of more
with which to berate him while she had the chance.
'And then you had the effrontery to tell them…oh, it's
too embarrassing. I shall leave first thing in the morning. I don't like it here. I should never have come but
for your interference. But for you, sir, I'd have been…'
She bit her lip, regretting the blunder.

'Yes? Where would you have been?'

She hesitated, then made for the gap between him
and the empty stalls, heading for the doorway. 'I've
managed for three years without a man to tell me what
to do, and I believe I can reach Winchester by the same
method.'

Sidestepping, he reached out a long arm, scooping it
around her waist and pulling her backwards into him.
'Perhaps,' he said, 'but you've had your say and you'll
go nowhere until I've had mine.' He swung her, off-
balance, into the nearest empty stall, slamming her
against its high side and taking her wrists in mid-air as
her hands aimed for his head. Holding them up on to
the curved edge, he stilled her struggles with his body
and, although she was not a small woman, or a weak-
ling, she was no match for him.

'Now, lady,' he said to her averted cheek, 'I don't
know what's going on any more than you do, but I
mean to find out. And, until then, you're going to have
to find some more trust in me from somewhere. Yes, I
can see you're full of hurt, still, though God knows it's
taking long enough to heal, isn't it?'

'With good reason, sir!'

'Well, I could think of far worse things that could
happen to a woman with as much property as you.
Keep your anger aflame with damp fuel, if you wish,
but it seems to me a pitiful waste of energy.'

'All yours, of course, being channeled towards interference.'

'Yes. So you'd better get used to it.'

'Let me go. I have my own plans and I shall keep to them.'

'So have I, and I've planned to escort you to Winchester so you'll follow my lead if I have to chain you to the saddle.'

She faced him at last, her eyes like sword blades clashing with his, steel blue and boldly unnerving. 'Then that is what you'll have to do, sir!' She pushed, but made no impression on the barrier of his body.

He continued as though she had not spoken. 'Furthermore, you will spread your civility more evenly…' he held her back as she made another attempt '…if only for the comfort of our companions. You think you have a right to embarrass them by your tantrums?'

'What tantrums?' she yelled. 'Would it have been a tantrum for a man to insist on continuing the journey whenever he wished? Would it?'

His eyelids fell, slowly, then lifted to introduce the obvious rejoinder with a hint of amusement. 'You're not a man, but you're in my charge and you'll bend to my will, as a woman should. Yes, I can appreciate your anger at my implication—'

'Implication?' The word emerged as a stifled scream. 'When you as good as told them we were…! Argh! I'd as soon have a *worm* order my life.' Lowering her head, she heaved, catching him unawares after her insult and releasing herself to hurtle across the stall, hitting her shoulder hard on its other side. She clutched herself, frowning angrily. 'The truth would have done perfectly well.'

'No, it would not. The truth is none of their business.

And whether you approve of my explanation or not, you're going to have to pretend some kind of truce from here to Winchester.'

'To save your face?' Her head came up, her eyes black, blazing like polished jet in the light from the doorway. 'Hah. Whatever revenge you're planning since your defeat of three years ago, Sir Rhyan, you won't get any joy in that direction. The spitfire tamed? Never!'

She had expected an instant denial, of sorts, or some kind of sharp retort for which she braced herself, ready for the shock. His silence made her uneasy and when she looked up to find a reason for the delay, she saw that he was regarding her with an expression far removed from anger.

'My God,' he said. 'You *do* hate me, don't you?'

She looked away again. 'You've noticed. Well done.'

'Why so much?'

It was absurd. Ironic. Incongruous. Here was the man who had stirred her heart to hate, fear and blame, asking her why, when that same heart was pounding out rhythms of longing and desire so strong that she could feel them in the soles of her feet. She was aware of its beginnings, this sickness, this trembling in her knees, but then her greater pain had been still too raw for her to recognise any other emotion and she had dismissed it as something an infusion of feverfew would cure. At his appearance in Canterbury, too sudden for comfort, she had tried to summon up the same dismissive thoughts, but the sleepless night and the furtively searching eyes during the journey, the tight breathless thud in her chest when he appeared at her

side in the chapel, these were symptoms which feverfew could not begin to cure.

Yet she must continue to hate him, to combat his
attempts to revenge himself. A man's honour was a
fragile and precious thing. Her lips trembled as she
willed herself to recall her sister's appalling stupidity.
She must never allow it to happen to her.

He saw the struggle, the trembling lip. 'Revenge?'
he said, softly. 'Is that truly what you believe? After
three years?'

'Deny it!' she spat at him. 'Deny it till you're blue
in the face and I'll not believe you. Your offer to take
Sir Adam's place is proof enough of your intentions.
Too busy, was he?'

'No, mistress. Too ill.'

Her eyes searched his mouth, then his eyes.

'He was ill. I went to Canterbury to complete some
business for him, as I told you. But I wasn't going to
give you any more details in front of that artificial little
pie-frill. With the king's ear practically in the lad's
pouch, Sir Adam's indisposition would be royal fodder
before the poor man has chance to recover.'

'Not the pestilence, surely?'

'God's truth, woman!' The palm of his hand slapped
the top of the stall-post. 'You think my so-called desire
for revenge is great enough to take you where the sickness is? You think that, too, do you?'

No, she could not believe that, but neither would she
say so. 'What is it, then? Serious? And what of the
babe?'

'Well enough when I left. The gripes, and gout.
Nothing serious, but painful enough to stop him climb-
ing into a saddle.' He saw how Merielle's hand crept
up to rest beneath her breasts. He had not understood

until their meeting yesterday how she still suffered over her own loss, how the physical contact with her own infant niece could fill a void left aching, how marriage to his uncle could put that on a permanent basis, even though Sir Adam was not what she wanted. 'I would strike a bargain with you, mistress,' he said, suddenly.

'No bargains!'

'Tch!' He sighed, barring her way with his arm as she dodged. 'If you can keep to a truce until we reach Winchester, then I will explain to the others that we cannot stay here another day but depart tomorrow. And I will escort you safely, find lodgings, make arrangements for your comfort. Could you agree to such a bargain?'

Merielle looked beyond him to the doorway, towards a lightness that had been missing until now. His words were incredibly sweet, taking away the responsibilities she had dragged heavily on to her own shoulders out of pique at his appearance. It was a tempting proposal. 'I fully intend to leave here tomorrow, sir, with or without your assistance. Chaining me into the saddle would cause an outcry, I believe.' There was a softening in her tone that conveyed more than the obstinacy of the words.

Sir Rhyan smiled, recognising some progress. 'I see. And what of the truce? For appearances' sake? For our companions' sake?'

'For your sake, you mean.'

'And yours. It's easier than fighting. Better for the digestion.'

The effort of maintaining her antagonism removed the smile that almost appeared at his persuasion. She must not give way. Given an inch, the man would take a mile.

But out there in the castle bailey was a group of men, each of whom was making some show of being absorbed in the king's business, measuring, theorising, each one waiting to see how accurate was Sir Rhyan's flippant description of her. Either way, it was doubtful she could undo the damage now, but what would serve her purpose best? Sir Rhyan would do the explaining and she would be sweetly apologetic and what would they make of that? That the spitfire was the tamer or the tamed?

'I can give you no guarantee that a truce would hold as far as Winchester, Sir Rhyan. Any pretence at a friendship I do not feel would be strained to its limits within the hour, I fear. But for the sake of appearances—mine, not yours—I will endeavour to be civil.'

'It matters not whose appearance it benefits, mistress, yours or mine. I take it you wish to avoid that crowd out there?'

Merielle turned her back on him, now sure of victory. 'Yes, I do.'

But she had reckoned on her triumph without him. Her shoulders were grasped and she was swung round hard into his chest, bound by his arms. His blue eyes, half-closed in anger, pierced hers like lances and as she turned her head away to escape his mouth, she was brought back roughly by his hand in her hair, tipping her towards him.

'You will endeavour to be civil, will you, lady? I see. Then perhaps a lesson or two in civility would not come amiss, do you think?'

There was neither time to escape him nor, if she was truthful, was there the will, for the scent of him already filled her nostrils as his mouth covered hers, and her lips had already begun to search for more, long before any sense of outrage had begun to stir.

Like a dry moorland roaring out of control at the first flame, the kiss caught them both unprepared and Merielle was at once enclosed within the furnace, unaware that she herself was responding, burning for those few moments with a white-hot intensity she had never experienced before. Matching him, she dug her fingers deep into his thick hair, her thumbs almost scorched by the softness of his ears, his hard jaws, his neck, her sense of touch leaping into the overpowering closeness of him, greedy for gratification. Better than sight or sound were the feel and taste of him, absorbing him through her skin and into her mouth, through every rib, quaking her thighs. Involuntarily, she pushed herself against him, trembling at his hardness and opening her mouth in an agony of desire; she flooded herself with love for him.

He swung her round again with a soft thud into the side of the stall, his arms slackening to begin a search over the full curves of her body, his mouth alone mastering her.

A shattering crash from the other side of the stall broke into the voiceless encounter, followed by a high-pitched neigh. The sound quenched the fire, waking Merielle to the danger within. Speechless, breathless, utterly confused, she twisted away and leaned against the panelling, her forehead pushing against the cool metal rim. 'Madness!' she whispered. Her legs shook, uncontrollably.

Sir Rhyan, who rarely registered shock, watched her but said nothing, indicating by his stillness that this was something he had neither intended nor expected. But more than this was his jubilation at the discovery that her protestations of hate were meant to conceal something far more powerful. His voice was subdued. 'Merielle? You're not weeping? I never meant that to happen. Can you forget it?' He bent his head to hers. 'Come, we'll give them the slip, through the wall and down the steps to the lakeside.'

'I'm not weeping.' She brushed her fingers across her eyes. 'Of course I can forget. It was nothing. A moment's madness, that's all.' She sniffed, smoothing her rumpled cote-hardie and rejecting his offered hand. 'No, I can manage.'

The group at the far end of the bailey, measuring-rods held like lances and with eyes as large as sauce-bowls, watched the two supposed lovers emerge, their arms around each other, her shoulder fitting neatly into his. From behind, they could see that the girl's arm was being held behind her back in mock-capture and, a few moments later as the curious crowd peered over the high wall, they saw that, down below them, the two were feeding the swans in unusual silence.

Chapter Five

Pretending a friendship Merielle did not feel turned out to be child's play compared to the pretence that she had forgotten his kiss or indeed that anything had happened that needed forgetting. Strangely, although she had heaped upon Sir Rhyan's head almost every delinquency she could think of, she could never have accused him of garrulousness, for when she had found it quite impossible to talk, he had matched her introspection with a calm reserve of his own. Only when they returned to the bailey did he resume his conversational tone to explain to the others that he had decided not to allow Mistress St Martin another day in their company since his uncle depended upon their return for his own affairs. As Merielle could not bring herself to smile apologetically, as she had meant to do, they seemed to assume that the decision was mutual as well as regrettable.

But the fear that Sir Rhyan might expect their so-called truce to extend to further public displays of accord whenever he felt it to be appropriate was never far from her mind, and so she took the earliest opportunity to make her feelings clear. Within the ice-cool passageway leading to the *gloriette*, out of sight of the servants, she detached her hand abruptly from his.

He caught her arm to hold her back when she would have moved on, waiting until she looked at him, albeit unwillingly and with some animosity. 'All right. Your feathers are ruffled. I know what you're telling me.'

In other circumstances she might have protested, but the eyes that held hers were unwavering and she knew that his understanding of her did not mean the same as acceptance. Given an inch, he had every intention of holding on to it.

'That's enough,' he said. 'You've made your point. Now give me your hand.'

With obvious reluctance, she replaced it in his, drawing herself to her full stately height as though the act was of no real consequence. 'For the sake of appearances, you said. Who's looking now, Sir Rhyan?'

'I am and you are. I also said quite a lot more.'

One beautifully arched black eyebrow hitched and fell again.

'I said that you would bend to my will while I was in charge. Remember that, mistress.'

'I agreed to a certain civility,' she replied with disdain. She did not like the uncomfortable sound of bending to his will. 'Civility is not mute obedience, sir. Remember *that*.'

'You wish to continue the debate?' Deliberately, he moved round to face her, watching the slow flush that flooded the wide neckline of her cote-hardie and followed it upwards to her eyes.

She turned her head away, even while gathering courage to reply. 'Thank you, no. Nor do I wish to lose my appetite for supper.'

He towered over her as no one else had ever done,

taking her chin in his hand and turning her back to
him, forcing her to meet his eyes. There was no trace
of the amusement she had half-expected. 'Your appetite, Merielle St Martin, is of great interest to me,' he
said softly.

Biting back the defensive insult that she had prepared, she jerked her head away angrily, fully understanding that his reference to her appetite had nothing
to do with supper. And that was the second time he
had called her Merielle.

The peaceful view across the lake from the window
of her chamber might have been the perfect antidote to
the turmoil of the afternoon, had Merielle given it a
chance.

'He's the same as all the others,' she told Allene,
glaring with distaste at a grey-bearded and decrepit St
Joseph who stood helplessly by his wife on the tapes-
tried wall.

'What others?' Allene countered drily, unlacing the
back of Merielle's gown. 'He's not like that Gervase
of Caen and he's not like—'

'Oh, don't go on. I meant men in general.'

'Ah, kissed you, did he?'

'Churl! Great lout!'

Behind her mistress's back, Allene smiled. 'Aye,
he's a big 'un and no mistake. Come on, lift your arms
out, lass.'

Dreamily, she stepped out of the blue-grey puddle
and went to sit on the cushioned step that surrounded
the bed. An early cuckoo called from the distant woodland, drawing her eyes to the window where clouds
hustled, filling the sky. Allene was right; he was not
like the other men she knew except that the same look

that Bonard had spoken of was there, behind the arrogant stare. Your appetite is of great interest to me, he had told her. He was a man. It would be.

Her appetite, she recalled, had amazed and disturbed her. Even now, she could hear the roar of the inferno, feel its searing heat as he had grasped her head, holding her lips under his and lighting a fire that she had never known lay ready, having submerged such conceptions in her loathing of the man. He had responded, of course, with his hands. What man would ignore her immediate interest? In that, he was the same, but he must never be given the chance again for, if he could seduce his uncle's new wife, he would believe himself well-capable of winning *her* over, especially after this. A man who could take advantage of Laurel's childish longing for approval was truly despicable.

Allene eased herself down by her side, folding a pair of woollen hose over her hand. 'Well, lass? Why so miserable? I thought you'd reached some understanding, by the look o' things.'

And that was something else he'd try to take advantage of.

Feeling that her control of the situation was less secure than she had intended, Merielle did what she believed most women would do in the same situation, dressing for supper in her brightest gown of golden yellow deepened with last summer's dyers' greenweed. That it also had the lowest neckline, resting barely on the points of her shoulders, was no matter when the surcoat of fur-edged tawny Italian velvet was what she knew would catch the eye, for it was skilfully woven, soft and luxurious. With its completely sideless bodice, the surcoat caught the men's attention less for its sumptuousness than for its facility to skim tantalisingly over the tight-fitting cote-hardie beneath, and there were few men in the hall who did not, at some point in the proceedings, envy that tawny fabric. Not even the chaplain.

Her determination to enjoy her last meal at the castle was aided and abetted by Master John Kenton, the king's official painter who was being borrowed by Sir Rhyan for a few months. To her relief, he was not in the least put out at having to miss the extra day, agreeing with Merielle that a painter's task would not begin until the new chambers were built.

He was darkly attractive, neatly bearded and with silky hair that lay in an obedient fringe around his head, skipping a beat here and there across a handsome brow. He was not as intense as Master Wykeham, his enthusiasm being reserved for those whose interest he was sure of, like Merielle and Sir Rhyan. His expressive dark eyes smiled in reassurance, wrinkling unexpectedly, prompting Merielle to suspect that he was older than his appearance suggested.

His smile was apologetic. 'Their talk is too technical for me, mistress. They're all master craftsmen of great ingenuity, so engrossed in their schemes they can talk of little else. I shall be glad to see more of the countryside after being closeted up in Canterbury for so long.'

Merielle saw Sir Rhyan on Master John's other side conclude his conversation and turn towards them, listening but making no contribution. 'But you're not a southerner, Master John?' she said. 'Do I detect an accent from the regions? East, is it?'

'St Albans is where I trained, mistress.'

Merielle's eyes lit up. 'Then you will have the great

works of Matthew Paris to live up to; no wonder the king values you.'

His eyes widened beneath the dark fringe. 'You know of him?'

'I've read his life of St Edmund and, yes, I know of him. But who doesn't?'

'A good many men here, I should think, let alone the women. You read Latin, then?'

She nodded, modestly, and without looking she could see that Sir Rhyan's eyebrows had lifted, then lowered.

'How so?'

'My father had two daughters but no sons, and he was a progressive man, in most things.' She aimed the last three words high. 'But tell me, if you please, about your remark just now. You seemed to be saying that your status as king's painter is of less consequence than the others here. Is that really so, or is that your humility?'

Laughing almost soundlessly, he leaned back to glance at Sir Rhyan. 'Beauty, learning and perception, too. What next, I wonder? Ah, mistress,' he gasped, trying to replace the laugh, 'it's not so much humility as a fact of life. Architects are born, mechanics, engineers, surveyors and masons get into deep trouble if their designs don't work. Painters are not quite in that class, except…'

'Except those who paint in the king's palaces, surely?'

'I was going to say except those who produce the illuminated gospels in the scriptoria of our great abbeys. Painters will never be as indispensable as those who build such abbeys in the first place. The fame of Matthew Paris rests on the fact that he was an exception: historian, artist and illuminator, goldsmith, Benedictine monk, traveller and diplomat.' He regarded her from beneath the fringe again, waiting for her comments.

'Even so, Master John, I cannot accept that a man of your calibre is not valued, as you would have me believe. What have you been working on at Canterbury? And didn't Sir Adam have you do some work for him? Are not those walls in my late sister's chamber of your doing?'

Three questions at once. He plumped for the middle one. 'Sir Adam did not exactly request me, mistress.' His smile was rueful. 'His grace the king sent me to Winchester to do the work for Sir Adam…'

'…As a reward for Sir Adam's services.'

He dodged around the implication. 'It was certainly a reward for *me* because I like Winchester and because there I met your delightful sister. It was so sad about her untimely death. Is that why you go…to see your young niece?'

The smile that washed over Merielle's face like sunlight could not have failed to convince both men that her eagerness was genuine. Her reply was no more than a breathless, 'Yes,' before the contest was resumed in which both players tried to steer the conversation away from themselves and towards each other. 'And have you ever made any cartoons for the tapestry trade?' she asked.

'Indeed I have; we painters never refuse work of that kind. I designed a series of four cartoons for your late husband. Before your time,' he added.

'For my…for Philippe?' Merielle looked at him, sharply. 'I didn't know…' She stopped before her astonishment could sound too much like ignorance. Before her time. Why should she have known? Her attempt to steer the conversation foundered.

Master John sensed her dismay. 'That's not so surprising, is it, mistress? How often do the designers of tapestries get a mention? Or even the workshop that made them, often as not. The only things you'll know for sure is where they're hung, who ordered them and how much he paid. You can always be sure he'll make that known. Eh?' He laughed, merrily, nodding towards the bluff Yeaveley and the gregarious Wykeham, 'That crowd get mentioned by name, but painters don't usually stick signs and epigrams all over their work like they do, where they're hidden till it's too late. We'd be told to paint 'em out.'

'So, do you do as Matthew Paris did and draw portraits of yourself into your designs?' The notion clearly delighted her.

'Yes, mistress. When I want to be associated with a piece of work, that's exactly what I do.'

'Really? So on whose wall do you appear in the St Martin tapestries? Some wealthy London merchant, was it?'

'No. The king's.'

Merielle stared, then looked away over the heads of the diners and across the smoke-filled hall. She saw entries in one of the old ledgers made before her marriage to Philippe St Martin, some mention of Master John, no more than that, certainly no Kenton or the name of the buyer. How long before her marriage had that been? Her eyes swivelled away and found those of Sir Rhyan, without registering his presence. 'The king's walls? Where?'

'That's not so easy to say with tapestries, is it, mistress? They could be in any one of his palaces by now, or in one of his houses, taken from place to place with the furniture. It's anybody's guess where they'll be at this moment. I simply had to design to the size of the loom. Do you still make them all at Canterbury?'

'Only the largest ones. But now I have several itinerant tapestry-weavers, Flemings, you know, who take the equipment to wherever they're required and work *in situ*.'

'You mean, they take the loom in pieces and assemble it when they arrive?'

'Yes, there's always a carpenter to do that. They take whatever materials they need and send back to the workshop for more. I have my own dye-house, and we have spinners, websters, finishers and carpenters.'

Master John nodded, sighing with something like envy. 'My work is almost always done *in situ*. I'd sometimes love to stay in my own workshop where it's peaceful and comfortable.'

Sir Rhyan unexpectedly broke in. 'You'll have peace enough up in Yorkshire, John. You've never been up there, have you?'

'No, but it sounds like my kind of place. Master Rutland was telling me you have some lead for his windows up there on your land. Is that so? It's a devil to get hold of the stuff nowadays. So expensive. Anyone who has lead mines is fortunate, indeed, with all this new building going on.'

Almost imperceptibly, Sir Rhyan's head dropped, then lifted, his eyes searching. 'Ye…es,' he said, eventually.

There was a pause, during which Master John appeared to expect more, but it was Merielle who broke the uncomfortable silence. 'No,' she said. 'Sir Rhyan means no, Master John. The lead-bearing land to which you refer is my property. It belonged to my late father, whose land I inherited. The old lead mines have been out of use for some years now, since the pestilence took so many of the workforce, unless my information is out of date. I shall have to do some checking, it seems.' Suddenly, she felt quite breathless and realised that, beneath the gaudy yellow gown, her legs had begun to shake.

The mortified Master John Kenton, king's painter, held his head as though it might fall off, his long fingers sticking up through his silky hair like spikes.

Watching the determined approach of Mistress St Martin towards the castellan's wife, Sir Rhyan tapped Master John on the shoulder. 'Come, John. Come with me,' he said, swinging sideways off the bench.

Master John sighed and straightened. 'If you're going to murder me, I need more notice than that.'

'You're safe till you've painted my walls, man.'

'Let's hope they're big ones, then.' He stood, unlinking his athletic form smoothly and pulling the inconspicuous brown woollen gupon down over his backside. He followed Sir Rhyan to a bench in a shadowy recess away from the clatter and chatter of the diners where the air was cooler and more breathable and from where Sir Rhyan could see Merielle.

'What do you know, John?' he said, as they sat together.

'About the lead mines? Nothing, except what Rutland—'

'Not about the lead. I can soon sort that out. The tapestries. You must have a good idea of where they are, or at least where they were intended for. And when.'

'Didn't I say?'

'You know you didn't.' Master John's reticence did him credit. He was not one to crow about his important commissions nor did he indulge in gossip, but Sir Rhyan wanted information. 'I know you keep your own counsel, John, but I have reasons for needing to know.'

Master John had only to follow the direction of Sir Rhyan's eyes to understand the reasons. 'Yes, she's very lovely. Probably the most beautiful woman I've ever seen. Intelligent. Sensitive. She deserves better.'

Sir Rhyan turned to look at him, sharply. 'Better than what?'

It had been an undertone, not meant for explanation. 'Better than having to chase halfway across the country to hold someone else's brat. A woman like that should have a clutch of her own by now. Did you not see her face?'

'Yes, I saw it. Now tell me about the tapestries.'

Anyone would have thought, John reflected, that the man was indifferent, but John had seen him drink in her loveliness and knew otherwise. 'It was November fifty-three, when his grace the king commissioned me to draw up cartoons to be made up at the St Martin workshop.'

'Why there, of all places?'

'Well, I suppose it was because of their reputation and because they were intended for the archbishop's palace in Canterbury. Quality and convenience, that's what clients want these days.'

'They were a gift to the archbishop, then?'

'Hah!' Master John gave a gentle bark. 'That's good. You know his grace better than that, I'm sure. He gives only when he wants something in return. The archbishop's rooms are used by the king when he's in Canterbury and very fine they are, too. You'll have seen the hall, I expect. The tapestries were in place two years later, behind the dais.'

'Before Mistress St Martin's time.'

'Just. She married St Martin late in fifty-five, didn't she? His grace had me painting the walls after that, which is where I first caught sight of the lady.'

'You mean, that's where she…?'

'…met the king. Right. Autumn of fifty-six, that was.'

Sir Rhyan nodded slowly, remembering the formal tone of his prosecution. He ran a hand through his hair and round his chin, unaware that Master John noted every move and gesture. 'So, you met her there, did you?' He returned the elegant hand to his thigh.

'No. Not so. Artists are invisible, I told you. She's never once clapped eyes on me till yesterday.'

'So how exactly did she get an audience with his grace? Does she know Archbishop Islip, is that it?'

'Most people of substance in Canterbury know Simon Islip, I should think, for one reason or another, but he doesn't make a habit of introducing beautiful women to his grace the king. He's quite capable of doing that for himself, as I expect you know.'

The hall became hushed as the first notes of a harpist floated up to the heavy beams and the silence between the two men was filled with the first few sweet phrases of a love song, of a wife's yearning for her absent husband. Sir Rhyan's question was whispered, and urgent. 'What are you telling me, John?'

'Shh! I'm not telling you anything.'

Rightly, Sir Rhyan suspected that Master John's revelations had taken him further than usual and that the artist was using the sweet music as an excuse to halt the interrogation. So he waited patiently until it was finished, then continued in the interval. 'Would Mistress St Martin have not seen the tapestries there, and recognised them?'

Master John reached towards the tray of clay beakers being brought round by a brawny kitchen-lad. He handed one to Sir Rhyan, sipping the frothy head off the other. 'No, they were not in the chamber where the king was but in the hall. Adam and Eve. The Temptation. The Fall. The Expulsion from the Garden. The usual stuff,' he added, dismissively. 'They like the same old stories.'

'So you had to work with Philippe St Martin for a while.'

'A few consultations, that's all. But I'd never have got to see the finished pieces if I hadn't been at the palace doing the walls in the archbishop's private apartments. Shh…listen.'

Again, the harpist claimed their attention with a song of battle and heroism and glorious death. The applause was tumultuous, flowing into a welcome as a group of musicians joined in with trumpet, tabor and two stringed instruments, a rebec and a cittern. The quintet was accomplished, the sound fruity, a song of summer and of love turning to apathy in winter.

'Tell me about him,' Sir Rhyan said, shivering a little.

Master John smiled, teasingly. 'You really want to know?'

'No. But tell me, just the same.'

'Excellent craftsman. Meticulous. Knew his trade inside—'

'Not *that*!'

The smile turned to a squeak of mischief and he

drank deeply into the cider, emerging with a moustache of froth. 'Pathetic,' he whispered.

'Eh?'

'Pathetic!' he yelled, as a crash of chords muffled him. 'Pitiful! No match for a woman like that.'

The music this time was loud enough to make conversation a possibility, boisterous enough to make the two men shout above the choruses of a hundred beakers clattering on the table-tops, and the words that above all others should have been hushed were yelled out loud.

'You mean he was…?'

'Oh, yes! Terrified of 'em. Shouldn't think he'd know what to do if he fell over one in the dark. High voice.' Master John jabbed his finger upwards to demonstrate.

'So why did she marry him, d'ye think? Money?'

'Well, she certainly didn't chase all the way down to Canterbury to find *him*, did she? Not from Lincoln, or wherever. He was probably sent up there to find *her*.'

Sir Rhyan frowned. 'Sent by whom?' He was obliged to lipread most of Master John's reply.

'Now that, my friend, would be pure speculation. As an artist, I can speculate in at least a dozen different directions at once, but I'm not going to on this. Work it out for yourself, if you please, sir.'

'Thank you, I will,' Sir Rhyan murmured into the din. His first attempts were in place before the noise had died down by which time he had deduced that an interval of two years between one marriage and the next indicated some extremely tardy wooing. Incompetent was the word that sprang to mind. As to who had made it worth Philippe St Martin's while to attempt such an unwanted mission, and for what purpose, his speculation on that theme took no time at all.

Master John felt that he had atoned for his innocent blunder. Brushing drips of water from his fringe, he looked at his hand then up at the rafters. 'It's pouring with rain through here. Was that thunder?'

'Hard to tell,' Sir Rhyan said, standing. 'Damn!'

'What? Are you wet, too?'

'No. She's gone.'

It was not easy to slam a door as thick as one's wrist, but Merielle tried it, nevertheless.

'Bolt it!' she said, curtly, to the startled Bess. 'I don't want that toad marching in here.'

There would have been some satisfaction to be had from such a defence had the deeply offending toad pleaded for an audience while she cruelly ignored him, but no such sound, contrite or otherwise, was heard, only the battering of rain upon the shutters. This was no time for common sense, logic or excuses. Already thrown this way and that by emotions she could neither explain nor control, Merielle attempted to blank out of her mind everything except the scene in which Sir Rhyan's floundering 'Ye…es' appeared to be the proof she needed, if she needed any at all, that his motives were entirely self-serving. From now on, he was the ultimate villain, and everything that had gone wrong in the last twenty-four hours could safely be laid at his door.

If it had been as simple as that, no doubt she would have fallen instantly asleep, but the shutters were opened enough to let in a blast of damp air and a ray of greyish light long before her pillow had had time to dry.

* * *

Again, it would have pandered to her sense of outrage if he had said something that she could have ignored with contempt, cutting him down to size. But he gave her no chance, addressing his questions on their readiness to Allene—who obliged, of course—and not to her. It was as though their truce had never existed. The closest he came was when he picked her up like a toy, muffled in thick woollen cloaks, and almost threw her into the saddle. Which said a lot for his strength but little for his manners.

The sleeting rain was merciless and their last view of the glorious castle was little better than their first, every effort being devoted to finding a strip of the track not filled by mud or water. The nightmare worsened.

She had thought of turning back, but that would have called for some communication, an argument at best, a showdown at worst, and she had no stomach for either. Anyway, why should she be turned from the tiny creature she wished to see beyond anything and whom, if she herself had not had a business to run, she would have seen long before now.

The Flemings were coming over in droves nowadays, since Queen Phillipa had fostered the connection, being one of them. They were the best, of course, but for conscience's sake there were also the widows of Englishmen who had died in the pestilence, women with families but no breadwinners. She could not ignore them, and any responsibility to her tiny niece at Winchester would have to take into account her duty to those women far worse off than herself. Even so, the yearning for motherhood tore at her heart, robbing her of reason. No man would ever understand it. No woman, either.

Chapter Six

The second stage of their journey from Canterbury was by no means comparable to the first relaxed and noisy departure when the sun had warmed the tops of their heads and whitened the May blossom into shimmering clouds. Nevertheless, there were rewards to be had for setting off before the skies had had time to clear, one of which was that their way would be less hampered by other travellers, at least until they reached Detling, about six miles to the north-west. Another was that their voluble friend, William Wykeham, the king's rising star, had opted for an extra day at Leeds Castle, after all, according to his master's instructions. His insistent conversation would not be missed.

Merielle rode in silence, coldly hurt and bitter. Having her doubts about Sir Rhyan's duplicity proved with such accuracy had done nothing to lessen the shock, and now she did not know how she could tolerate the pain of it for the rest of the journey with his company to reinforce its significance. The long hours of night had refused to accommodate her denial that his kiss had meant anything to her; her tears had been for all the things she had missed and was destined to miss for ever. The furnace would have to burn itself out unattended. In the blustering rain and the hard facts of day, her conjecture about what his next affront would be dogged each soggy hoofbeat, thankfully eliminating future hospitality from the list, for surely there could be no more of the king's properties needing renovation on their way.

Snatches of the haunting love-song from last evening's minstrels broke into her grey thoughts, hummed by Master John who rode at her side. He stopped humming as Merielle looked his way, blinking at the rain and tipping his hooded head towards his young assistant, Padraig, who held the rope of their packhorse on one side and the hand of Bess on the other. His dexterity was commendable.

Merielle dropped her head, laughing.

'That's better,' Master John said. 'My lad and your maid. That gives us something else in common, mistress.'

The idea warmed her, but she did not pursue it. 'You should see the young men with broken hearts, Master John. What's one more?'

The redness around her lovely eyes was not caused by rain, that much Master John knew, but why these two should be so much at odds with each other was beyond his understanding. Their pretence at amity had not fooled him as it had the others, and now his blunder had wrecked even that. He looked ahead at the broad erect figure on the black stallion, impervious both to the weather and, seemingly, to the lady's aloofness. But this did not deceive Master John either, for he had caught Sir Rhyan's darting glance towards her from beneath black brows and knew that her manner disturbed him more than he was admitting. As an artist,

Master John was as expert at observation as he was at speculation.

Determined not to experience the same fiasco as on Saturday when they were stuck at the tail-end of an accumulation of travellers, Sir Rhyan had issued instructions that, on catching up with a slower-moving party, they must make their way round it to the road ahead. In theory, this should have worked satisfactorily, but by now their own party numbered about twenty-six horses, including pack-animals, and the track was not always wide enough for this manoeuvre. Consequently, there were two occasions when he had to come to Merielle's rescue and drag her by the bridle through the crowds. The second time was on the approach to Detling.

'There's no need,' she told him, stiffly. 'We're almost there.'

'Where?'

'Detling. We'll be dismounting soon. What's the rush?'

'No, we won't.'

'Well, I will, sir!'

'We've only been on the road an hour or so,' he said to his stallion's ears. 'We stop at Snodland to eat, not before.'

She glared as he pulled out the leather purse-thong and threaded it through her cob's bit again, but was obliged to look away as he glared back as if to challenge her from his greater height. 'The usual gallantry,' she muttered, clenching her teeth.

'Yes. I'll explain things later.'

'Save yourself the trouble of concocting a story, sir. I understand perfectly already.'

'No, you don't.'

In the event, they stopped long enough at Detling for the women to make themselves more comfortable, then they were off again, passing a bedraggled group of rain-soaked pilgrims who slithered ankle-deep through mud, their long staffs sounding the depth of each watery hole.

Along the forested hillside, a group ahead of them peeled away to visit Boxley Abbey where the Rood of Grace would no doubt move for them if their donations were acceptable. Others left the track to visit the small Carmelite Priory at Aylesford, none of them hearing Sir Rhyan's cynical remark that they'd never reach Winchester or anywhere else if they stopped at every abbey along the way, quite missing the point of their venture. Maidstone passed them by in the distance, washed by a pale light through the clouds, and by the time Snodland appeared, the marshy valley was alight with sunshine and hoods had been pushed back. The swollen Medway glistened, lapping over its banks.

'The ford's going to be too deep,' Sir Rhyan said to his men.

'Of course it isn't,' Merielle said. 'We can pull our legs up if it comes any higher than the horses' bellies. We shall have to go miles further upstream to find another place. Come, we've done it before.' She leaned forward. 'And let go my bridle, damn you! I'm not a child!'

Descending sharply towards the thatched rooftops of Snodland, they found a sandy loop where locals were already crossing the river, thigh-high, carrying sacks of flour on their shoulders and children on their backs. There the riders entered, with the water pushing past aggressively just below their feet, the clatter of the mill-wheel echoing across the swirling surface. Master

John helped Allene, Padraig helped Bess, Sir Rhyan would have helped Merielle, but she ignored all his offers and suggestions. Finally, in exasperation, he descended upon her, splashing noisily and catching at her bridle, almost yanking the reins out of her hands.

'*This* way, woman! D'ye want to get sucked into yon whirlpool? For pity's sake!' He hauled the cob alongside. 'You've made your displeasure obvious enough to everyone, now give it a rest, will you?'

'For appearances' sake?' she snarled, angry at her own ineptitude.

He reined the stallion in, still knee-deep in water, his leg hitting hers as he swung round. He was almost black with wet, his hair cutting swathes like daggers across his forehead. 'Merielle,' he said.

Her heart ached, briefly, then snapped shut again.

'Merielle, we have several more days of this. Is this how you want them to be? Is this what contents you? Can you not wait for an explanation before jumping to your own conclusions? It's not what you think, you know.'

'And you're so sure of my thoughts, are you?'

'On this, yes. You're not so hard to read as all that, you know. Come, can we not continue the truce we started? It was not so very uncomfortable, was it?'

Twisting the greasy reins and feeling the cold trickle of rainwater down her neck, Merielle experienced a desperate need of some small grain of comfort and, coinciding with his conciliatory tone, the persistent urge to relent washed away the groundwork of the night. Her mind was apparently as readable as he had said it was.

'Merielle? A short truce, until we've had a chance

to talk? Re-negotiable? I know you can concede no more than that.'

'No more than that,' she agreed, watching his beautiful hands. Their backs glistened with wet dark hairs, and the memory of their pressure on her body was a sweet one never to be repeated. She supposed he had already put it from his mind, along with a hundred others.

He nodded in satisfaction, turning both their horses and leading her safely towards the shallow bank. 'We need to get at our dry clothes and some food,' he said. 'Come, I know of a place.'

'You're regretting we didn't wait until tomorrow.'

'On the contrary, I was as eager to leave the place as you were.'

Steaming with damp, but nourished, the party took once more to the high ground out of Snodland up on to the edge of the woodland, the land rising steeply on one side, catching the sun and the freshness of scented rainwater on every surface. White and pink hawthorn blossom dripped heavily into spumes of cow-parsley, with stitchwort and eyebright winking from between their leggy stalks. While the diamond-studded countryside enclosed them and stretched ahead, one might have been deceived into thinking that their comforts were completely restored, but the comforting of the heart required a different kind of solace and, communication being what it was, the pretence strained at Merielle, even on such a day.

She did her best by talking to Master John, and when Sir Rhyan joined in it gave her a chance to hear his voice in peace instead of discord. When thatched roofs appeared in the distance, the leaders halted at the steep downward path, calling to Sir Rhyan, 'Kemsing, sir?'

'No, we go on a bit round the corner. It's Otford tonight.' He held the hint of a smile in his eyes as he turned to Master John and Merielle. 'The archbishop's palace. That all right?'

Master John scoffed. 'You jest. You mean his stables?'

'I mean his palace.'

After that he would say no more on the subject and Merielle took it for granted that he must have good reason for being so sure of his welcome. At Otford, the archbishop's palace courtyard teemed with liveried men, their mounts, packhorses, servants and house officials whose faces registered disbelief and consternation at the arrival of another party seeking hospitality. At the sight of the white homespun habits of monks amongst them, Merielle was ready to turn away. 'Oh, no,' she said to Allene, 'the men can stay here. We'll go on. Come.'

Sir Rhyan stopped her. 'No, mistress. Wait. Leave it to me.'

'But it's an abbot's party,' she argued. 'We can't possibly impose ourselves upon the Cistercians. They won't want…'

He laughed. 'That's a risk they have to take when they travel. And anyway, I'd know that face anywhere.'

At the top of the stone steps leading up to the first floor hall, a lean white figure emerged with the chamberlain, deep in conversation. The monk did not look up until he reached the bottom, then his lined face broke into a network of cracks as surprise and pleasure lit his deep eyes. He held out his hands in welcome to Sir Rhyan. 'My son! What on earth do you do here so soon? I understood Sir Adam's party would not be here till tomorrow. He's not with you?' He glanced over Sir Rhyan's shoulder.

Kneeling briefly to kiss the abbot's fingers, Sir Rhyan explained, 'I come in his place, Father Abbot, to escort his sister-in-law. My timing went askew, I fear.'

'Ah, no.' The gaunt abbot stopped the apology with a hand. 'Mine, too, my son. I should have been here on Saturday, is that not so, Edmund?' He brought forward the chamberlain who had stood to one side in the hope that the two friends could solve the dilemma better than him.

'That's so, Father. And Sir Adam informed me it would be Tuesday, at least. Instead, you're both here together. It's going to be a tight squeeze. Just as well the archbishop's not here, too.'

The abbot threw back his head, revealing an Adam's apple of immense proportions that plummeted and rose like a yo-yo. 'Now that,' he said, spreading his hands, 'would have been the tightest squeeze imaginable.' His laugh was a wheeze: his coughing lasted too long. 'Never mind, we'll make do. You must stay, my friend. We insist, do we not, Edmund?'

With little choice, Edmund agreed. 'Er...oh, yes, indeed we do, Father. Is this Sir Adam's sister-in-law?' He peered sideways. 'She's not staying with us?'

Sir Rhyan turned. Merielle was already doing the same, her ladies and grooms with her, heading for the gateway. He ran, catching at the cob's bridle and pulling it round again, then he held up his arms to her.

Before a courtyard full of curious men, any decision of hers was expected to be terminated in favour of his, which was even more irritating than a simple change of plan would have been. She frowned down at him, but he stood firm.

'Come, it's all right. They'll make room for us. He's Robert Monkton, the Abbot of Fountains, our neighbour.' And when she still hesitated he took hold of her wrists and pulled gently until she relented and lost her balance.

Although unaccustomed to the company of women, Abbot Monkton was as charming as any courtier, and if he found anything disturbing in Merielle's sunripened beauty, he gave no sign of it. Rather, the astute abbot saw that the shoe was on the other foot and so he did what he could to put Merielle at her ease with, 'Mistress St Martin, it has long been an ambition of mine to meet my other more elusive neighbour. You are missed up in north Yorkshire, you know.'

'Thank you, Father. I'm happy to meet you at last, but we cannot stretch the archbishop's hospitality like this. I shall—'

'Mistress St Martin, my monks require nothing more than a dry floor to sleep on. Nor do I require the king's bed that Edmund insists on foisting upon me. A straw pallet will do perfectly well. See, Edmund?' He turned to the relieved chamberlain, who smiled at the instant solution. 'Take the ladies through and put me in the day-parlour. Plenty of room there.'

Merielle's colour had drained away, though he appeared not to notice. She swallowed, hearing a rushing waterfall inside her head. 'The *king's* bed, Father Abbot?'

With an eloquent gesture, then tucking his hands away, he invited her to follow him up the steps to the hall. 'His grace stays here several times a year, doesn't he, Edmund?'

Beaming with pleasure, Edmund agreed. 'The whole court had Christmas here ten years ago and we're only just recovering from it.' He laughed, leaving his guests in no doubt how the purse-strings had been stretched at the archbishop's expense in spite of the hospitality allowance. 'But the king's solar is reserved for the archbishop's special guests like yourself and the abbot.'

The lightest possible nudge in the small of her back was intended to move her on, but still she balked. 'Father, I could not…' But the nudge then became a strong arm that encircled her waist and, unable to resist it, she was propelled forward to follow in the men's footsteps against every scruple she could summon. Unable even to turn and protest, but with a rage mounting at every step, she found herself inside the great upper hall that smelled of sweet rushes and beeswax.

So, this was his latest provocation. Despite his desire for a truce, he was not going to let up. One each day, so far.

The best chambers used by King Edward and Queen Phillipa were situated in a complex of buildings leading towards the quieter side of the manor overlooking the archbishop's garden. Previous occupants had added to and altered it as the need took them, and here they entertained visiting prelates, held council, and rested from administrative duties. Although most of the rooms in the palace were used for a variety of purposes, there was no real shortage when all but the archbishop's most prestigious guests slept in the great hall, the stables, stores and outhouses.

The large solar into which Merielle and her ladies were shown was a square tower adjoining the main building that faced south and east, well away from the busy hall. But none of this registered with Merielle through her indignation at being thrust yet again into the memory of an incident she had tried hard to forget. To drag her back once more into another of the king's chambers suggested malice, no more, no less; the desire to rub her nose in the fact that she had sought the king's help against an absurd injunction.

He would have her believe that Leeds Castle was to have been Sir Adam's first stop, but Sir Adam had not used Leeds on their journey last year. It *must* have been his doing. Then he had appropriated her lead mines. Now this. What next?

She threw her vexed question at Allene, with another 'How could he?' along with a distasteful glance at the massive bed, equally as large as the last one. Covered with fine white linen sheets, white woollen blankets and folded-back furs, it had already been prepared for the abbot who, as a Cistercian, would prefer to do without the costly and exquisite covers woven with the king's cypher, though he could not escape the bed-curtains. These hung from the suspended canopy to the floor in heavy folds of red silk embroidered with gold. The absence of any pillows or matching cushions was another indication that the abbot's needs had been regarded.

'How could he, love?' Allene straightened with a groan and turned from the pannier, hobbling across to the window- enclosure where her mistress stood like a caged bird. 'Nay, I think it's time you and he had it out, don't you? You're sure all this is intentional, but unless you find out exactly what he's up to, you're going to have another night like the last one, aren't you? And tomorrow, you're going to be daggers drawn again. Why not ask him?' She turned Merielle as if she

were a child. 'Come on, lass. Let's get you out of these
damp things and into something dry. You'll be getting
elf-shot like me if this damp gets into your bones. Bess,
lass,' she called, 'find something warm for the mistress
to wear. Doesn't matter what as long as it's dry.'

Allene's lumbago had always been attributed to the
northern dampness, and who could argue when the be-
lief was as old as the description 'elf-shot'?

Allowing herself to be peeled of her damp leather
chausses that now stuck to her legs, then the service-
able surcoat and cote-hardie, Merielle wound a thick
blanket over her linen kirtle until something could be
found. 'What difference will it make?' she said, sulkily.
'He'll deny it, of course, which is all he's ever done.
And he expects me to believe him. The *monster*!'

Allene tucked the blanket around Merielle's legs and
under her feet. 'Bess,' she said, 'take this damp pile
down to the kitchens or find the laundress, if there is
one. Tell them they must be dry before dark.'

Obligingly, Bess turned from one task to the other,
opening the heavy door only to step back with a squeak
as it pushed against her of its own volition. The hand
on the heavy iron ring at the other side was that of Sir
Rhyan, but the faithful Bess held fast. 'Sir, ye can't
come in. The mistress…is…dressing…'

But the door eased her backwards, and he stood
aside, ushering her out, and she was obliged to leave
with an apologetic glance at the two women.

'Get out!' Merielle ordered, refusing to look in his
direction. She saw, however, that he had wasted no
time in removing his damp upper garments and now
wore only an unfastened gupon over his white linen
chainse that showed an expanse of neck and chest hith-

erto concealed. His hair had been rubbed into a damp
mass of untidy waves that tippled onto his forehead.

The door closed quietly, and when Merielle turned
to look, she found that Allene had gone, leaving her
alone with him. 'I meant you, sir, not Mistress Allene.
Get her back, immediately. I cannot talk to you here
alone.'

Unhurriedly, and looking about him, he came to sit
opposite her on the stone window-seat, spreading his
hands across his great thighs set wide apart, unknowing
or uncaring how intimidating this could be at close
quarters. 'You see, Mistress St Martin, how easy it is
for things to be misunderstood?' he said.

'No, I do not, sir,' she replied, thoroughly nettled by
his intrusion, as though he had timed it deliberately to
embarrass her further. 'I see how your manners are as
bad as ever. And if you've come to offer me more
piddling excuses why I'm humiliated yet again in *this*
place…' she indicated the room with a toss of her black
head '…then spare me the sound of them; they grow
more tedious and unconvincing by the day.'

'I'm a northerner, Merielle. Remember? How am I
supposed to know where the king stays? I certainly
didn't know he stays here.'

'Well, of course you'd say that, wouldn't you? So
by the same token, Sir Rhyan, who invited you to stay
here in a place reserved for the archbishop's own
guests? Did he invite you?'

'Neither the archbishop nor the king,' he said,
watching the blurred shapes beyond the greenish glass.
'Interesting, isn't it? It was my uncle's instruction I
followed. As Master of the King's Works at Winchester, it's where he would have brought you if he'd been
here instead of me. It's on his list of places to stay.

Apparently, he was expected here with you tomorrow, which means he must have expected to stay at least two days at Leeds Castle. This is why we've run into my neighbour, the abbot. I've no more idea than you why you were supposed to come here. If you think—'

'Yes, Sir Rhyan. That's what I do think. That you have it in mind to repay me yet again for asking the king's aid to resist your claim. It must have bitten you very deep for you to go to all this trouble to vent your spite, for it can be nothing else.'

He leaned forward, filling the narrow space, his blue eyes suddenly flashing as hard as hers. 'I have more things on my mind, mistress, believe it or not, than indulging in petty spiteful acts against a twenty-year-old widow from Canterbury.'

'Twenty-one!'

'Ah, my mistake. We cannot afford inaccuracies at this stage, can we? But *you* mistake if you think I care a damn about revenge. I thought we'd had all that out, once. You harp on the same string till it wears thin, woman.' He leaned his large frame against the wall, his chin set firm, the muscles of his cheek rippling in annoyance.

'I harp on that string, sir, because that's the tune. You'll be telling me next that it's Sir Adam who's taken my lead mines to supply the king's glazier with lead for his windows. Forgive me for harping on that string, but I had always believed that they were on my land, not yours. Was that something in the contract I overlooked? Have I got that wrong, too?'

'Well, you've done extremely well, so far, in getting as much wrong as one could conceivably manage in three days,' he said with biting sarcasm. 'The king's beds suddenly become instruments of revenge, despite the fact that they're the most comfortable in the land and any woman would think herself fortunate…'

Merielle saw red. With a surge of fury, she burst through the blanket's overlap like a butterfly from a chrysalis in a flurry of new vigour, her hand making loud contact with Sir Rhyan's cheek well before the impulse could be controlled. Exultant, yet horrified, she saw his head swing sideways, yet she could never have moved fast enough to evade his leap towards her, or the sudden pull on her arm that jerked her upright. The rest of the blanket slid to the floor, leaving her standing in her sleeveless linen kirtle.

She dared not allow him time for a counter-attack. 'That's exactly what a man like you would think, isn't it? That as long as a bed's comfortable, it doesn't matter whose it is. No honour, no principles. Those are for men, are they not?' She pulled, then pushed, but both wrists were held fast. 'And what's your holy neighbour going to say when I tell him how you might acquire *his* land, despite the king's command to stop interfering? Let me *go*!' There was not the slightest give in his arms.

'He'll probably tell you, woman, to get your facts straight before you fly off the handle every time you hear something you don't understand. Ask him, by all means, if you want him to think you foolish.'

'So Master John was hearing things, was he? I'm wrong about the lead mines belonging to me, then?'

'Yes, you are wrong. Very. The lead mines I've recently opened are new ones on my land, not yours. Lead veins run through my property, too, and you could have kept your workings open if you'd been there to attend to things.' He released her wrists with an irritable shove. 'Your mines are still disused whilst

mine are now producing lead for the roofs and windows which I shall be selling for the king's building
programme. That's why I'm down here instead of up
there. Now, lady, misunderstand that, if you will.'

'Master John said—'

'He said that the lead was on my land, and it is.
Your mines will continue to fill up with dead sheep, as
they are doing.'

Stunned and chastened, Merielle stooped to retrieve
the blanket that kept her feet imprisoned. What he had
said made sense, as did everything else, if only she had
been less prejudiced. It was Sir Adam, his uncle, who
had arranged the accommodation for himself and her,
not Sir Rhyan. It was not her land which was producing
lead but his: veins of lead ran vertically, not horizon-
tally, so she could not even claim that *they* were hers.

Holding the wayward blanket, she straightened, turning away quickly as her kirtle sagged at the neckline.
'I'm sorry. I misunderstood,' she said, quietly, hugging
the blanket to her.

'Yes, Merielle. So you have. As you've misunderstood everything about me, so far.'

She could feel his warmth on her back. His hand
came to rest gently on her waist, as light as a butterfly,
and there was nowhere for her feet to go. 'Please…'
she whispered, releasing the blanket unwillingly into
his other hand.

His mouth moved like a summer breeze over the
back of her bowed neck beneath the loose knot of hair,
sending a spasm of fear through her thighs that quick-
ened and set alight once more the dry tinder of her
longings. His hand came round to hold her, his thumb
between her breasts, and she gave a cry that began in
her womb, out of all reason.

'Yes?' he said, into her neck, his arms now tenderly enclosing her. 'Yes? Is there something you might understand, for a change, my lovely Venus? Is there?'

There was so much she ached to understand, so much that kept her sleepless at nights. No longer could she hold those faults against him which relied on revenge for a motive, but there were others—her sister, for one. She had become used to dwelling on his treachery; the letting go would be madness, as she had discovered only yesterday. Madness.

'Let me go. This is unfair. I have accepted your explanation, I can do no more than that, sir.' Her voice was breathless, but she felt the pause of his mouth upon her neck and, with all the strength she could command, she prised away his hands, holding his thumbs like staffs.

He lifted his head. 'You *can* do more than that, Merielle.'

'No!' Anticipating his next words, she held to her defence.

Quickly, without allowing her argument to develop, he turned her to him, holding her arms on the soft flesh above her elbows. 'Yes, you can. You can begin by admitting your feelings for me. Yesterday, you…stand still, woman…yesterday you showed me something of it. Or can any man light your fire so soon, eh?' This time, he was prepared for her reaction to his deliberate provocation and caught her hands, clamping them cruelly behind her back, holding her in to his body. 'Well, mistress? Are you as hot for that pretty lad you left in Canterbury? Were you on fire for your…?'

'Stop it! Stop!' she croaked, twisting her head. 'Stop!'

'Answer me!'

'Yes, I am. I *was*! Anybody! There, does that satisfy you?'

The words satisfied neither of them, for they were untypical of Merielle's usual honesty, their sound foreign to her, nor did they foster the air of exclusivity she had nurtured so carefully since widowhood. Far from being anybody's, she was nobody's. Yet there was not, nor had there ever been, a man like this one who made her heart lurch into her knees at the mere thought of him. At close quarters, she took in his warmth against her stomach and thighs, his male smell, the way his thick hair settled closely above his ears, the smooth skin over the point of his jaw. She was close enough to have touched his throat with her tongue. Had her sister done so?

'You lie, woman. I do not believe you.'

Nor would she have believed him if he'd denied being her sister's lover, which he would, naturally. They were even. To think ill of him, falsely or not, was the safest course. She saw the anger in his narrowed eyes, the compression of his well-formed mouth.

'I do not believe you,' he repeated. 'Whatever you hold against me now, Merielle, has nothing to do with your fear of reprisals. There's something else eating at you, I can see. Is it pride? Is that it? Or is it Sir Adam's infant that's closing your mind to everything else?' His voice softened to a whisper. 'I can give you bairns of your own, Merielle.'

His tender offer took her breath away, pulling at her deepest parts and opening up her empty chasm of despair. The hands that released hers slid to her buttocks, caressing and holding them to him, melting her.

Unable to reply with words, her mouth sought his with a cry no one could have misinterpreted, and she clung to him as if to tell him of her desperate need. The time for words had passed.

Deftly, he caught the key which she tossed to him in her moment of yearning and, lifting her without a moment's hesitation, carried her to the king's bed. Nor was there time for a lengthy or gentle wooing, no time for him to do more than throw off his gupon and undo the points that tied hose to shirt. Kneeling astride her to prevent a sudden change of heart, he recognised both the submission and the urgency in her eyes, the pleading of her hips as she moved to meet him, the wild unbridled searching of her mouth, the deep moans of ardour.

For Merielle, the only need was for possession and consummation: his hand playing upon her soft tender parts tuned her to a pitch she could bear no longer. Clinging to his head, she spread herself beneath his weight, whimpering with joy as he plunged into her with a total lack of reverence. It was the experience she had dreamed of during lonely nights when hidden thoughts had been at their most wilful, except that even then, it had never compared to this.

Immediately engulfed by the vortex she tossed, moaning, not knowing how to stave off the end before the beginning, for this had never happened to her before. Stormed by the quickening pace of his powerful loins, she cried out in ecstasy, gasping at his fierce and absolute possession of her and, while it lasted, she was a feather in a whirlwind. Something within her exploded in slow-time and she reeled beneath him, unable to think or move but, faraway, hearing his muffled victory-shout into her hair. The shortest loving had been the most intoxicating.

He rested inside her while she listened to the thud

of her heart echoing in his chest and turned her head
to seek his lips. Instantly, he responded and, instead of
withdrawing from her as she had expected, began
gently to move upon her again as if to comfort them
both for its short and fiery duration.

At her tiny sound of surprise, he lifted his head and
studied her darkly, moving more purposefully while he
watched for her reaction. 'A man's performance,' he
whispered, kissing her nose.

Unbelievably, he led her back to the beginning
again, this time persuasively and with tenderness, caressing and consuming at the same time, arousing her,
step by step, to a different glorious height. Wave upon
wave of pleasure washed upon her shores, her body
responding to the skilful search of his hands, and when
the last wave sucked her far out into the depths, the
drowning was the sweetest thing that washed her up,
shuddering, back into the haven of his arms.

The contented hum of diners in the great hall and
the easy conversation closer at hand faded and returned
with alarming regularity as Merielle struggled in vain
to re-focus her attention. Sharing her dishes of food,
Robert Monkton, Abbot of Fountains, dipped his bread
in the gravy, left-handed as etiquette required, and took
the sop into his mouth. His reply to Sir Rhyan's enquiry left Merielle bewildered. 'Hardly notice it here
in the south,' he said, smiling tooth-gapped.

Merielle's vacant stare at Sir Rhyan was a plea for
help until she caught his signal, a tapping on his chest
with fingertips that went on to toy with buttons as small
as peas. 'Even so, my lord Abbot,' she said, 'you must
allow me to make you an infusion of ground ivy to

loosen the phlegm. There's sure to be some in the archbishop's garden.'

The abbot inclined his head. 'My thanks, Mistress St Martin. If the archbishop's garden is anything like mine, it'll be hard to miss it.'

Again, the sounds receded as she watched Sir Rhyan's hand reach towards the dish of roasted vegetables. Only an hour ago those same fingers had explored her in a manner she had been sure would never happen. He offered her a chunk of spiced parsnip, drawing her eyes to his. 'Come on, dreamer. You must eat, you know.' His eyes twinkled, knowingly.

Automatically, she took it, tasting little as she slipped back into a reverie that encompassed an hour within the space of one heartbeat, an hour that had been all the more remarkable for its silence. There had been fears, both during and afterwards, that he would try to explain, justify, gloat, or even make light of it, but he had done none of these. He had held her close while she wept silent tears of emotion and guilt, gently rocking her and wiping her cheeks. There had been a scratching at the door to which he had called, 'Yes, all right,' before swinging his legs off the bed so that his broad back blocked out the light from the window. He had heaved a sigh as he ran his fingers through tousled hair, then quickly turned to catch the hand that moved stealthily on to his thigh, pressing it beneath his. He had kissed her again as if reluctant to leave her, pulled the fur rug over her, dressed himself and bent to the bed again. 'I'll send Mistress Allene in to you,' he said, caressing her face.

Allene's head had been barely visible above the pile of pillows that billowed into the solar like white windfilled sails. 'Just as well supper's ready,' she had mut-

1st

IRST PAST THE POST

cratch & Win...
up to 2 FREE BOOKS
and a FREE GIFT

See inside ↗

Race to the finish and get up to
THREE FREE GIFTS!

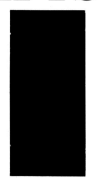

NO RISK, NO OBLIGATION TO BUY... NOW OR EVER!

HERE'S HOW TO PLAY:

1. Flip that lucky coin in the air and scratch off the silver boxes. Now, depending on where you finished in the race, you will receive up to two specially selected Mills & Boon® novels from the Historical Romance™ series.

2. Simply return this card and you will receive up to two Historical Romance™ novels. These books have a cover price of £2.99 each and are yours to keep, absolutely **FREE**

Why Would We Offer Such A Deal?

The editors at Mills & Boon simply want you to enjoy what thousands are already enjoying: the convenience of home delivery of the latest Historical Romance™ novels. Imagine receiving the best romance novels at your door before they are available in the shops. And better yet, postage and packing is entirely at our expense.

FREE Books
A FREE Gift
and more...

Scratch here to reveal your FREE Gift.

Scratch off the silver box to see if you were 'First Past the Post'

SEE CLAIM CHART BELOW

YES! I have scratched the silver boxes above. Please rush me all the free gifts for which I qualify, as shown on the claim chart below. I understand that I am under no obligation to purchase any books, as explained overleaf. I am over 18 years of age.

HOAIA

MS/MRS/MISS/MR _____ INITIALS _____

SURNAME _____ BLOCK CAPITALS PLEASE

ADDRESS _____

_____

_____ POSTCODE _____

| **CLAIM CHART** | For 3rd place you get **1 free book.** | For 2nd place you get **2 free books.** | For 1st place you get **2 free books & a Free Gift!** |

MILLS & BOON READER SERVICE™
FREE BOOK OFFER
FREEPOST CN81
CROYDON
CR9 3WZ

NO
STAMP
NEEDED

tered, 'or I might have been standing out there for another hour, I dare say.' Which had made Merielle smile
at last.

'That's better. Was that a smile?'

Her eyes lowered, then sought his again. 'Sir Rhyan,
you know I didn't want...' Guiltily, her sideways
glance acknowledged the poor timing of thoughts she
could no longer contain.

'Shh...I know you didn't. But I did.' No such guilt
clouded his direct stare that held something of the ar-
rogance she remembered so well and which had once
angered her. Now it was teamed with an intimacy that
stirred her woman's parts, making them tighten upon
the cushioned bench. She took the slice of venison he
offered with a word of thanks that might also, she
thought, have done for his reassurance.

Turning to Robert Monkton on her left, she enquired,
'Do you have lead mines on any of your lands, my lord
Abbot?'

The abbot mopped his purple-tinged lips with his
napkin. 'Sadly, no. Though even if I were as fortunate
as Sir Rhyan, there'd be little chance of getting at it
with my dwindling workforce.'

'You mean the sickness that took so many of them?'

'Not only that, mistress. Our problems with labour
go back earlier than that, I fear.' He noted her raised
brows and was neither too old nor too monkish to be
flattered by a lovely woman's attention. 'Raids, mistress,' he continued. 'Scots from the borderlands. Terrible damage they do; if my abbey were not one of the
largest and strongest, we'd have gone under like some
of the others.'

Merielle studied his gnarled and blue-veined hand
upon the silver goblet where one finger explored an

unlikely combination of monkeys and hares chasing each other around the rim. The problem of labour had occupied little of her attention until Sir Rhyan's mention of it, for women seeking employment in Canterbury had not been hard to come by, nor had the Flemings. Yet here between her two northern neighbours she felt compelled to demonstrate an awakening interest. 'But you have lay-brothers, do you not, Father?'

Glancing across her at Sir Rhyan, he shook his head, smiling ruefully. 'I can see you're a little out of touch, mistress.' At her expression, he added kindly, 'But no one can be in more than one place at once, and a woman must continue her husband's business, of course. Stewards need watching like hawks, don't they? There's no reason at all why you should know of our troubles.' It was a charitable excuse and nowhere near as brutal as Sir Rhyan's reasoning. 'It's true that we had a large number of lay-brothers to man our granges up in the dales where the sheep are, but that was well before the Scots' raids. Since then, the granges have mostly been demolished, one by one, the sheep stolen, men killed, until we had to abandon them. Our last abbot had the granges staffed by bailiffs who manage them for us, wearing our livery, but there are still some years when we cannot fulfill our obligations to our customers who've bought our wool in advance. Then we have to make up the deficit from our other funds, robbing Peter to pay Paul, as always.'

Sir Rhyan leaned forward, enclosing Merielle with an arm along the back of the bench. 'Then why not lease them out, Father?'

The silver goblet which had almost reached the abbot's lips was lowered slowly to the table. 'Lease?' he said. The deeply etched lines of his face indicated a terrible acceptance of events rather than an imagination to seek a way out of them.

'Yes. Convert them to manors. Allow the tenants to sell their own wool and produce on the open market instead of to the abbey. That way, you get a steady rent each year equal to the wool-clip, and no responsibility to speak of. Nor would you have to pay the occupants. And as for not having the wool, well, you can keep as many sheep as you need nearer to home, can't you? And anyway, there's more money to be had in breeding warhorses at the moment. That's what I'm doing.'

'Very true, but the idea of leasing property to tenants goes against the original concept of monastic self-sufficiency, Sir Rhyan. It's something we've always strived for, you know.'

'Times change, Father. We didn't always have the Scots to contend with, did we? Or the recent sickness taking the last of our workers. Or the murrain. Or the drought one year and floods the next. Or bad harvests four years in a row. We must seek every opportunity up there, or we don't survive.'

'You've suffered from the Scots, too, I believe?'

'Several times. I'd have been here sooner but for them. There's hardly a village or a manor that's escaped their attacks. Some of us have built special defences, you know. Towers, gatehouses. Moats.'

'And some of us run away from the problem altogether.'

Both men turned sharply to catch the expression accompanying the softly spoken words which were overlapped by the harsh blare of a trumpet heralding the last course. Merielle was relieved that neither man suggested any excuse, as if they understood that the remark had been a thought spoken out loud, no more.

Not even she, at that moment, could have devised any excuse why she should be sitting there in the archbishop's palace at Otford, of all places, whilst repeated raids were taking place on land she was supposed to be protecting. A sudden and heavy wave of exhaustion coincided with the trumpet's strident call, swamping her with a drowsiness that closed her eyes against the swimming shapes before her.

'I'm so tired,' she whispered into the din.

But Sir Rhyan saw and heard. 'That, mistress, does not surprise me.' His tone was severe, but when she looked she saw that his eyes held a wicked sparkle, brimming with laughter.

Chapter Seven

'Well, John. Don't tell me you painted the archbishop's walls here, too. A dossal for the altar, perhaps? A tryptych?'

'No.' Master John Kenton smiled at the teasing. 'Never been here before. I knew the king stayed here, of course, as he does in other bishops' palaces. They're the ones who can best afford it.'

It was on the tip of Sir Rhyan's tongue to ask the king's painter why he hadn't told him, but knew the question to be unfair. He himself had only told them of the hospitality as they approached Otford, and Master John was not being employed as wet-nurse. After what had happened at Leeds, he should have been more on his guard. 'What about Guildford, then, John?'

'That's our next stop?'

Sir Rhyan nodded. 'It's quite a step, but we should be able to make it, barring accidents. Care to make a guess where we're to stay?'

Master John sniffed, watching the changing interplay of light and shade amongst the leaves on the trellis. 'Guildford. Then it must be the manor of Clandon, I suppose. Yes?'

'How in hell's name d'ye know that?'

The brown eyes remained steady beneath the silky fringe. 'Well, we appear to be making a beeline for the king's beds, do we not? And the next one's at the royal manor at Guildford, not far removed from the track. Didn't you know that? The king has them everywhere.'

The sharp expulsion of air through nostrils was almost a snort. 'I've only got the directions, not the details of who owns them. And he doesn't have so many of these places scattered around the north as he does here. What's going on?'

Master John's eyebrows were as expressive as words, but they were well concealed and he was as discreet as any man who wanted to remain in the king's service. 'I don't suppose anything is, Sir Rhyan. The places Sir Adam suggests to you are no doubt where he would have stayed if he'd been here. He is, after all, the king's Master of Works, and it may be that he's required to check them over with a view to suggesting renovations, alterations, additions. Painting, even.'

'And tapestries?'

'Why not? Sir Adam would not be averse to putting a little business in Mistress St Martin's way, presumably.'

'And does this place need tapestries, d'ye think?'

Master John smiled to himself, thinking how easy it would be to give a facetious reply out here in the dusky garden that tinkled to the sound of water from the fountain and the last call of doves from the rooftop. The leafy greens wove their own tapestry more beautiful by far than any woollen ones covered by emblems and coats of arms. 'Oh, it doesn't matter much whether a place *needs* tapestries, does it? It's not like a new roof or a water-system, exactly. If Sir Adam told the king

he needed tapestries, he'd have them. You know how
he loves that kind of thing. Why d'ye think I'm doing
so well?'

'Because you're a good craftsman, John.'

'Because the king appreciates beautiful things, that's
why.'

Sir Rhyan swung his long, tightly clad legs up on to
the turf-covered bench and slid a hand over his thigh
where Merielle's hand had been trapped only a short
time ago. She had wept at her own capitulation, angry
and ashamed at being caught in a moment of weakness,
and he had known better than to offer defences for
either of them. She was proud. She would not have
accepted any reasoning except that of his purposeful
hands over her soft skin, his lips lapping over her moist
cheeks, his body holding her under him. The king and
his painter were not the only ones who appreciated
beautiful things.

A sudden thought occurred to him. 'The king's at
Windsor, is he not, John?'

'He was when we left Canterbury three days ago.'

'And how far is Windsor from his royal manor at
Guildford, do you think?'

'The way he rides, less than a day. It's the nearest
one he has to Windsor.'

'And it's en route from Canterbury to Winchester.
Convenient, eh? He could even be there by now.'

'Overcrowding the place already,' Master John
mused. 'I stayed at a quiet little place called Shere last
time I came this way. There's a comfortable guesthouse
for pilgrims there.'

'I stayed there, too. Shere. Not as far as Guildford,
John.'

'Nor as crowded.'

'Mmm…good!' Sir Rhyan swung his legs down and stood. 'Shall we walk on, Master Painter? Look here; white roses already open. They'll not be out for weeks up in the north.'

The dew fell in a shower from the bowed heads of white blooms, narrowly missing Merielle's leather-clad feet. She was dressed for the day's travel but her thoughts had been heading in a different direction since waking from a deep and dreamless sleep and were now already phrasing the argument which would inevitably follow her announcement. Perhaps another half-hour before the sun would rise above the tree-tops in a chaste grey veil, before he would come to find her, and she would either have to plead or demand.

The thoughts had been in place long before this, but the conversation at supper had been the catalyst which had made some kind of decision essential; the growing recognition of her own selfishness giving her little choice about how to proceed. How could she, how could anyone, follow the needs of her heart when there were those who needed her aid on land she had suffered so much to retain? What was the sense of fighting to keep it and then choosing to ignore it, allowing it to waste away for lack of attention? The bailiff and steward appointed by her father had let her down, then died.

She ought by now to have appointed official receivers, as others were doing nowadays, responsible men who would keep her informed, week by week. She ought to have been to see, to re-open the lead mine and arranged more outlets for the sales. She ought to have put as much effort into defending the villages against attack as she had into her tapestry workshop

and the poor women who had begged her, as one of
the few women employers, for work.

The business in Lincoln was in the safe hands of her
first husband's family, who were glad enough to manage it for her, but Sir Rhyan's claim on her northern
properties had been one loss too many and she had
clung to it on principle.

She heard him approach, too soon, and whirled to
face him, already defensive and halfway through her
reasoning. 'Why did you not tell me how things are?
The whole story. Why wait until I'm three days from
home before telling me of the raids? I could have been
halfway there instead of halfway to Winchester.' She
slapped at a tall foxglove heavy with buds, sending a
shower of dew across Sir Rhyan's brown leather gupon, where it hung like pearls.

His blue eyes narrowed. 'Yes,' he said, as if talking
to a young squire, 'attack is an acceptable form of defence, but only if you keep your head. Now, mistress…' he took a stride forward upon the straw-
covered path and scooped an arm around her waist
before she could retreat '…allow me to show you how
to aim accurately.'

Infuriated by his flippancy and by his assumption
that she could be diverted so easily, she proved to him
how little she needed his advice. 'Is this how you
taught my sister, Sir Rhyan? In the garden between the
rose bushes? Or did you have as easy access to *her*
chamber as you did to mine?' She leaned backwards
in his embrace to watch the shockwaves spread across
his handsome face.

The arrow found its mark. His arms slackened and
dropped. 'What?' he whispered, a look of sheer incredulity in his eyes. 'What? Is that what you believe?

Truly? That I seduced your sister, a child of *fifteen*? God's truth, Merielle, now I've heard everything.' He took a step backwards. 'You need no lessons in attack, I see.'

She did, though, for she had no idea how to follow it up, already regretting the hasty accusation that she had not meant to use until the proof was great enough for her to fall over. Now it was out, and of no more use than a broken sword, for she could tell by his re-action that the doubts she had nurtured since Laurel's marriage were without foundation. No one could have faked such dismay.

Lamely, she blundered on. 'She told me.'

'Told you? Told you what?'

'That…that she was in love with you.' She lifted her chin, hating the words and dreading the tell-tale soft-ening of his eyes.

But they were like blue steel. 'So? Did she say I seduced her?'

'Not…not exactly.'

'Not exactly? Then what did she tell you? *Exactly!*'

'She implied…she made it sound…she wanted me to *believe* that you were…had… She told me…no, no I cannot!' Her attempt to turn away was intercepted and she was caught, pulled back and held to face him.

'What, Merielle? What did she tell you? I have a right to know what I'm accused of.'

'That…that the child was not Sir Adam's.' She heard the weight of her words drop and echo, round and round, sounding far worse than when she had said them to Allene.

'She told you that? Whose, then? Did she tell you it was mine?'

Merielle shook her head and, in trying to remove his

tight grip on her arm, found her wrist caught instead.
Then both wrists. 'No, we were not close enough for
her to tell me more,' she whispered.

His voice was loaded with scorn. 'Saints alive,
woman! You were close enough for her to tell you the
state of her heart and that she'd been unfaithful to her
new husband, but not quite close enough to tell you
the name of her unborn child's father. Do I read the
situation aright? And you...you believed every word,
did you?'

'Please. You're hurting me.'

Brutally, he pulled her wrists into his chest. 'You
did! Every bloody lying little word, and not only have
you believed her all this time but you've held it against
me without the slightest proof and without giving me
an inkling of what was eating away at you. You believe
me to be the brat's father, is that it? And that's what's
been nagging at you, is it, woman? That was the cause
of the tears?' He shook her, angrily. 'Was it, eh? You
believe I make a habit of taking sisters?'

'Stop it!' she yelled. 'What was I to believe? That
you were a saint in disguise after what you'd put me
through? I didn't *want* to like you, as she did, and
heaven knows you spent enough time together. I had
your prowess drummed into my ears morning, noon
and night by both my sister and your uncle. For all I
knew, you could have been doing him a service—'

'*What?*'

She looked away, choking on the rest of the sentence
and bracing herself for another fearsome defence.

'What are you saying to me, Merielle? Explain it!'

'I didn't mean...I meant that Laurel had told me Sir
Adam had not...didn't...' she stuttered, losing her way.

'Didn't what?'

'Consummate their marriage.' At last her hands were released, together with the words that limped out on crutches instead of being shot from a bow.

His reply to that was suitably scathing. 'I see,' he said, slowly. 'And my being there was quite enough for you to believe that your young sister's disappointment, re-directed towards me and turned into some kind of fantasy, was evidence enough that I was the one to be blamed. Well, somehow she managed to get herself with child, didn't she? With or without my uncle's assistance. And since you believe your sister, I'm to be the obvious candidate, despite the fact that she stopped short of naming me. Well, at least I have that much to be thankful for. And you, mistress, are no doubt relieved that your sister's romantic fantasies centred around men rather than women or heaven knows what *you* might have been accused of.'

'She didn't accuse you.'

'No…she'd have damned herself for a liar if she had. She got her elder sister to do it for her, didn't she?'

'I'm sorry.' The words sounded pathetically inadequate. 'I had not meant to say any of this.'

'I see; you'd rather have continued to…?'

'No…no, that's not what I meant.' She stood, waiting, stiffly uncomfortable with this large and powerful man, the events of last evening now far away, insubstantial as a dream. She could not find a way forward. He had denied her accusations and she believed him, but what now could she hold against him except that which no one must ever know of? The silence between them stretched, and the moment was lost.

His tone was abrupt. 'I came to escort you to the courtyard. We're ready to depart. Come, mistress.'

Reminded of what she had intended to say at the

beginning, she shook her head and held back. 'No. I'm returning home.'

She heard his deep breath and braced herself once more.

'Mistress Merielle St Martin of Canterbury, you are *not* returning. You are going with me to Winchester. Is that clear?'

Making no reply, she ignored his outstretched hand.

'I know the reason for this change of heart,' he said, more kindly. 'But you cannot reach your Yorkshire lands any quicker by going back to Canterbury than by going forward to Winchester. Quite the reverse.'

'I can appoint men to…'

'You can do that just as well from Winchester. And if you then want to travel north, I will escort you.'

'Despite what's happened between us?' she whispered.

He dropped his offered hand and studied her at length before answering. 'You think I've come so far to find you, only to leave you now, woman? Perhaps you'd better learn to trust me a little. Come, we can discuss what needs to be done as we ride.' He turned on the narrow path, knowing that she would follow.

Not knowing what he meant by coming so far to find her, nor wanting to ask for an explanation, she remained silent and with no heart to prolong any argument. The scent of him lingered in his wake as she trod in his footsteps, her head bowed, her plan demolished.

He stopped suddenly and turned, catching her in his arms. 'Does that put your mind at rest?' he said, grimly. 'Or would you rather continue to see me as a villain? Are there any skeletons in *your* closet, mistress, or are they all in mine?'

'Yes,' she said, purposely ambiguous.

'Good, I like to know where I stand. But know this. I am not a seducer of fifteen-year-old girls, or of newly married women or of my relatives' wives. The only part of your sister's anatomy I ever kissed was her hand. Not even her cheek. Now, have we put that particular ghost to rest before we set off, do you think?'

She nodded, savouring the warmth of him through her woollen surcoat, but unable to resist using the moment to regain some of the advantage. 'Yes, I believe so. But at the same time, Sir Rhyan…' she gently removed herself from his arms '…what happened last evening must never happen again. You do understand that, don't you?'

'Oh, I understand perfectly what you're saying, mistress. But it *will* happen again. Believe me, it most certainly will.' And before she could think of any reply to that, he was leading her by the hand out of the archbishop's garden towards the courtyard where her chestnut cob waited on three legs, half-asleep.

Naturally, the one thing she had believed would be totally unnecessary on this journey was the one thing she was desperate to have; her charm against conception which, although in one sense too late, might have been better than having nothing at all. Being fully aware of the cause of Merielle's concern, both Allene and Bess were on the lookout for suitable alternatives and, even though it was too early in the year to find exactly what they were looking for, Bess managed to collect the wall-pepper from the low-hanging shingled roof of the stone porch. But she did not manage to prevent young Padraig from questioning her purpose.

'Taken after Easter,' she told him, pertly, 'it makes people both blind and dumb.'

'But it doesn't even have flowers on it, yet.'

'So it won't make you deaf then, will it?'

'Someone got a sore head, then?'

'Not yet!' she snapped.

Ever caring, she had passed on the cargo to Allene who had stowed it away next to her green tangle of mugwort. 'Let's hope we don't need it,' she whispered. 'We don't want to go through all that again.'

This sentiment was precisely the cause of Merielle's heart-searching, for while she could hardly revert to the blatant animosity of the last few days, neither could she allow the madness of last evening to extend into the days ahead. Therein lay dangerous waters which she had no wish to test a second time. Yet, ironically, she could not help but visualise what it might be like to bear his child, which was something she had not considered with anything like the same equanimity two-and-a-half years ago in respect of the king.

On the few occasions when her thoughts demanded some explanation for his sudden interest in her—apart from the usual male interest, that is—the possibilities became so confusing and contradictory that she was brought back to his initial argument at Canterbury when he had insisted she would not be allowed to marry without his consent. In other words, he was going to see that she kept to the letter of the contract. And if the thought flitted through her mind that his prompt collaboration last evening when he had given her no chance to reconsider might have something to do with this, one way or another, she shied away from dwelling on the finer points. Either way, it must *not* happen again, whatever his views on the subject.

This resolution did nothing to prevent her, however, from reliving in minutest detail all that had passed be-

tween them there upon the king's great bed that had
been so starkly prepared for the Abbot. Comparisons
with previous partners were so absurd as to be unthinkable, and it was in this state of contemplation that her
journey progressed towards Winchester. The three who
understood the reasons for her pensive mood left her
alone with her thoughts. The one who guessed was
wise enough to do the same and, by the time they had
traversed the forested hillsides, mile after mile, Merielle was ready to rest.

'Look,' she said, pulling up the cob on a downward
slope, 'Mistress Allene's had enough for one day and
Guildford's still miles away. Can we not stop soon?
What's that place down there?'

'That's Shere,' Sir Rhyan said, shading his eyes. 'I
think.'

'Then that'll do, won't it? I can see a church, so
there's sure to be an inn. Isn't that where those last
pilgrims had been staying?' A silver glint of water
where a stream widened was speckled with ducks and
children, and smoke rose steadily from a cluster of
thatched roofs.

'I believe so. But if we don't reach Guildford today,
it's doubtful we'll reach Winchester tomorrow, mistress.'

But Merielle was already continuing her descent and
so missed the lift of one darkly expressive eyebrow in
Master John's direction.

The stop-over at Shere passed with only a minor
turbulence. Visiting the little church of St James to
offer prayers for a safe journey, Merielle and her two
women were followed by what appeared to be an army
of Sir Rhyan's men. When she questioned the captain,

a kindly but burly Welshman who would have deterred
an ox on the rampage, he told her he was obeying
orders and tipped a nod towards four unmistakable figures who lounged in a group outside the alehouse,
watching them.

'Nay, they'll not be a nuisance, mistress,' he
grinned. 'But don't go off anywhere by yourselves, will
you?'

The visit to the church took longer than Merielle had
allowed, owing to her discovery that an anchoress lived
in a small cell built into the north wall, taking mass
via a tiny hole through which she would speak to anyone who wished it. Merielle wished it, but had no way
of beginning a conversation of an intimate nature with
her mind still in turmoil and so, kneeling before the
square aperture and seeing only darkness beyond, she
could only say, 'Lady, will you speak to me, of your
mercy?'

There was a long silence, and Merielle was about to
leave, thinking that the recluse was perhaps unwilling,
or asleep. Then a voice spoke to her so closely that at
first she believed it was inside her head. 'You are full
of doubts, daughter. You doubt everyone, even me.'

'Yes, mother.'

'Then learn to trust.'

This time, it was Merielle's turn to be silent, the
woman's first observations having found their mark so
immediately.

'You hurt, child. Why do you hurt so?'

'Ah!' Stifling a cry with one hand, Merielle groped
with her other through the small space into the blackness, seeking contact. Her hand was caught in a warm
grasp strong enough for her to feel the gnarled bones,

the soft fingers, the thumb moving over her skin in an age-old comfort.

The anchoress waited until Merielle could bring her sobs under control, then spoke again, very softly. 'Yes, I see. You still suffer, do you not? But you must not hold it against them, daughter. They will never understand the pain. They have no losses like ours, nor would it be right that they should: they would not be strong enough.'

'What am I to do, mother?' Her voice was barely audible.

'Do, my child? Why, nothing except trust again. That is all we women can ever do. The salve *you* seek is already there, in place.'

'But I'm—'

'Shh. Be still. The pain was not of your making, but your fears and doubts are. They are inside you, my daughter, not out there. Accept what is offered as a comfort, not as a penance. You may not turn a loving gift into a reproach.'

'Loving, mother?'

With a pat, her hand was tenderly folded up into a fist and returned to her with the ghost of an audible smile. 'Aye, child. Love. Hold on to it. It's precious. God be with you.'

There was more Merielle could have said and far more she wanted to hear, but sounds at her back came from a queue of women anxious to take their turn and whose problems, for all she knew, might be greater than hers. 'Will you take this ring, mother, as my thanks?'

'No, child. Make a donation to the church in the chest over there.'

'Thank you. God be with you.' Her face still wet

with tears, she made her way past the line of sympathetic faces towards Allene and Bess and the great iron-
bound chest where a tonsured cleric stood waiting to
receive the ring.

Together, they knelt in the little chapel dedicated to
St Nicholas, patron saint of children, where Merielle
tried to recapture the anchoress's words of consolation
and encouragement. Already there, in place. Her niece,
undoubtedly. She must not turn a loving gift into a
reproach, but accept her as a comfort for past hurts.
How did the wise woman know of her doubts, her
fears? The child was Laurel's loving gift to her, a childless widow. What else could it mean?

Yet, when she had become calm, left the busy church
that thronged with pilgrims and taken a deep lungful
of the cool evening air, the first person she met was
Sir Rhyan waiting for her on the pathway with his men.
There was no disguising the traces of tears from him
but he said nothing, taking her hand and drawing it
through his arm and walking slowly back with her to
the guesthouse. And at that moment, she wished with
all her heart that the anchoress had said something different.

Chapter Eight

It would take more than twenty-four hours for Merielle to learn the trust that both the anchoress and Sir Rhyan had recommended, but it was not in her nature to finish the journey in the same contentious spirit which had accompanied her departure from Canterbury. The truce agreed at Leeds Castle stayed in place. Things had changed, certainly, but the journey offered no facilities for a greater understanding of their exact nature: she would have to wait a while longer for that.

Guildford was bypassed without notice except for some straining of eyes to find signs of the royal manor; whilst this was hidden from view, the three royal water-mills were easy enough to discover along the water's edge.

'For corn, malt and fulling,' Master Kenton told them. 'Built about a hundred years ago in the king's park and still going strong.'

Sir Rhyan's estimation of their timing had been correct, for the village of Aylesford was as far as they could travel that day, the women half-asleep in their saddles and too tired to protest at the cramped quarters already packed with travellers converging on the route from London to Winchester. If sleeping spaces were in short supply, food answered loudly to the talk of money and it was in this area that Sir Rhyan's party scored over many others. Brought out to the large group under the trees and away from the crowds were roasted chickens and spiced bacon, broth, pasties, hard-boiled eggs and new-baked bread, honey and cheese, apples and frothing ale.

By mid-morning on Thursday, still scratching at new flea bites, the party descended the steep chalky slopes of St Giles' Down. Although they had left Aylesford early, many others were just as eager to reach Winchester, blocking the bumpy track with wagons and carts, herds of sheep and strings of merchants' pack-horses loaded with goods. Merielle recognised some from earlier in the journey, but was now too intent on the view below them to begin conversations. Shading her eyes, she peered through the layer of blue wood-smoke to pick out the short spire of St Mary's Abbey where her sister Laurel had been laid to rest a mere nine months ago.

Master John Kenton moved his bay gelding closer to Merielle, squeezing out a cheeky young squire who had been gazing at her too long, he thought. 'Anticipation, is it? Or trepidation? Or plain and simple relief?' he smiled.

'All three,' she replied. 'My niece will have grown apace. She was such a new little thing last time I saw her.'

The king's painter knew nought of infants except that their method of communication seemed to be out of all proportion to their size. 'And you'll be fully oc-

cupied with her, mistress? I had hoped to show you the
new windows in the cathedral, among other things.'

'I shall have time for that, Master John, before you
continue up to Yorkshire. How long will you rest?
Three days?'

Sir Rhyan's black stallion moved up close to her
other side just long enough for its rider to make the
reply. 'We shall wait upon your pleasure, lady. As soon
as you're rested, we'll be happy to escort you once
more, will we not, John?' He moved on ahead, controlling the great beast with one hand and not waiting
to see the expression on Merielle's face.

She would like to have deflated his assurance. At no
time had she agreed to gallop off up to Yorkshire in
his company. She would follow when she had ascer-
tained, once and for all, exactly what Sir Adam was
offering her, and though she had no wish to delay at-
tending to her property in the north, she did not intend
to be manipulated either by Sir Rhyan or Sir Adam.

Traffic flowing through the Eastgate in both directions gave them time to accustom their ears, eyes and
noses to Winchester's busiest thoroughfare, Cheap
Street, the street of the cheap, or market. Constantly
awash at its eastern end with brown and stinking water
from the tanners, dyers and fullers whose workshops
depended on the supply, the road here was particularly
foul beneath the feet of those who waited to cross the
bridge. A mat of soggy straw was supposed to alleviate
the problem, but the previous day's garbage added yet
another dimension and, nearer the meat market, offal
from the butchers' stalls already swarmed with flies and
bold daytime rats large enough to fight off cats. If anything, Merielle thought, Winchester was worse than
Canterbury in this respect, though she liked the place

well enough for other reasons. For one, there was a large Chapman's hall here that sold good white linen straight off the loom. She would stock up while she was here.

Through the stone-arched gateway they passed un-hindered along the wide main street, bounded on the left by the solid wall of St Mary's Abbey, of which only the shingled roofs and spire were now visible. Behind the shop fronts of the meat, wood and corn markets, the cathedral slumbered, tolerating the inter-ference of men like a benevolent giant. But watching over the whole town from its high vantage-point in the far corner was the Norman castle towards whose ram-parts the party progressed, uphill.

Out through the Westgate, Sir Adam Bedesbury's manor was barely a quarter of a mile into the leafy suburbs on Wood Street, the road to Romsey. Here the properties were larger and less densely packed, each one surrounded by a cluster of outbuildings, stables, kitchen, storerooms, their gardens and orchards spread-ing backwards at ease into the rolling hillsides. The manor Sir Rhyan's uncle leased from the Bishop of Winchester was one of the finest, a timber upper-storey built on to a stone ground-floor, an L-shaped building with a great hall over vaulted storerooms, a solar, chapel and guest-chambers with an imposing round tower added to one corner, the late Lady Bedesbury's private chamber. This, Merielle knew, was where little Joanie would now be, probably asleep.

Her smile broadened at the thought and, without waiting for Sir Rhyan's help, she swung herself out of the saddle and into the excited flurry of grey and white gazehounds who bounded and pranced around the horses, yapping their greeting. The hounds, however, were alone in this.

'Where is everybody?' Sir Rhyan yelled above their din.

The empty courtyard came to life as grooms ran from the stables at one side to take the horses' heads, their faces unsmiling and half-apologetic. Performing their tasks, they replied in monosyllables to all queries, except for the head groom who complained that no one had told him to prepare for Sir Rhyan's party till the weekend and he didn't know where he was supposed to put so many 'osses.

Brusquely, Sir Rhyan snapped at him and turned to look for Merielle.

On the covered stone steps that led diagonally up to the door of the hall on the upper floor, a man flattened himself against the wall as Merielle bounded past then, recovering himself, came down to meet Sir Rhyan. He held up the hem of his charcoal-grey gown, reaching out with the other hand. 'Ah, Sir Rhyan…back already! Did you not see Sir Adam on your way through the town?' He glanced towards the heavy gates as if expecting his master to follow close behind.

'See him where, Matthew? Did he come out to meet us?'

'Er…no, sir. You were not expected for a day or two, I believe. Sir Adam and the rest of the house… er…' he looked about him, uncertain how to proceed '…are at…er…the abbey.'

'Yes? At the abbey. What is it, Matthew? What's amiss?'

'It's the child, sir. A burial, I fear, sir.' He shook his black-capped head, sorrowfully, his lower lip trembling.

Sir Rhyan frowned, taking the man's arm and drawing him away from the others. 'Matthew, what are you telling me? That the infant has died, is that it?'

Grey-bearded and grey-faced, Matthew nodded. 'Two days ago. They've taken her to the abbey to lie with her mother. This morning. I thought you might have seen…'

'My God…Merielle…she's gone up to see…'

He took the steps two at a time and caught up with her as she emerged from the tower chamber through a short passageway in the thickness of the wall. 'You… you've seen?' he asked.

'No one there. Nothing to see,' she replied, slipping past him. 'Where on earth is everyone? Where's Matthew?'

Sir Rhyan stepped ahead of her into the great solar. 'Down in the courtyard. Merielle, wait…I have some news.'

Startled, she turned back to him, her dark eyes wide open in the shady corner, and though the room was still warm from the mound of white wood-ash in the wall-recess, goosebumps were rising along her arms. 'Is it Sir Adam? His illness? The little one's not there either, or her nurse.'

'Merielle, come. Sit here, in the window-seat.' Leading her up the steps into the deep V-shaped enclosure, he pushed her gently down on to the cushioned ledge and opened the window shutters, letting in a stream of light and cool air.

'What is it? Tell me, I beg you.'

He took the ledge opposite her, holding both her hands between his. 'The child, Merielle. Sir Adam's down at St Mary's, burying her alongside your sister. I'm so sorry, sweetheart. I don't know what happened, but I'll find out.' Not for all the world would he have wanted to wound her in this way.

Predictably, she stared at him, uncomprehending, while meaningless words sought a way through the protective barrier of her mind. Then she stood, pulling away, making a dash towards the tower chamber once more. It was useless to try to prevent her.

The wooden cradle contained only a folded linen sheet on the goosefeather mattress and, on the small table in the centre of the room, a pile of white napkins, each with a yellow stain in the centre. The silver feeding-spoon she herself had given the child at its christening was there, too, and the bone-handled rattle, the coral teething-ring and a small white linen cap still rounded from the infant's head. Slowly, as though in a dream, Merielle picked it up and brought it to her face, breathing in the lingering scent of downy hair, her own skin now as white as the cap itself. Without resisting, she allowed herself to be lowered on to the joined-stool that stood in the corner.

The room filled with people. Allene and Bess, Master John, Sir Rhyan and Sir Adam's chamberlain, Master Matthew, who spoke to them rather than directly to Merielle.

'How, sir?' He shook his head again with a sigh of bewilderment. 'It seems that the child fell, though the lord knows what the nurse was doing to allow that to happen. She placed it here, on the table, to…er, do whatever it is they do to them.' He cleared his throat, pointing to the oaken surface no wider than the cradle. 'The maid says that, while the nurse was turned away, the child rolled and fell to the floor.'

'Fell off? God's truth, what was the maid doing at the time? Gossiping?'

'She was not here, sir. She was only repeating what she found out from the nurse.'

'So the nurse didn't tell you at first hand?'

'No, sir. Went off her head, she did. You must have noticed how strange she was when you were last here. I wanted her replaced with someone more reliable, but Sir Adam would not hear of it.'

'Where's the nurse now, Matthew, at the funeral?'

'Nay, sir, they took her off last night to the Sustren Spital just outside the King's Gate to be looked after by the sisters. She was demented; just screamed non-stop. Terrible.'

Allene, almost as pale as her mistress, threw her cloak around Merielle's shoulders. 'Bess, go down to the kitchen and bring up a hot posset for Mistress Merielle. Hurry, lass.' She turned her attention to the chamberlain. 'Master Matthew, who saw the child after this accident? You? Did she die instantly?' She nudged a deep pile of rushes with her toe, wrinkling her nose at the dank smelly mess. 'And how often is this place cleared out? Has it been done since we were here last August?'

Master Matthew, who was responsible for the chambers and their occupants, pulled himself erect and glanced for moral support towards the two men. He and Mistress Allene had never seen eye-to-eye about what constituted good hospitality, for his master had been a carefree bachelor for many years before his recent venture into matrimony, and Matthew had not welcomed the changes, whether to his master or to the rest of the household. Ignoring her criticism of the room, he replied with some asperity, 'Of course I saw the child, briefly. The screaming was impossible to ignore, but I know nothing of infants. It looked all right to me.'

'Whose screaming? Little Joanie's?'

'No, the nurse. It was she who yelled. The babe was quite silent.'

'So she returned it to its cot, did she?'

'I believe so, but she kept up the yelling that it was God's will and none of us could shut her up. Demented, she was. Sir Adam had the chaplain to say the last rites. So white and still it was. Poor little mite,' he whispered, looking at the cradle.

Tapped by Merielle's fingers as though the child still lay asleep inside, the cradle rocked soundlessly upon the heavy mat of rushes. The tiny cap was still held to her face. She had said not a word.

Allene took charge. 'Leave us, masters, if you will. My mistress needs some attention and privacy. Have our beds made up in here, if you please, Master Matthew, and in the solar for the mistress. And let's have some fires lit.'

Even with the fires and the soothing drink of milk and ale, the trembling in Merielle's knees persisted, making it difficult for her to rise in greeting as she had done at Canterbury at the expected arrival of Sir Adam. Different for so many reasons, this meeting was silent and far from eager, for neither of them had experienced such an untimely death of this nature, though it had occurred frequently to others of their acquaintance. Nor had Sir Adam ever expected it to happen to him.

He shook his large sandy head, avoiding Merielle's eyes, but gripping her hands more tightly than he realised. 'I don't know,' he whispered. 'Really, mistress, that's the truth. The woman looked after her from birth, you know that. You saw her. I believed she was competent, but...' His hands began to shake and finally released hers to grab at a log and throw it on to the already blazing fire as a diversion.

He was as tall as Sir Rhyan but less robust, and already showing a thickening of the waistline where a gold-buckled belt sagged beneath a corpulence of cashmere folds. He wore his fine, deeply dagged black gupon longer than Sir Rhyan's, though there was no shortage of gold-embroidered edges, buttons, chains, clasps and rings to compensate the eye for his lack of good looks. He was known for his astute business sense, his wealth and ambition, his loyalty to the king, and, only a year ago, for his young and lovely new wife. At forty-two, it could only have been his wealth and standing that remained attractive to a young woman straight from a convent.

Seeing him again after the deliberations of the last eight months, Merielle was concerned to see how the lines around his eyes had deepened and the folds had become hoods, the pouches sagging on to his cheeks. Another two teeth had disappeared and the newest white hairs paled what had once been a rich tawny head of hair, his best feature. Obviously his illness, whatever it was, had taken its toll.

No doubt he had seen a change in her, too. 'The coroner?' Merielle whispered. 'Did he have an opinion?'

'He looked, but found nothing significant except a bump on the forehead where she must have hit the foot of the table. He obviously saw no reason to disbelieve the woman's story. He agreed that she was damned careless, but he said it was not uncommon. Delicate little things, infants. Might have been different if she'd still been swaddled, you see, mistress, but she was being changed-over, or whatever they call it.'

'Changed, yes.' Mentally, Merielle saw the soft pink folds of flesh, the sporadic kicks and jerking waves, felt its warmth, heard its squeaks and gurgles. Turning, she bumped blindly into Sir Rhyan who caught her on one arm, both of them missing the appraising glance of the bereaved father.

Until she could bring her breathing back under control, she accepted Sir Rhyan's support, not caring that he would be able to feel her shaking. Willing her mind away from the tender scene, she noted instead how Allene, in the space of one hour, had had the house-servants clear the debris from the solar and tower-chamber, make up beds with clean linen, light fires, sweep floors and change the rushes, replace the sconces with new beeswax candles and half-unpack their panniers. She was now noisily scouring the garderobe, having declared that no lady could be expected to use that filthy hole. If Sir Adam noticed her less-than-subtle comings and goings, he made no comment, but studied instead the piles of clothes that littered the chest and bed.

'It's a blessing that my nephew was visiting, mistress. Without his help, you'd not have been here when you were most needed.'

Sir Rhyan replied for her. 'Matthew tells me we were not expected today, uncle. How long did you think it would take us? A week?'

'Well, yes, I suppose I did. I take it you followed my suggestions for accommodation along the way?'

'Almost, sir.'

'Almost?' The question was sharp. 'You stayed at

Leeds Castle first, surely? I expected Wykeham and
Yeaveley to be with you, as well as Master John, here.'

Sir Rhyan led Merielle to the bed and seated her
carefully on the ledge that surrounded it. 'Yes, Leeds
first, then Otford. But we missed Guildford out, because…'

'Eh? Missed…tch!' Sir Adam looked at Merielle and
then swung irritably away from the illuminating fire,
stalking to the door. 'Come, nephew, if you please. I
wish you'd kept to my list. Let me have the details of
this journey.' He paused long enough for Sir Rhyan to
open the door for him, bowed to Merielle and left the
room before Allene's next noisy outburst of disgust.

In the window-recess, sitting with his knees under
his chin, Master John felt the silence more keenly than
Merielle, who was already in a silence of her own.
'Would you prefer it if I left you in peace?' he said.

Trance-like, Merielle located the sound. 'Ah, Master
John. No, I thank you. But this has been a subdued
homecoming for you.'

His home was neither as fine nor as much in need
of a thorough clean as this one. While Merielle's sister
had been alive, the place had been spotless. The lithe
young man swung his legs down and came on silent
feet to seat himself at arm's length on the low edge of
the bed-platform. 'This must be the worst possible tid-
ings for you, mistress. I'm so very sorry.'

'It seems to be getting a habit with me,' she whispered. 'I cannot begin to understand it. What have I
done?'

Her sorrowing words made Master John hesitate. 'A
habit, mistress? How so?'

'Just after my husband died, I lost the child I was
carrying. I had hoped to foster my little niece: it would

have been the perfect salve. And then...no.' She brought her memories under control and hoped her slip would have no meaning.

Master John would not pry, even if the facts that lined up in his own memory seemed too unkind to be true. Two infant losses could hardly be called a habit.

For Merielle, the salve that the wise-woman had spoken of had been removed even as the words had been offered, and now the void left behind was something which Merielle could not begin to replenish with alternative interpretations. The ache of motherhood that she had carried this far now threatened to overwhelm her as, blank and stunned, she stared at the flames and accepted the balm of Master John's silent presence.

'It appears, John, that we were expected to have stayed at the royal manor at Guildford for at least two or three days. That is what Sir Adam intended to do if he'd been escorting Mistress St Martin instead of me. Now, what d'ye make of that?'

'So, we *were* expected there, then.'

'Apparently.'

'Then Sir Adam, presumably, will have to make his apologies to someone for not arriving. Do we know who?'

'The same person who went there from Windsor, expecting to meet him and his guest.'

'Oh, dear.'

'Yes. Oh, dear. Yet I cannot believe that, in view of the reluctance of a certain member of our party to be housed under royal roofs, the meeting would have been equally welcome on both sides, John.'

'And you would rather suffer your uncle's censure than the certain member of our party.'

'Certainly I would. Less exhausting.'

'Any explanation given, sir?'

'Not the slightest. The strange thing is that *either* I'm not being expected to see the point of all this *or* that I'm being expected to work it out for myself and go along with it. What's more, far from being a list of suggested stops, it was in fact a list of commands, something I failed to appreciate.'

'But your uncle was ill when he gave it to you, re-member.'

'I reminded him of that.'

'And he agreed…?'

'He didn't agree at all. He was more put out than I can remember. I think I may need your assistance, John. Are you with me?'

'Certainly. But in what manner?'

Sir Rhyan peered out across the vista of green fields and rippling woodland behind the manor house, leaning on hands splayed across the stone window-sill. 'My uncle,' he said, quietly, 'has just lost his most precious bait, and that is a sad blow to him. Now he discovers that a certain meeting he was eager to bring about did not occur. He will no doubt find other enticements which he hopes will prove irresistible, and I shall have to do my damnedest to counter them. By hook or by crook, John, I'll not go back empty-handed again.'

'How long do we have, sir?'

'Hmm. That's a good question, master painter. This business is something of a setback none of us could have foreseen.'

But Master John was by no means sure of that.

The welcoming supper that was supposed to have been a celebration by both parties was a subdued affair at which the central figure, Mistress Merielle St Martin, was absent, having pleaded to be allowed to keep to her own chamber at least until tomorrow.

Her earlier visit to the Abbey of St Mary, where a fresh mound of dark earth lay on Lady Bedesbury's grave, had brought back to Merielle the startling picture of the infant in its mother's arms at last, where Laurel had no doubt wanted it to be. Once again, Merielle was at a loss to understand how the anchoress at Shere could have been so mistaken: the infant was supposed to have been a gift to her as a comfort for her own loss, so why this sudden change of plan?

She had knelt to touch the earth with the flat of her hand, whispering words of solace to the departed ones and feeling a guilty pang that it was her, not they, who needed solace. But Allene and Bess and Sir Rhyan had been standing by, and she had forced herself not to give way to the shattering waves of grief, and the single white eglantine rose from the garden was laid upon the mound without a tear being shed to water it.

When she had told them of her intention to visit the child's ex-nurse at the Sustren Spital, they had persuaded her that it was too near supper-time: the nursing sisters would probably prefer her to go in the morning. Sir Rhyan had felt her shaking like an aspen leaf as she rode pillion behind him, and he had later conspired with Mistress Allene to put her to bed with an infusion of lemon-balm leaves.

'She's not wept, Mistress Allene,' Sir Rhyan whispered at the door. 'Would it not be better if she did?'

'Aye, sir. It'll all come out in a day or two, I reckon. It's the shock, you see. It was like this before.'

He nodded and left them alone, hoping that events would not precipitate a return to Canterbury and wish-

ing most fervently that he had been allowed to share
in Merielle's grief.

The Sustren Spital was easily reached from Wood
Street by taking the southern fork of the road that
skirted the city wall and following it till just past the
King's Gate. Here, the overspill of dwellings spread
into the southern suburb within easy reach of the cathedral, a most convenient arrangement for the brothers
of St Swithun's Cathedral Priory who managed the
hospital's spiritual and financial affairs. The nurses,
Benedictine lay-sisters mostly, had dwindled in number
since the great pestilence ten years ago and were now
only eight, with some fifteen women-patients between
them. Hard work, but they managed.

Once inside the gates, one could see how the hospital
building was surrounded by a network of walled gardens, a pond yard for fish, a piggery, hen-coops and
stables, vegetable plots and daisy-covered lawns where
elderly patients sat in half-sleep or quiet contemplation
in the morning sunshine. Beyond were the well-tended
gardens of St Swithun's Priory and, on the water-
meadow, a herd of white goats mingled with two
white-clad women gathering armfuls of plants. Beside
the building, an orchard was loaded with blossom that
pulled the branches down to meet the creamy platters
of angelica.

In the courtyard, the sister at the water-pump arched
her back after hauling at the dead weight of the bucket,
pushing her sleeves further up her arms. 'You may
leave your horses over there in the shade, mistress,'
she said, eyeing them calmly. 'I take it you're visiting,
not staying?' Her habit was something between a nun's

and a servant's, her wimple and veil caught back behind her shoulders, an apron tied around her waist.

Allene and Bess tied the horses and followed Merielle and the sister into the cool building. Shafts of light fell across a large hall divided into cubicles by white curtains that floated in the draught from the door, hiding and revealing the rows of bedded occupants. At once, the sister who had shown them in withdrew at the approach of an older woman, white-clad, tall, elegant and dark-eyed.

'Good-day, mistress. How may I help you?' she said, softly.

'Good-day, sister. I come from Sir Adam Bedesbury to enquire after his child's nurse, Mistress Waterford. I am the child's aunt, sister.' She saw the beginnings of a refusal in the experienced eyes and watched how they changed to acceptance at the mention of a relationship. A careful guardian indeed.

'Ah. She was brought in on Wednesday. You were there…?'

'No, sister. I arrived in Winchester only yesterday.'

The sister nodded, noting the expensive fabric of her visitor's blue-grey surcoat and the gold nets that held the heavy plaits of hair. Nor did she miss the pain in the eyes, the pale complexion. This woman cared, but for the lost child rather than for the demented woman in their charge. 'I see. Will you follow me, Mistress—?'

'St Martin of Canterbury.'

The sister's fine eyebrows twitched. 'Ah…the tapicier!'

'You know the name?'

'I should. My late husband, God rest his soul, was Philippe of Canterbury's partner until he died in the

summer of fifty- five. I moved back to my home town
to take up God's work here.'

'Master Robert of Whitstable!'

'That's right. I'm Edith of Whitstable, except that
I'm not, I'm of Winchester.' She smiled at last.

'And that was the year I married Philippe. October,
it was, so I never met your husband, Dame Edith. My
Philippe died the following summer.'

'I heard. I'm sorry. You were married less than a
year.'

'As I was to my first husband. And less than a year
as aunt to my…' She took deep gulps of air to steady
her lungs. 'Forgive me.'

Dame Edith placed a hand over Merielle's arm and
squeezed gently. 'We shall have to talk one day, my
dear. Come. Follow.'

Mistress Claire Waterford, the child's nurse, was not
in the larger ward, but in a small chamber to one side
where her ramblings could not disturb the other patients. The room was stark and peacefully white with
only a crucifix to adorn the wall, but sunlight filtered
through boughs of pink blossom, dappling the sheet
and textured coverlet. The patient's head was enclosed
in a white coif, her body in white linen, the only colour
coming from flecks of bright red blood being wiped
from her lips by a young sister.

'The wasting sickness,' Dame Edith whispered.
'We've not made much progress so far. She's not been
able to make her confession yet, so we know nothing
of what might be troubling her mind.'

'Wasting sickness? Is that what they call the lung-
pox?'

'I fear so. We're giving her mallow-root, figs and

elecampane in honey, and a sedative at night. She's still very poorly.'

'She's taking food?'

'Only a little. Baked apples and goat's milk, that's the traditional remedy, but I believe the pox may have spread too far.'

'Has she spoken of the accident, Dame Edith?'

'She rambles a great deal, so it's difficult to know what she's trying to say. A day or two of rest and she may become more lucid. They often do, you know. Bouts of alternate strength and weakness.'

'They tell me the child fell while she was being unwrapped and changed. Does that make any sense to you?'

Dame Edith studied the sleeping face on the pillow. 'Overcome by a bout of coughing, there'd be little the poor creature could do except turn away from the child and cling to some support. The one thing that surprises me, mistress, is why on earth she was alone with the child. There should have been at least two, if not three, nurses on hand. It might be worth trying to find the answer to that.'

'It seemed strange to me also; I'll find out what I can. Is there anything I can do to help? Would a donation be out of order?'

'On the contrary, we rely on donations as much as on the St Swithun's clergy, so I never refuse offers of help, whatever form they take. It usually helps those who give as much as those who receive.'

Merielle opened her pouch and brought out a handful of gold nobles, taking Dame Edith's hand into her own and placing them in her cupped palm. 'I would like to visit again, if I may,' she whispered, close to tears.

Their common bonds brought them together as if

they'd been friends for years and their arms reached
for each other in an embrace of sisterly affection. 'They
won't prosecute her, will they?' Merielle asked.

'Hardly. She'll have gone to her Maker before they
can make out a case against her. Did you know her
well?'

'Not well. My sister died from milk-fever within a
month of the birth and Mistress Waterford has attended
the child from the beginning. There was a wet-nurse,
of course, who lived in, and a maid, but my brother-
in-law seemed to think that that was as many women
as he wanted in his house. She never liked me very
much, I'm afraid. I don't know why.'

'Mmm. Nurses are sometimes possessive. Is there no
Master Waterford? She wears a ring, but...'

'Oh, yes. She's the wife of Sir Adam's house-
steward, Brian Waterford, an Irishman. He's been with
Sir Adam for years. He's not been to see her?'

'No, not yet. Are they childless?'

'Er...as far as I know. I'll make enquiries.'

'And I'll do the same. That'll answer some questions. They don't tell you these things unless you ask;
they just dump them on the doorstep and go. You're
the first person to come from Sir Adam to find out how
she fares. Ah, here's your lass with the horses.'

'I'll come again tomorrow, dame. God be with you.'

'And with you. Maybe we'll have had some sense
from her by then.' She tapped her white-coiffed head.
'Many illnesses begin in here, you know.' The soft
dark eyes remained steadfast until Merielle had
mounted, warming to a smile as her visitors passed
beyond the gateway.

Sir Adam's distress at the loss of his infant daughter,
to whom, it must be admitted, he had not paid as much

attention as he might have done to a son, could not be expected to last much beyond the funeral. So, by the time Merielle returned from the Sustren Spital, he was quite ready to get down to serious talks about their future together, apparently seeing no reason for her lack of interest.

Merielle had some trouble swinging his mind back to more immediate matters. 'Sir Adam, did you know that Mistress Waterford's husband has not yet been to see how she is? Isn't it time he went?'

'Brian? Well…' He scratched at his sandy head with a rasping sound and then studied his fingernails. 'He knows she's safe. It's a case of fitting it in with his duties here, you know. Extra guests make more cleaning, beds, fuel, food…'

'Most of that was done before he showed his nose on the scene, Sir Adam,' Merielle said, sweetly. 'His wife is extremely ill.'

'She deserves to be,' he said, moving one of his sleeping gazehounds from the hearth with his foot. 'The damned woman dropped my child.'

'No, sir. The damned woman, as you call her, dropped your child *because* she was ill, not the other way round.'

'Eh? Oh…yes, well that's as may be. The thing is, mistress, have you considered what we…?'

'Sir Adam,' she interrupted, 'did you have any particular reason for continuing to employ Mistress Waterford as little Joanie's nurse when you suspected she was unwell? And did you have any particular reason for not employing more help in the nursery? Three nurses would not have been too many, you know.' Instinctively, she knew that two questions were too many for an interview of this nature, and for a man suffering from gout.

Sir Adam pinched his nose in annoyance and rubbed at it, peevishly. 'Oh, rubbish! She had a cough. So do we all at this time of year. And I don't particularly want a house full of w—er...' He sniffed, totally lost down the wrong track. 'No...er, well...oh, but I didn't mean...'

Merielle almost bumped into Sir Rhyan on the way out of the hall but didn't stop to greet him or to explain that she was of the wrong gender, that his uncle was little interested in the reason for his daughter's untimely death or in the well-being of his employees. Quite aware that her behaviour would be seen as typically unreasonable and that it would thereby add credence to Sir Adam's opinions, she chose not to return and apologise but took the nearest passageway that led down a spiral staircase in the thickness of the wall and out through a door that only a midget would have appreciated.

She found herself at the side of the house in a narrow space between the dung-heap and the vegetable garden that led directly into the field beyond, an enticing view of cool greenness topped by darker trees. Thirsting for isolation, she walked on.

Beneath her bare feet, the bluebell carpet was cool, and sounds receded as she moved through the embrace of the fully flowering elders that deadened the din from the noisy manor. Here was the silence of the wind high in the trees, the chink-chink of alarmed blackbirds, the mad ticking of crickets. And here was also the deafening silence of confused thoughts, of suppressed anguish, of a heartache that welled up into her throat with each running stride. With no one to see or hear her, she could no longer hold back the contorting grimace of pain or the whimper that came with it.

Each step took her deeper into the mottled shadows where the play of light made her stumble and catch her hair on the lowest branches that bent to her advance. Wading waist-high through bracken, she was oblivious to the sharp stalks on her feet, aware only of the renewed pain of loss that tore loud sobs from deep within her. They rose to a wild howl like a creature caught in a trap, echoing through the woodland and lifting the heads of the gentle deer until, blinded by tears and by the sudden brightness that pooled around her feet, she sank down into the cool flowers, howling like a child.

The infant who now lay in the cold dark earth would never take its own knee-high steps amongst the bluebells or lilies-of-the-valley, nor would she herself ever suckle as even the smallest woodland creatures did. To relieve the heavy ache in her breasts, she held them, rocking, overcome by the primitive urge to conceive, bear and nurture. So private a moment of unconcealed longing was it, that when the rattle of a horse's bit revealed the presence of one who stood at the other side of the clearing, outrage brought her instantly to her feet with a roar.

'No! Leave me, damn you! Leave me!' Fury brought a fresh bout of tears as Merielle leapt away, crashing back the way she had come, picking up her skirts and wading once again into the waving ocean of bracken.

She knew she was being pursued and that she would eventually be caught, but not so soon. A woody stem jammed between her toes as a hand caught at her arm, and she was brought down, twisting and fighting, deep into the miniature forest of ferns. Held hard against his chest, she could only cry, 'No! No!' but could offer no effective resistance to the strong arms that lifted and carried her back to the glade where the black stallion waited.

The experience of being weightless, even for that short time, combined with her exhaustive weeping to disorientate her, so that when the trees tipped to a strange angle and a coolness pressed against her back, she was overcome by a sudden inevitability and a lethargy she could not combat. When she opened her eyes, his bare arms resembled those same tree-trunks braced on each side of her, his head and shoulders blending into the canopy of fluttering leaves. He had thrown his cloak like a net over the sea of bluebells, made a pillow for her with his clothes and now, stark naked, he lifted her on to them, removing her surcoat and cote-hardie with deft and knowing fingers.

Protestations and resistance were redundant. Helplessness became acceptance, and compliance became rapture when, turning her into his arms, he took her breast into his mouth and gently suckled, massaging the inexplicable tension beneath the skin with his tongue and lips. Tears of relief and gasps of ecstasy mingled with her sorrowing and then replaced it altogether as the suckling continued, sending messages of tingling excitement into her womb. She cradled his head in her arms, caressing his neck and ears, slipping her fingers through his thick hair and burying her nose amongst its dark waves. His shoulders were smoothly mountainous and wide, the hands that captured her breasts large enough to cover them; when he raised his head to look at her, she saw how the muscles of his great chest rose like two mounds and sloped to meet his collarbone. Mottled with light and shade, his body covered and warmed her like a blanket of comfort.

'Shall I go on?' he whispered.

She could not answer except by offering him her swollen lips.

'Sweet, sweet thing. Weep if you must. I can see your pain. Share it with me, Merielle. I'll take it. I'll carry it for you, if you'll let me.'

His kisses were heady, coaxing and masterly and Merielle's responses were heightened by her need of comfort and of him. The reasons she had held so securely for not allowing him into her life, reasons to do with the very pain he was offering to carry, were being released far beyond recall. She did need him. She had needed him long before this and he had already tried to respond, as much as she had allowed him in her anger.

Before her sanity lost its footing, it reminded her, in the space of one mini-second, how a man could remain emotionally uninvolved far longer than a woman, and how he could walk away whenever he was ready, leaving her with the consequences of a bruised heart and body, and perhaps more. But his knee took advantage of her procrastination and nudged itself with resolve into her groin, allowing her no more time to deliberate. His kisses melted her and she opened to him, already lost.

Just as the first time had been tailored to her fierce mood, he took his second possession of her more gently, for he could see that weeping had sapped her energy. And if Merielle had any doubts about whether he was about to give or take, they were dispelled instantly when his deep and delayed penetration drew from her equally deep and audible sighs, taken up in chorus by the trees above them. Gentle it may have been, but no less effective, for the woman who had been moaning in distress only a few moments earlier now tossed obliviously beneath him, her unloosed hair spilling like black water over her skin. Incredulous, she gave herself up to his slow and seductive domination.

Almost, but not quite, he withdrew from her. 'Look at me, Merielle,' he commanded.

She shook her head. 'Come back. Please, come back.'

'No! Look at me.'

Prepared to plead, she opened her eyes, blearily.

'You're mine, Merielle. Do you understand? Mine!'

'Yes.'

'My name.'

'Rhyan.'

'Again.' Still he held off, demanding her acceptance.

'Please, Rhyan, I want you. Help me. I need you.'

He slid back into her with a masculine grunt of triumph, relief and effort, taking him further, further, bringing down a shower of stars upon their heads that changed into green dust on contact with his back. At one with the earth and its growing things, with its sounds and scents, the two lovers made long, slow forays that changed pace time after time until a rush of exhilaration took them over the edge, drawing cries of ravishing pleasure from them both as they fell, in harmony.

Chapter Nine

She awoke to the caress of his hand over her hips, her face turned into the warm angle of his chin and neck. His cloak had been pulled over them both, his legs entwined with hers, and she was loath to move, so long had she wanted this. She tried to recall what he had said during their rapturous loving, whether it had been significant enough to change anything between them, and then decided that it must have been, or she could not have been so at peace.

'What was that you said, knight?'

His hand dipped into the deep valley of her waist and up the other side. 'I said, woman, that you're mine and that I'd be very much obliged if you'd make an effort to remember it. Did you think you'd dreamed it?'

A dried-up sob made a late exit as her lips played over his throat. 'No, I remembered that bit.'

'I'm relieved to hear it. What, then?'

'About helping me?'

Trying not to dislodge her, he propped himself up on one elbow to look down at her face, brushing away the damp strand of hair before placing a tender kiss on her spiky-wet eyelashes. 'I have been trying, Merielle of Canterbury, to help you for the last seven days. Has it taken a whole week for you to accept it and ask for more?' Then, instantly relenting at her expression of contrition, he told her what she needed to know at that moment, above everything else. 'Sweet thing, there is no need to take on each problem single-handed. Share them with me. Trust me, Merielle.'

Recalling certain advice so recently given, some of which she was sure had been mistaken, she reserved her reply to his last request while searching his eyes for honesty. She saw nothing there to make her doubt, yet she had already been touched by his considerable power and, in a way, still feared it.

'You said, last time we did this, that you could give me babies.'

He touched her cheek with his thumb. 'I can.'

'Then what if that were to happen? Now. Had you thought of that?'

'My lovely Venus. You have an appallingly short memory regarding certain matters. I told you, earlier, that you belong to me. I intend to keep you by my side until you learn to trust me, and when you give me that trust, I shall make you my wife. So it's up to you, sweetheart, to start learning before those bairns appear. Which they will.'

Tears started again and had nowhere to go, so he put his lips to her eyes and licked them away.

Tenderly, he rocked her in his arms. 'I know that something happened, sweetheart, to tear you apart. The miscarriage and then my ill-timed lawsuit, your appeal, and I know that somehow you hold me responsible. Maybe one day you will be able to tell me what it is so that I can put it right. I was never your sister's lover, as you believe—'

'Believed,' she cried.

'Good. I'm glad that's agreed. I am not eager to repossess your lands in Yorkshire although I do want you to manage them properly. I want you and only you. Do you believe that?'

'Is that why you will not allow me to marry without your permission?'

He smiled into her eyes, wickedly. 'That made you angry, didn't it?'

'Yes, it did; and it'll make Sir Adam angry, too.'

'I can deal with my uncle. I can deal with you, too.'

'You took advantage of me once again, knight.' She hid her face in his neck.

'So I did. What did you expect me to do, wait till you were strong? We're encouraged to be chivalrous, sweet thing, not to take leave of our senses.'

'A chivalrous knight would have given a lady some choice.'

His laugh was almost silent, showing his perfect teeth. 'Don't you believe it. Any knight with his wits about him makes sure that the choices are with him. That's how he wins.'

'And you believe you've won, do you?'

'Getting there,' he whispered against her mouth. 'Wouldn't you agree?'

'I agree that you're extremely arrogant, sir.'

'Inherited, like my size.' He robbed her of the last word.

If any man had asked her to explain the incredible foolhardiness of wanting her offspring to be fathered by a man in whom she had not yet learned to trust, she would have had to fall back on the unconvincing but well-worn excuse that women in love did strange and foolish things. No woman, of course, would have needed to ask. Fortunately, Sir Rhyan did not need an explanation, nor did he view her new acceptance of him with anything but relief, delight and a certain natural pride in his achievement.

Merielle, however, viewed it as a personal failure. 'I never meant this to happen,' she whispered, fingering his strong jaw and chin. 'But there are times when...'

He caught her hand and kissed its palm. 'Shh...don't feel sore about it. I love your fierceness. You would have held me off longer, I know, had it not been for your grief, but I would have won, sooner or later. And anyway, you left your protector, your faithful Bonard, behind, didn't you?'

She smiled at that. 'He's so good. So loyal.'

'And in love with you.'

'He's one of those rare characters who sees the good in everyone. Even you,' she added, remembering their last conversation.

'Even me? Then he's more perceptive than I thought. I shall make an ally of him, Mistress Merielle of Canterbury.'

'You don't use my married name.'

'Then you'll have to change it, won't you?'

'I have not agreed to do that, knight.'

'You will, woman. The contract...remember?' He levered her up and reached for her clothes, revealing to her his beautifully muscled body that tapered towards narrow hips, the dark downy covering over his legs and arms. Even with the fine white lines of scars on his neck and shoulders, he was flawless.

She rode pillion behind him, grateful for the extra time over a devious route that approached the manor

from the side courtyard. It had taken them some time
to locate her shoes, but even that had not been the
aggravation it would have been if she'd been alone.
His closeness warmed and calmed her, as he had said
it would, and although her grief was no less, the suf-
focating blackness of it was.

There had been a few times, during the winter, when
Merielle had fancied herself as mistress of this place,
but now she was hard-pressed to remember why, except for the escape it offered, and the child. In the nine
months since the death of her sister, it had lapsed into
a scruffiness for which Mistress Allene had a more explicit name; the servants, all men, less aware of their
duties than when there had been a woman to carp at
them. Compared to her well-run establishment at Canterbury, Sir Adam's large manor displayed a lamenta-
ble lack of domestic management about which the Irish
Brian Waterford was as little concerned as he was
about his sick wife at the Sustren Spital. Hardly a
chamber was without its festoon of cobwebs, without
the stink of filthy squelching rushes or sooted and dusty
walls and window-ledges. And though Sir Adam was
Master of Works at Winchester, the case of the cob-
bler's family going barefoot was never more applicable
than here.

The outside was no better: heaps of kitchen refuse
buzzed with flies near the doorways to the pantry and
dairy, the waste from the garderobes still smeared
down the stonework into the open cesspits, and the
granary nearest the brewhouse was awash with grain
from burst sacks that tempted hoards of rats, even in
the daytime. If Sir Adam wanted her to stay here for
some time, Merielle thought, the reason was not hard

to find, for even her younger sister had imposed some standards.

On the stallion's black rump, their back-to-front conversation was both intimate and practical, Sir Rhyan seeing the issues from a broader standpoint. 'If my uncle suspects that I intend to have you for myself, he'll probably send me packing. And I mean to stay long enough to find out what he's up to.'

Merielle, her cheek pressed against his back, pretended disinterest. 'I have no more intention than you, knight, of telling the world how I've been rolling about in bluebells with a man. I'm a respectable widow.'

Sir Rhyan smiled and ventured a hand out behind him to caress her thigh. 'So you are, woman. So you are. A beautiful, desirable, respectable widow that I can scarce keep my hands off.'

'I shall return home soon.'

'You're going up to Yorkshire with me as soon as I've found out what I want to know. If it's really marriage my uncle's offering you, I shall be the one to forbid it.'

'You don't think I should accept him, then?' She smiled into his back.

'Discuss whatever you wish, woman, but that subject will be a waste of time.' He would not tell her of his interview with Sir Adam regarding the planned route to Winchester from which they had digressed, or of Sir Adam's barely suppressed annoyance that they had missed meeting the king at Guildford.

'He's looking to appoint a royal tapicier, lad. For the first time ever,' Sir Adam had told him. 'If I'd been there, it would have been sewn up by now, but I thought I could rely on you, of all people.'

Sir Rhyan had had the temerity to answer back.

'Then why didn't you say as much before I set off?
And why did she have to be delayed along the route?
You knew how eager she was to see the child. That
was why she agreed to come, wasn't it?'

'There were one or two other reasons.' He had not
elaborated except to say that the gatherings of those
who were to be involved in the refurbishment of the
king's residences would have been a perfect chance to
whet Mistress St Martin's appetite. 'I was trying to do
her a favour, lad,' he said. 'To put some important
commissions in her way. Royal ones.'

Sir Rhyan had not been totally convinced by that
seemingly artless explanation, but he had left it at that.

Having almost lost interest in Sir Adam's plans,
Merielle was more concerned about little Joanie and
her nurse, and about Laurel's boast that Sir Adam was
not the father. If not his, and not Sir Rhyan's, then
whose? To voice these concerns to Sir Rhyan again
might imply that she still had doubts about his denial.
It would also show that she wished to pursue the matter
of Sir Adam's inability to father a child, something
about which she was unlikely to acquire proof. These
were not concerns about which she could ask for his
help, except in a roundabout way.

'Could you find out what you can from Master Waterford about his wife?' she asked, as they approached
the courtyard.

'The child's nurse?'

'Yes—if they have a family; how long they've been
married; what her experience is as a child's nurse; who
recommended her? That kind of thing.'

'How often they make love, without prying, you
mean? Certainly, mistress. He'll be within his rights to

tell me to mind my own business, but I'll ask, just for you. Look who's here.'

The courtyard was crowded with horses, barking hounds and the familiar figures of Master Henry Yeaveley, the king's mason and architect, and Master William Wykeham, the king's surveyor at Windsor. Surrounding them were their assistants, apprentices, and panniers full of equipment. There was no escaping their notice.

The mid-morning meal was a lively affair for which Mistress Allene's excursions into the kitchen garden had not come a moment too soon. Neither of the two extra guests were insensitive men, but the news of Sir Adam's infant daughter saddened them only temporarily and, though Master Yeaveley had lost several infants of his own, his preoccupation with his craft soon eclipsed the event from his mind, as it did for the others in a way Merielle was not able to do. Sir Rhyan shielded her from their good-natured but inappropriate heartiness and then, with Master John, accompanied Merielle to the tower chamber where the brightly painted walls were lit by the full mid-day sun.

With the wooden rocking-cradle replaced by Mistress Allene's canopied bed, the chamber had become less of a reminder of the tragedy and more a reflection of the lovely fair-haired girl for whom this had been an ivory tower, her personal place of escape. The deep lancet windows looked out from the front corner of the house where the tower had been built-on to enlarge the existing sunny chamber, and the inner walls were alive with patterns and scenes from floor to ceiling.

The ceiling itself was painted an intense blue and littered with stars, suns and moons, crosses and fleurs-de-lis of gold, white and yellow. Below this, the scenes of every wall were an unusual medley of stories that appeared largely to concentrate on women's biblical and mythological exploits.

'Hardly suitable for a nursery, surely,' Sir Rhyan murmured. 'Who suggested the subjects, John?'

'Lady Bedesbury herself, sir. The king's orders to me were to paint whatever Sir Adam and Lady Bedesbury wished, though of course there was no talk of it being a nursery at that time. It took me well over a month to do this place.'

'With assistants, surely?' said Merielle. She had seen the room, newly painted, while her sister was alive, and had thought then, as she did now, that the subjects were typical of the romantically inclined and somewhat frivolous girl, a fifteen-year-old married to a man in his middle age. Master John's figures were almost life-size, enclosed within scrolling vines and set against diaper-patterns of chequers, chevrons and lattices. 'They must have had to prepare a great deal of paint, Master John.'

He nodded, flipping his dark silky fringe. 'I remember we used about two hundred leaves of gold on those stars and suns,' he laughed. 'I had Padraig do those. We used almost twenty pounds of white lead and six pounds each of red lead and vermilion, about five of blue, I think, and the same of verdigris.'

'That's for the green?'

'Yes, and there were others. Charcoal and lampblack and ochres are cheap enough, but some are very expensive, which is why we must reserve them for the most important bits. The blue, for instance.'

'And you use oil to bind them?'

'Not on plasterwork, sir. Linseed oil we use on woodwork, but limewash must be damped as we go along, and then the colours are bound with lime-water and skimmed milk.'

'I thought you used egg whites,' Merielle said.

'Not on limewashed walls, mistress. The lads grind the colours on stone slabs, just as much as I'm going to need that day. What d'ye think of the subject matter, then? Does it remind you of your sister?'

'Well, the mermaid and the centaur were certainly favourites of hers. She loved mythical beings, and I think she used to see herself as a mermaid when she was very young.' The pink voluptuous, ogling creature with the tail was similar to Laurel only in the abundance of flaxen hair, but it was the centaur facing her that caught Merielle's eye more than the mermaid, for his sudden resemblance to Sir Rhyan could surely not be accidental or imagined.

'And who's the centaur?' she asked. 'Anyone we know?'

The men laughed, exchanging glances. Sir Rhyan's arm stole around her shoulders, drawing her close to him. 'It must be Master Wishful-Thinking,' he whispered loudly in her ear. 'A supposedly lustful wretch with a bow and arrow ready to pierce the imagination of mermaids. No one can get more fanciful than that, sweetheart.'

'You mean—' she turned to Master John '—she actually asked you to make him look like Sir Rhyan? Really?'

'At the time, mistress, I had not met the one she was describing to me, so it was not until Sir Rhyan and I met in Canterbury last week that I realised who she had asked me to paint. However, might I point out that Lady Bedesbury's instructions were inaccurate. She naturally assumed that her centaur, like those from an-

cient Greece, would be hairy-chested, when I have seen
from my own observations that he is not.'

Without comment, Sir Rhyan moved on to the sections between the windows. 'Who are these two? Ah,
let me guess. Adam and Eve. Yes?'

Disinclined to doubt Master John's explanation, or
indeed Sir Rhyan's, Merielle nevertheless experienced
something of her previous annoyance at Laurel's girlish
crush on the dark and handsome man with whom, unlike Merielle herself, she had been on cordial terms.
To have been so brazen as to have him depicted on her
walls was, Merielle thought, disturbing to say the least,
though the centaur's decidedly hairy chest gave her
some consolation. Had it done the same for Sir Adam?

The naked figures in the Garden of Eden were indeed
those of Adam and Eve, but here was a discrepancy
that Laurel had vaguely explained away as the artist's
apprentice's fault. 'Why is Adam offering the apple to
Eve instead of the other way round?' Merielle asked.

'Because that's the way Lady Bedesbury wanted it,
mistress.'

'It was her suggestion?'

'It was her command. I didn't argue.'

Needless to say, Eve's hair was, like the mermaid's,
long and blonde, while Adam's was the same colour
as his namesake.

The next space between the windows was taken up
by Judith and her maid striking off the head of the
commander Holofernes, which came in for no comment except about its savagery, and Master John's, 'I
believe she admired the lady's courage,' before moving
on to the next mural. This one showed Salome dancing
before King Herod. The woman's posture, bending
backwards to make an arch over the floor, was common

enough with female dancers whose tantalising displays were often more acrobatic than artistic.

It brought a frown to Merielle's brow, for now she was beginning to see undertones she had not previously noticed during her sister's dismissive interpretations, and though Master John's only wish was to oblige the patron, Laurel's intent appeared to be of a different nature. The large adjoining wall seemed, after that, to be a natural progression of the same womanly theme.

'The wise and foolish virgins,' Master John told them, tenderly fingering the surface to test its stability.

'Another strange subject. Especially for a new married woman,' said Sir Rhyan.

'As are they all, sir, if I may say so.'

'And where are you, Master John? Did you not say,' Merielle asked, 'that you painted yourself in somewhere, as a signature?'

They might have expected a grin of mischief, of which the king's painter had a good store, but he looked instead as if he had hoped Merielle would not ask. 'I'm here,' he said, evasively.

'Where?' they said, in chorus, realising he was not going to show them. But he was not so very hard to find, standing as a small man behind King Herod's chair, peering cautiously round to watch the dancer's bending figure whose semi- transparent shift was responsible for the king's glazed expression.

'Did my sister notice you?' said Merielle, low-voiced.

'No, mistress. As I said, artists are invisible.'

Master John's account of the decoration of the tower room did nothing to clarify Merielle's thoughts about her sister's relationship with Sir Adam. Already in no doubt that Laurel had desperately been seeking another

dimension to the marriage for which Merielle herself
had partly been responsible. She had, after all, not
made it easy for Laurel to refuse the offer, having persuaded her that marriage to Sir Adam was a small price
to pay for independence from a sister. Never having
met the man recommended by the king, Merielle now
saw what she had pushed her sister into, selfishly
grasping at the offer before having assured herself of
Sir Adam's suitability. Not that it would have made
any difference. In the turmoil that had followed her
interview with the king, Merielle had dismissed that
part of the proceedings from her mind, little realising
how quickly he would set the wheels in motion, nor
how dearly it would cost them both.

On the next day, rejecting Sir Rhyan's offer to accompany her to see Mistress Waterford at the Sustren
Spital, she accepted instead his proposal to appoint receivers and stewards to travel to Yorkshire and make
a detailed review of her property there.

With the weight of that responsibility removed from
her shoulders, she took Allene and Bess with her to the
whitewashed hospital, loaded down with baskets of
eggs, butter, cheeses, new bread, herrings, honey and
last year's apples and a large bundle of baby clothes
which the two women had secretly collected together.

Dame Edith of Whitstable had seen them coming
and crossed the courtyard to meet them, her arms ready
to embrace and draw the women forward into the cool
building. Her face lit at the sight of gifts. 'A little progress,' she said. 'Mistress Waterford's taken some food
and has been awake once or twice. Come, she may
even recognize you.'

'Her husband's not been yet?'

The deep-set eyes drew heavy lids over the word as if no alternative existed. 'No.'

'He will,' Merielle said. 'If I have to drag him here myself.'

A fine net of wrinkles enclosed the eyes. 'His wife won't care how he comes,' she said, chuckling at the improbable image.

Following Dame Edith across the dormitory, Merielle was surprised. 'You mean, she wants to see him?'

'Aye, she does. All her talk's been of him, so far. Dotes on him, by the sound o' things.'

'No family, then?'

'Don't think so. I'd swear she's not borne a child. Not a sign.'

Exactly what signs were revealed when one had borne children Merielle was uncertain, unless they were signs of happiness. A jug of blue cranesbills and creamy meadowsweet filled one corner of the small chamber where the white-coiffed head of the drowsing patient rested, her face towards the sun-filled window.

She turned at the almost soundless approach and her eyes, pale and sunken in pools of brown skin, watched Merielle in particular, recognising her. 'Her sister,' she said.

Merielle came forward, sitting lightly on the white bedcover. 'Yes, Lady Bedesbury was my sister. You cared for my niece.'

The voice became a whisper. 'Look after her...the little one. She's precious to me.'

Merielle, uncertain how to proceed in the change from past to present, looked to Dame Edith who took her patient's hand and encouraged her to continue. 'Yes, she'll look after her. You love the little one, do you not?'

'As my own.' The sound was now so insubstantial that a draught might have carried it off. 'And Brian… he'll…'

'Yes?'

'He'll want to see her. He was fond. Let him see her.' Her eyes closed with the effort, missing the exchanged glances of her two guests.

'Your husband?' Merielle willed the woman to explain.

But the patient had said enough, and spoke as though in sleep. 'He never had one from me. Black-haired little darling. Just like her father, she is.'

Hair stood on end along Merielle's arms. 'Her father?'

'Aye.' The sound was so faint that they had to lean forward to catch it. 'Her father. My Brian. Make sure he gets to see her.' Her head turned away from them and it was clear that the effort of speaking had exhausted her.

Dame Edith signalled Merielle to leave her, shepherding her through the door. 'She's had enough,' she said, taking Merielle's arm.

Beneath the heavy boughs of cherry blossom, Allene and Bess talked to a group of elderly patients and helped them shell peas while Merielle, dazed and incredulous, was drawn down on to a stone bench along the wall side to sit with Dame Edith. The water in the courtyard trough stretched like a satin skin across the stone, mirroring the sky and the dance of a mayfly, and a grey-patterned cat twisted and rolled in a pool of sunshine, displaying its pure white vest to the sun.

'What's she saying, Dame Edith? That…?'

'Nah!' The older woman lifted a hand to halt the useless probing. 'I told you, she rambles. Of course her husband's not the father. How could he be? Take no notice, m'dear.'

'But little Joanie did have black hair.'

'But hair colour doesn't prove…' Her assurance tailed away before the next attempt. 'Listen. The poor woman's mind is troubled. You cannot make anything of what she says when she's in this state. Give her a few days to settle down. She'll improve, I'm sure of it.' She watched Merielle's troubled face. 'You have reason to believe her, do you?'

Merielle nodded, biting her lip. 'Something my sister said, once. I've nothing to go on. Nothing definite.'

'Heaven forbid. She was not promiscuous, was she? A convent-bred girl? That would be sad indeed.'

'No, dame. Not promiscuous, but out of her depth, I fear, as I was when I first married. As I expect you were also.'

Dame Edith's warm hand reached out to cover Merielle's. 'Indeed I was, though I had time to get used to my man, which you did not. Still, there was no one more amazed than my Robert when Philippe of Canterbury began chasing up to Lincoln to court you. So you see, the attraction was very great.' She smiled, remembering. 'He told Robert he was going up there on business, at first. In winter, I ask you!'

'Amazed? Why?'

At once, Dame Edith squeezed the hand under hers, realising how her words must have sounded. 'Ah, no. But Philippe had never shown the slightest interest in women until that moment. And we had so much work on hand, it seemed the oddest time to choose to be absent, time after time.'

Memories began to connect in Merielle's mind.

'Was that the time Master John Kenton designed a set of tapestries for the workshop?'

'Oh, Master John had done them by then. They were already on the looms by the time Philippe began his trips to Lincoln. For the archbishop's palace, they were. A very important commission.'

'From the archbishop himself?'

'More important than that. From the king. My Richard…' she chuckled '…began to think there was some connection between that and the sudden interest in the opposite sex but, of course, when he heard of your beauty, he understood why Philippe had waited, for no one loved beauty and perfection more than he did. There was never a man prouder of his achievements than Philippe.' She looked across to the sunny orchard where a burst of laughter rippled through the dappled grass. 'It all seems so far away, doesn't it?'

But to Merielle, it seemed like yesterday.

'Interesting. Very,' was Sir Rhyan's response when Merielle told him of the mysterious interview. 'She might have been rambling, but that doesn't necessarily mean she was talking nonsense.'

'Whatever it means,' Merielle said, holding his wandering hand still over her belly, 'it's useful that you should know what she's said before you speak to her husband. You might also send him to visit her.'

'Master Waterford is my uncle's man. I cannot send him out of the house without his permission.'

'Then I'll send him myself,' Merielle said, shrugging him off.

But she was caught and held against the wall by the great laughing man whose teasing she had not yet learned to understand. 'No, you won't,' he said. 'You go and keep my uncle talking awhile. And understand this, my spitfire, there'll be one commander around here, and only one.'

She glared at him, loving his strength. 'You!' she snapped.

He nodded, once. 'Good. Remember it. It'll save time.'

'Short of that, are you?'

Bracing himself against the wall with a hand on either side of her head, he looked down pointedly at the place where his hand had recently lingered. 'We'll see who's shortest of that in a month or two, eh?' His gaze travelled slowly upwards to find her eyes, but by then they had flinched and sought refuge in the darkest corner of the solar.

Chapter Ten

The two gazehounds, usually so curious, rolled their soft dark eyes and slunk away to safety behind the cushioned stool where their master sat, his bare feet propped up before the fire. The pungent smell surrounding the bowl on the floor was obviously not for them.

'What in pity's name is it, mistress?' Sir Adam spluttered. 'God Almighty! It smells like cow-sh—'

'It is,' Merielle said, unintentionally completing the word. 'Sweet herbs and wheat-bran, too, salt, and wine-vinegar. Come, hold your nose and allow me to plaster you. Heavens, sir, these toes are so swollen.'

This was an act of contrition as much as mercy, for Merielle's previous rudeness was not something she wanted to be remembered for, and while she smeared linen cloths with the healing gunge and laid them tenderly around the inflamed joints, her apology was taken as said.

'You should rest them, you know. Look, here's a bunch of gout-wort to keep in your pouch. Carry it around with you; it'll help to keep the pain away.'

He took the green and white bunch, sniffing at it.

'Can't rest,' he said. 'Too much to do. What did you say it is?'

'Ground elder.' She took more strips of linen from Bess. 'You should keep off the venison, you know. And why can you not delegate? Others do.'

'I do delegate,' Sir Adam replied. 'It's not the venison that makes it worse, it's that damned inferior red wine. But I'm not giving wine up.'

'Rubbish! It's the meat. Why are men so stubborn?'

He pondered the question, unused to having his pronouncements challenged, especially by a woman. His breath was sucked in sharply as the plaster touched his skin. 'Resolute!' he blew out the word. 'Resolute, mistress, not stubborn.'

'I beg your pardon, Sir Adam. Of course, I should have remembered, it's resolute *women* who are stubborn, isn't it? Now, if I bind these gently, we can perhaps have supper in here instead of in the hall, then you won't have to walk, will you?'

'Just we two?'

'No,' she offered the word with a smile. 'With Sir Rhyan and my ladies and your other guests. You'd not desert them so soon, I'm sure.'

He grunted, watching the coils of thick black hair glisten in the firelight. 'And you'll wear the green again?'

Merielle handed the bowl up to Bess, scooped up the linen strips and stood in one graceful movement, knowing that Sir Adam's eyes had not strayed far from the deep scoop of her neckline. She also knew that his request for the green gown was a prelude to the talk he had tried to initiate earlier when she had left him too abruptly, so she made no reply but waited for Bess to leave before drawing up a stool and seating herself

near his propped-up feet. 'Now, Sir Adam.' She
smoothed her skirts, primly. 'You gave me the winter
to think about things, but so much has happened since
I was last here that I've almost forgotten what it was
that you wanted me to decide. Will you refresh my
memory? You could not have offered me marriage, I'm
sure, or I would have remembered that.'

There was a pause in place of an immediate denial,
during which Merielle could almost hear the words being shuffled into position. Even so, they were out of
step. 'Er…yes…no, well, things have changed, you
see, haven't they? Recent events…' He cleared his
throat. 'There was a time, last year after Laurel…
er…went, when I believed you might do far worse for
yourself than take her place, the bairn needing a
mother, and all.' He sighed. 'But even now, without
the little one, you might consider the advantages of
having two homes, one in Canterbury and one here, a
kind of working partnership where you could be mistress of my home and accompany me as my lady. At
the same time, I could help you with important con-
nections that would mean a vast amount of new business for your workshop. You might even want to set
up another branch here in Winchester and bring over
more Flemings to man it. We have everything you'd
need here, dyers, loom-makers, websters. And I can
offer you my protection, companionship, if that's of
any interest to you. Sometimes…' he leaned forward
to search her face '…an older man is more reliable than
a younger one for a woman such as yourself.'

'As a widow, you mean? A widow of means?' She
had meant the qualifying words to amuse him, but saw
that they had missed the mark.

'Well, it's three years, isn't it? And for all I know

you may have given up the idea of raising a family to concentrate on your business. As you know, the St Martin workshop has no parallel in this country. Clients are having to send to Flanders when they would much rather have their tapestries made here, to order. In my official capacity, I can get you commissions from all the royalty and the nobility, mistress.'

'In return for…companionship, was it?'

'A man in my position needs a lady by his side.'

'Yet you were many years without one, sir.'

'I'm choosy. That's why I'd prefer to have you than one I don't know. I've seen how you conduct yourself. I'm impressed: you would be an advantage to me, and I to you.'

'You didn't know my sister too well, did you, Sir Adam?' The question was more a sad comment than a rebuke, and he took it as such.

'No, more's the pity. I was very fond of her. Would you be shocked if I told you I was growing to love her?'

'Would you be shocked, Sir Adam, if I said that the position you are offering her sister sounds remarkably like that of official mistress to Winchester's Master of Works?'

He sighed again and touched the sleek grey head of a sleeping gazehound with his fingertips. 'No, I was aware of how it would sound. I would have offered you marriage, mistress, indeed I would, but it would hardly be in order for my wife to have her own business four days' ride away, would it? That makes little sense of a marriage, I'm sure you agree. A wife must put herself entirely at her husband's disposal, and I could not ask you to forfeit the prestigious St Martin workshop. I prefer to help you build it up, not to sell it off.' Waiting for some response, he read into Merielle's hesitation what he assumed to be the problem. 'Is it me, mistress? That need not trouble you. I can wait for your affection, as I did for your sister's.'

Having half-expected this proposal, Merielle could hardly pretend to be surprised. What did surprise her was the depth of her own revulsion at the business-like manner of it, its calculated cold-bloodedness, as if the next step might be a written contract or a bill of sale. One expected a certain formality over the arrangement of a marriage, but surely the bond between a lover and his mistress was of a different nature from that. A declaration of love, desire, devotion? Was it any wonder that Laurel had fallen in love with Sir Adam's nephew or sought a kind of relationship with his house-steward? Whilst never made public, such things were far from uncommon.

'It's not that,' she said, lying. 'I was wondering how I could share my time between here and Canterbury without spending half of my life in the saddle. Four days travelling is four days lost, you know, and I can ill afford that.'

'Mistress St Martin, if my nephew had done what was expected of him, you would have had the answer to that by now. Those venues to which, but for this—' he pointed to his toes '—I would have escorted you, were all places which require your expertise. Of course, if I'd been there with you I could have shown you what I had in mind, but they're all en route, are they not? Places at which you could stay, do business, meet clients, oversee your itinerant weavers and then move on to the next. That way, you make use of the journey, you see. Leeds Castle, for instance. Now that lovely place needs years of work on it.'

Merielle agreed: she had been left in no doubt of that.

'And only a day's ride from Canterbury, like Clarendon from Winchester.'

'Where?'

'Clarendon. Just west of here, in Wiltshire. That's where Yeaveley and Wykeham are going on Monday. I'll have to go, too. Will you come?'

The king's master mason, his surveyor, his Master of Works; what else could this place be but another of the king's palaces? Alarm bells rang. 'A royal palace, is it? I think not, Sir Adam, I thank you. I have almost decided to return home next week, then to make a visit to my northern properties. They're having a hard time of it, due to my neglect.'

He ignored her excuse. 'Glorious place. On a hillside overlooking New Salisbury. Been neglected. Walls crying out for tapestries. Years of work for you already. Dozens of rooms. Good hunting, too, and hawking. You enjoy the falcons? Massive new kitchens and gardens. The daffodils will still be out. Only a day or two, that's all. Less than a day's ride. You can't pass up a chance like that, surely?'

Merielle had come away from that discussion quite sure that she could pass up another visit to one of the king's palaces as easily as hell itself and, expecting Sir Rhyan to support her distrust of all Sir Adam's suggestions, she was more than put out to discover that he did not.

'I shall be there to protect you,' he said, taking her shoulders.

She could have hit him, but dared not. 'He believes

you to be leaving for the north on Monday,' she said, icily.

'Then he believes wrong. Where you go, I go.'

Testing him, she pushed him further. 'Yes…well, I know you want to make sure I don't commit myself, or fall headlong into his arms in a moment of utter spite, don't you?'

'Come here, woman.' He placed his arm across her back and pushed her gently but firmly towards the sweet-smelling stump of a sawn-off oak, easing her on to its creamy surface. A tabby cat watched them settle, then did the same, wrapping its tail neatly over its paws. 'Tell me, did you reject his offer outright?'

'No. I don't think he'd have noticed if I had.' She leaned back against him, savouring his firm warmth against her back. Hidden from the house by a tangle of honeysuckle over the trelliswork arbour, she trembled as his arms enfolded her and his fingers began to caress her throat. 'I think he's expecting me to be won over at this place called Clarendon, but I'm not going. It's another of the king's.'

'But his grace won't be there.'

'It makes no difference. I'm not going, Rhyan.'

'Yes, sweetheart. You are, with me.'

A day or so earlier, this overbearing decision-making would have sent her flying into a rage; now, she almost revelled in his impending persuasion, prolonging her intransigence so that he would have to work harder at it.

'No,' she said. 'I'm sorry, but I'm going home and then up to York. My reason for being here has gone, and time is important to me.'

Sir Rhyan placed his nose against her cheek and

lapped at her earlobe with his bottom lip. 'Why? What are you afraid of?'

This was a mite too far. She twisted away but could not release herself and was pulled back, protesting and suddenly fearful at the possibility of having to explain. Not to him. Of all people, she could never explain to him. 'I'm *not* afraid. Let me go! I'm far more interested in finding out about my niece's nurse than in traipsing over to Wiltshire. *You* said you'd speak to Mistress Waterford's husband.'

'I did.'

Merielle relaxed and turned her head up to look at him. Her eyelid reached his lips and she felt his breath upon it as he spoke.

'He tells me his wife has been ill for some time.'

'Then why did he allow her to continue as little Joanie's nurse?'

'Because they cannot have a family of their own. She's had a string of stillbirths and he said it seemed a kindness to suggest her for this position, even though he knew she was hardly the most suitable applicant. No recommendations except his own. He said my uncle didn't appear to mind, at the time.'

'You believe what he told you?'

'Mmm. Not sure about his motives, though. Kindness doesn't seem to be one of his redeeming features, I must admit, though, he and your sister were apparently on good terms, and that I can vouch for. In fact, I felt that she was perhaps over-familiar with the man at times.'

'What, enough to…? Oh, surely not.'

'Oh, I don't know about that. His wife is probably seeing things, in her illness, that are not there to be seen. She desperately wanted children.'

'I know how she feels,' Merielle murmured. The words escaped before she could stop them.

Sir Rhyan's hand slipped beneath her surcoat, fondling her breasts and circling their fullness. 'You are not of that mould, Merielle. With you, it's been lack of opportunity, till now. You are ripe for breeding, my lovely Venus. Perhaps you are already. Shall we see?' Expertly, he pushed away the sideless surcoat and eased the wide-necked cote-hardie off her shoulders before she could protest. His great hand delved, freeing one superb breast to rise between layers of fabric, cradled by his fingers.

Startled by his boldness, Merielle watched as his thumb brushed across the nipple, causing a crease to appear between her black brows at the deep rosy brown which had spread into a wider circle than usual, raising a ring of nodules into a swollen mound.

His thumb moved again, tenderly, feeling the resistance. 'Well?' he said.

'No,' she said in a small voice. 'My courses are due, that's all.' She turned her burning face into the darkness of his chest, not wanting to look but aware of the warm hand that migrated into the warm and soft inner regions of her thighs to where she held her secrets close. The hand paused, holding itself ready, waiting for the reluctant signal to proceed, then began its own brand of lovemaking which was entirely new to her, ending with a moaning sob into his mouth as he teased her lips into submission.

Skilfully, his fingers plunged, then eased, hovered, and slowly withdrew, wiping themselves on the linen of her kirtle, and Merielle clung to him, admitting by her silence that she was a stranger to almost everything he had showed her, so far.

* * *

Understandably, she was unwilling to give the impression that she could be won over in this fashion on every occasion, but the argument about Clarendon Palace was not resumed, though neither of them doubted the outcome. Even so, the incident in the garden stayed in the forefront of her mind throughout the green-gowned supper in Sir Adam's solar, and the guests, so intent on their own affairs, thought nothing of her preoccupation.

Common sense told her that the symptoms she had witnessed were indeed more to do with the time of the month than with anything else and that no signs of pregnancy would be visible so soon, anyway. Yet the more she thought on it, the more likely it seemed that she could have misunderstood what the anchoress at Shere had told her and that, in her distress, she had applied the wise-woman's words to her own plans instead of to what was in her heart.

The salve you seek is already there, in place.

Was this what she meant? Not her sister's infant who had already been lost to her by then, but Sir Rhyan's, which was a gift he seemed determined to give her, the salve she secretly craved.

You are full of doubts, daughter. You doubt everyone, even me.

She had not only doubted the anchoress, but had been quite sure she was mistaken. Even that, the old woman had known. She doubted Sir Adam and the direction of Sir Rhyan's motives. Knowing of her strong objections to the king's properties, why had he not offered to take her up to Yorkshire immediately instead of accompanying her to Clarendon Palace? Why was it so necessary for them to go? When she had asked him if he believed Sir Adam's offer to help her secure large orders for her workshop, his reply had been immediate.

'That, my beauty, is the one thing I *do* believe.'

The rest of Sir Adam's ridiculous proposal made little sense in view of the bachelor existence he had lived for much of his life. Nothing about his lifestyle—or about his response to losing an only child, for that matter—convinced Merielle that her brother-in-law could no longer manage without a woman by his side, or that Winchester itself was not teeming with eligible candidates. Most men would prefer their own offspring to inherit, rather than a nephew, but if Sir Adam suspected that little Joanie was not his, his lack of grief would be understandable. But then, if he did have doubts, why had he taken no action against the one he suspected?

With an unexpected suddenness, she longed for Bonard, the only one in whom her trust was absolute. Why, oh, why had she left him behind?

The visit to Winchester's great Norman cathedral, which Master John had been so eager to arrange, arranged itself on the following day, which was a Sunday. By coincidence, the west front was undergoing a transformation like the nave of Canterbury, an imposition, Master John told her, that each successive bishop apparently felt duty-bound to prolong. Mark his words, he told her, young William Wykeham would be the one to make his presence felt here.

'You believe he'll be the next bishop after Edington?' She glanced at the intelligent animated face of the king's surveyor and wondered at his ambition. 'Architect to bishop? Is that usual?'

'Architect to chancellor to bishop, certainly. Astuteness, ability and loyalty are required more than holiness

these days, mistress. But then, they always were.
Crawling under St Swithun's shrine to kiss it is all right
for pilgrims, but you don't catch the king's surveyor
doing it. He'll get to the top without that kind of crawling. The king already takes his advice on many matters
which have little to do with buildings.'

It was after mass, when she stood in a group beyond
the intricate network of scaffolding, that she felt a
touch on her elbow, a gentle pressure which was main-
tained until she responded. It was the black and white
figure of Dame Edith Whitstable, custodian of the Sustren Spital.

'Dame Edith, forgive me, I didn't see you at mass.'

'No, I took mass earlier at the hospital. We have our
own chaplain, you know. I thought I might find you
here. May we talk?'

By the slight turn of her body, Merielle realised she
needed privacy so she linked her arm into the dame's
and strolled apart from the others. 'What is it, dame?
Good news?'

The older woman tightened the clamp of her elbow
on Merielle's wrist. 'The worst,' she whispered. 'The
very worst.'

They came to a halt where the grass was less worn,
reading each other's eyes.

'Yes, she died early this morning, my dear.'

Bereft of words, Merielle closed her eyes against the
intrusive sight of the swarming crowds in the cathedral
precinct, shaking her head at the news she had not expected to hear for many months. 'Why? I thought she
was recovering. You said…'

'Yes, I know. So did I. But this is a fickle disease,
Merielle, and we had no way of knowing the full extent

of it. At least she was able to see her husband before she died.'

Merielle's eyes opened wide. 'He visited her, at last?'

'Indeed he did. Apologetic, naturally. Took her some wine. With his master's approval, I expect,' she added wryly.

'Wine? She drank it?'

Dame Edith blinked. 'A little. We recommend it. Why?' Her eyebrow twitched at the grip on her arm.

'Then for pity's sake, don't allow anyone else to drink what's left before the coroner has had chance to test it. It may have been—'

'But we shall not be calling the coroner in, Merielle. When a patient's complaint is known, to those who nurse her, to be a fatal one, there's no need for anyone to investigate the cause. And I didn't keep the rest of the wine; it would not have been proper for anyone to consume it, in the circumstances. Surely you cannot think her husband would…no, I won't believe that. He was most concerned.'

'Yes,' Merielle said, 'so concerned that it was three whole days before he could walk a mile to visit her. And even then he had to be prompted.'

'You?' Dame Edith remembered Merielle's threat.

'No, not I. Sir Rhyan spoke to him.' The eyes of both women alighted on the handsome figure clad in madder-red, violet and silver grey, at his beautiful dark head thrown back in laughter at someone's remark, his hands splayed low over hips, feet apart. Merielle's innards churned at the sight of him. 'Did you tell her husband that she'd been rambling?'

'He'd already been told of that: oh, heavens, lass—' she placed a hand on Merielle's arm '—not what she'd said about the bairn. Not that. We'd never divulge a confidence of that nature to anyone, not even to a husband.'

Merielle experienced a pang of guilt. '*Especially* not to a husband,' she murmured.

She would have liked Dame Edith to return with them to Wood Street to break her fast, but she seemed eager to go, even refusing to be introduced to Sir Adam. 'No,' she told Merielle, 'it's not my place to seek an introduction to him, but his. Not once has he been to see how his employee fares, nor even has he sent a messenger, and now it's too late. You have done more than any of them, my dear. I'll see you tomorrow, perhaps?'

'Indeed you will, Dame Edith. At the abbey.'

It was left to Merielle to break the news of Mistress Waterford's death to Sir Adam. She found it strange, even slightly eerie, that his florid, sagging face was unable to hide the relief that washed over it before concern took a hold. And whilst she tried to exercise some Sunday charity, she could not dismiss his words of yesterday about the damned inferior wine making his gout worse. Nor could she help wondering if the wine had also been the cause of the illness that prevented his journey to Canterbury.

Sir Rhyan, who had shown some sadness at the poor woman's demise, went missing after the mid-day meal.

The black-haired house-steward's forehead hit the stone wall with a sickening thud, his nose squashing flat with the force from behind. His two fists were held up somewhere behind his shoulder blades in a grip that hurt even his shins, though the more recent pain was cancelling that out. In an agony of blackness, he was slewed round to face his assailant, who then delivered a blow to his stomach with such force that the floor came up to meet him. He hardly heard the words.

'Get up, you whey-faced little rat. Get up, or I'll find another way to release your sudden memory loss.'

Master Brian Waterford, recently bereaved, clawed his way obediently up the wall of his room over the stables, more concerned now about whether his mouth could be made to deliver anything coherent before the next assault. 'No…don't…oh, God!' For his pains, he was hurled sideways into a corner, just managing to stay upright. Wrong words, obviously.

'It's not God we're concerned with, you turd, but your woman. I told you to get down there and *visit* her, not kill her,' Sir Rhyan snarled. 'Now, tell me what happened, or I'll stick you head first into that—'

'No…no,' the man moaned, clutching at the hand twisting his tunic into a noose beneath his chin. 'No…I'll tell you, sir. I took her some wine, that's all. Honest.'

'You told Sir Adam what I'd said to you about her rambling, didn't you?' He slammed the man backwards again.

'Yes…yes, sir, when I asked him if I could go. He said I was to take her some wine.'

'So you laced it with something.'

'No…no, sir, I didn't. I swear. It was the same that had made Sir Adam ill. He'd told me to put it on one side.'

'That was the one he told you to take?' Sir Rhyan frowned.

'Yes, sir.' He felt at his nose to see if it was still there, and his hand came away, sticky with blood. 'It was rancid, that's all, but I never thought she'd want to drink it. She never gets to drink real wine, sir, only ale.'

'Well, she did, didn't she? And now she's dead, thanks to you. So what was it Sir Adam was afraid she might say in her ramblings to Dame Edith or Mistress St Martin? Eh?'

'Honest, sir, I don't…argh!' The man doubled up again, clutching at his stomach. Then, after a suitable pause and a dowsing of cold water, he discovered the rest of his memory. His place at supper-time was taken by a young man who was smart enough to say that Master Waterford, due to his sadness, was indisposed.

'You'd make him a lousy wife, anyway, sweetheart.' Sir Rhyan held Merielle against the wall at the side of her chamber door. 'You'd make him a lousy mistress, too, for that matter. He likes women to be more compliant than you.'

'Then it's as well that he knows, isn't it? I'm not going to be told what to do by my brother-in-law after all this time. I shall do as I wish.' She swung her braided head away in an anger that had lasted during an hour's argument, but Sir Rhyan brought it back to him, enclosing her face in his hand.

'He needs you to…'

'He doesn't *need* me at all! He wants me to go so that he can show off his tame tapicier, a woman, his late wife's possible replacement. Well, I'm not, and I won't. I intend to go to Mistress Waterford's funeral whether he likes it or not, and I shall explain to everyone how Sir Adam was too busy to attend his child's nurse's funeral. I'll shame him, I will.'

'But you'll go on Tuesday.'

'Why must I?'

'Because I told him I'd escort you.'

'And he could barely manage to stop himself telling you it's time you cleared off home, nephew,' she mimicked Sir Adam's pompous tone.

Sir Rhyan's mouth lifted at the corners, then straightened into a more acceptable seriousness. 'I don't care a damn what he wants me to do. I'm staying by your side and you're staying by mine. I shall take you to Clarendon Palace on Tuesday.'

'I'd rather go to hell.'

'Not there, either. On Monday night, while he's away, I shall sleep with you.'

She peeped at him from beneath lowered lids. 'Sleep?'

The corners lifted again. 'No, not sleep.'

'I want to go home. People die here.'

'Sweetheart.'

'Take me home, Rhyan. Or up to York.'

'I will. When we return, I will.'

'Now,' she said, petulantly, teasing him, almost smiling.

'Shh...stick your lips out, like this...'

But she could not do it and laugh at the same time.

Chapter Eleven

The funeral at St Mary's Abbey was another harrowing affair that brought back into sharp focus the losses that were inflicted on all families with monotonous regularity: family, infants, friends, employees. Old age was rarely the commonest cause; mostly it was illness or accident, the result of fighting or too-severe punishment. It was accepted, though the pain was the same.

Merielle was shocked to see the stooping form of Master Brian Waterford at the side of his late wife's bier, even more shocked to see the mass of bruises on his previously attractive face, one eye completely closed, his nose swollen. 'In God's name,' she whispered to Sir Rhyan, 'what's happened to him?'

'Banged into a wall.' His eyes followed the man impassively.

She turned to him, expecting him to do the same, and when he did not, knew that it was his doing. 'Oh, Rhyan. Was that necessary?' she said, her voice reprimanding.

'Yes,' he said. 'It was.'

She asked no more questions, assuming that the man had been punished for hastening his wife's death with rancid wine, wittingly or not. The question of his being her sister's lover was now something that would never be known, except to himself. Secretly, Merielle doubted it. His condition was noticed (how could it not be?) by Dame Edith, who stood on one side with the abbess of St Mary's. The two were old friends, whose mutual support was a joy both to themselves and to their establishments, and three of St Mary's oldest nuns had now retired to the Sustren Spital to be treated for the pains of life's twilight.

Abbess Margaret de Molyns, still only in her early forties, had held office already for almost ten years after the death of her predecessor from the pestilence. She was a beautiful woman, with heavy-lidded serenely blue eyes and a wide full-lipped mouth that smiled gently and often with a hint of sensuality where the corners dimpled. Her pale brows were delicately arched and Merielle was sure they had been plucked. No one, she thought, could look more becoming in the Benedictines' black habit than this woman, though traces of silk and a sparkle of jewels and gold provided an unorthodox touch that softened the harsh contrasts.

Merielle and the abbess had met previously at Lady Bedesbury's funeral here last year, and now there was a chance for the two women to note how the nine intervening months had wrought no change to either of them except, in Merielle's case, the glow which a growing love imparts. The abbess's eyes darted like flames to where Sir Rhyan stood and, even with her discipline, she was unable to prevent an inner gasp of admiration at the sight of wide shoulders and well-muscled legs. Then the heavy lids eclipsed the interest in her eyes and, with all outer tranquillity, she continued her conversation with Merielle and Dame Edith.

A group of nuns stood silently in the background in the angle of the north and west walls. With them was a young woman in a plain gown of deep russet and blue, a white veil over her head doing little to conceal the heavy auburn plaits that hung, braided with blue and gold, over each shoulder as far as her knees. For a moment, Merielle's attention was arrested by the girl's loveliness and by the conviction that she had seen her somewhere before, but there was no opportunity to ask about her, nor did one come later, for the nuns did not linger in the growing dusk.

'Dame Edith asked about Master Waterford's condition,' Merielle told Sir Rhyan. 'She said he looked as though he'd been set upon.'

'And you said he had?' He looked at her through narrowed eyes, unsmiling.

'I think she might have guessed. What *was* it about, Rhyan?'

He smoothed his knuckles thoughtfully over the soft skin of her neck, holding up her chin, his eyes drinking in her beauty. But in them was something else that Merielle had not seen before, not even in his anger— a coldly murderous glint that she understood to be a recollection of his mood when he had beaten the man. Then it disappeared, and he bent to kiss her with an unmistakable possessiveness that took her breath away and made her hold on to him for support.

'Forget it,' he told her between kisses.

But she did not.

Without Sir Adam and his architect friends to share their supper, they ate alone in Merielle's solar. 'There'll be talk,' Merielle said.

'Undoubtedly. There's little else for them to do.'

'Is that why you left when Laurel became pregnant? Because of the talk?'

'I left *before* she became pregnant.' He held her eyes, boldly.

'You didn't return for her funeral.'

'No. She was nothing more to me than my uncle's wife.'

'Besides which, you knew I would be there and you didn't—'

'You had nothing to do with my decision not to attend. It was the Scots. They raid in the summer months.'

'Ah. The Scots.'

'Anything else?'

She nibbled at her lower lip, shaking her head.

'Then what?'

'Madness,' she whispered, looking away, using the same words she had used before. 'This is madness.'

He stood, taking her wrist and drawing her up with him. 'No, it's not. You are safe, Merielle. I've told you that you are mine. Can you not learn to mix some trust with your passion?' He drew her into the softest embrace, tipping his head to see her eyes. 'It was never my intent to hurt you so. I wanted you from the very first, nor have I ever stopped wanting you, not even while we were so far apart. Night and day you've eaten at me, at my guts, woman. I'll never forgive myself for causing you pain, even though I don't understand how it occurred.'

'No, you could not have wanted me from the very first. You scarcely spoke a word.'

'I didn't speak because I knew you already hated me. You would not even look. I knew I would have a hard time of it, after that, but I swore to win you, somehow. And now I almost have, but not quite. What's stopping you? For pity's sake, tell me what it is so that I can put it right. Is that so bad? Is it so painful, Merielle?'

How could she expect him to understand? He was the king's man, had fought with him and Prince Edward, the king's mighty warrior son. In his eyes, the king was incapable of an unworthy act. He was a hero, a paragon of virtue. For any woman intentionally to abort one of the king's own progeny would seem to Sir Rhyan like the act of a madwoman, especially one as desperate to bear a child as she was. As for accepting some of the blame for his part in the sordid events, why should he? It had been her decision to seek the king's aid, at Gervase's suggestion. She could have paid a fine many times over if there had been the slightest chance that he would have accepted it from her. Which he would not.

He intended to make her his wife and had experienced her quick arousal, her fierce passion; he would take some convincing that she had not recognised, even at eighteen, any signs of the king's impending interest in her. What man would ever understand her revulsion? As for the possibility of him discovering what had happened, that was something she could not live with, and now was the time to make a decision, now, before she became pregnant again. And if she was already, he must never know.

'Come, sweetheart.'

'No, Rhyan, I cannot.'

'Cannot? Of what are you afraid? Me?'

'Of ghosts,' she whispered. *Of pain. Unbearable pain.*

And so it was that the intended night of bliss during

Sir Adam's absence was spent in wakeful isolation by both of them until just before dawn when Sir Rhyan let himself into her solar and into her arms, lacing himself around her and promising celibacy. She was damp with weeping.

'Just hold me,' she sobbed.

'Yes. No more than that, I promise. Hush…sleep now.'

'I don't want to go to Clarendon.'

'Hush, sweetheart. There's nothing to fear. I shall be there.' He hated to insist, but there was more to be discovered, and wherever his uncle was, there was the information he sought.

Their first sight of Clarendon Palace, specks of white on the wooded hillside, dispelled any remnants of the foreboding Merielle had had about the place being a fortress. It sprawled like a gaggle of white geese hoping to escape detection in a forest of new greenness, a froth of pale leaves and powdery yellows sprinkled into a shaft of evening sunlight. From this distance, the only sign of life was the few vertical columns of smoke rising from the kitchens, splitting the pale pink sky into sections. A flock of white doves swooped and circled, then settled into a dovecote hidden by the trees.

Sunshine and the journey itself, the peace of the open countryside, rolling hills and the freshly washed colours of spring, had helped to make the expedition more acceptable to Merielle. That, and the knowledge that business for the workshop was sure to follow. Nearer still, they caught glimpses of hedged parkland where herds of deer grazed, paler lawns through the trees and close-walled gardens hugging the white walls of the buildings. Blossom softened every corner except

the pointed gables where extravagantly carved and colourful finials were linked by the peaked ridge-tiles.

Merielle's curiosity was aroused. 'What a site,' she
said to Allene.

'Aye, lass,' her old nurse replied. 'Room for a fair
few wall-hangings there, I dare say.'

Perched on the brow of the wooded hillside, the palace commanded a magnificent view over the river basin
where the town of New Salisbury nestled, its new white
cathedral spire marking the spot like the point of a
dagger. A solid stone gatehouse gave access to a wide
courtyard surrounded by stables, storerooms, a blacksmith's forge, kitchens and paddocks and a complex of
whitewashed buildings tiled with red and lichen-
coloured ochre, with oak shingles, cushions of moss
and bright stone-crop. Liveried men stood in clusters,
arranging, unpacking waggons, hauling boxes of ice-
covered fish and meat, baskets of flapping chickens and
geese and sacks of grain towards the kitchens, past
clerks loaded with lists checking casks of wine and
tripping over yelping hounds.

At the noisy greeting, Sir Adam emerged from the
great porchway over to the left, blinked, and saw them
slowly pour towards him, a large group of armed men
before and behind whom Rhyan would not travel without. Wearing a harmony of browns, oranges and
creams, Merielle was the one to whom he made his
way, reaching his arms up to support her to the dusty
ground and keeping his hands on her elbows and waist.
Relief showed in every line of his face. His compli-
ments were not exaggerated, for her apricots and burnt
oranges were warmed by the late afternoon sun and her
hair, threaded with gold, was piled up in an intricate
nest of plaits, framing her face. She smiled because his

greeting was exactly how Sir Rhyan had told her it would be when he had warned her not to relent.

'My dear Mistress Merielle—' she smiled again at the predicted dropping of the St Martin part '—come; you will wish to rest. Your rooms are prepared; bring your ladies; refresh yourselves. Is this not the most beautiful place? Wait till you see the gardens.'

From the first, Merielle could see that Sir Adam had not told her the half of it, for inside the sprawling buildings were the most beautiful rooms she had ever seen, despite their need for restoration and refurbishment. Between rooms, courtyards and lawns were pockets of privacy and sun-soaked warmth. Wooded and trellised pleasances tinkled to the sound of fountains, channels and ponds. Pathways led to herb gardens and secluded enclosures where roses already raced to reach the top of tunneled arbours. Tiled pentices like open passageways shielded guests between one building and the next, creating a cloistered effect where vines writhed sinuously around pillars. But outside became inside when the vines found their way on to the walls, painted over a hundred years before into the Labours of the Months. Leeds Castle had held an air of watery exclusivity, but Clarendon Palace unfurled itself into the surrounding parkland in a way that Leeds could not, tumbling its rooms wantonly out of doors until Merielle had to look up to see whether she was indoors or out.

Many of the floors were patterned with colourful tiles made in the estate's tile-kilns, and the royal apartments had been painted in rich greens and expensive blues, gilded with leaden stars and moons and bordered with royal heads. There was stained glass in the chapels, carved fireplaces, pillars of white marble, wainscotting of Norwegian fir, mermaids and mermen, a world map and a Wheel of Fortune carved on the chimney-pieces. There were sumptuous bedcoverings embroidered with peacocks and trees, Catherine wheels, suns and silly little garters. Merielle looked away but was lured towards the royal wardrobes (rooms, not cupboards) where all the clothes of the household were stored, fabrics made up by the dressmakers, valuables kept and accounts made. The need for tapestries had been no pretence: even Master John agreed that what the flaking walls needed were not his ministrations but a layer of woollen hangings to keep out the hilltop draughts in winter.

By arrangement, Merielle and Sir Rhyan kept well apart when in Sir Adam's company, hoping that their otherwise friendly ease towards each other would suffice to keep Masters Yeaveley and Wykeham from commenting to him on the previous stormy relationship. Had they known how far the two had progressed since Leeds, they would probably not have held their peace so easily, but they had plenty to do in planning new staircases, extensions, conversions and enlargements, pacing, measuring and drawing plans with little time for hunting in the surrounding forest.

Never one for hunting, Merielle borrowed a young and eager clerk and went with Allene and Bess to measure the walls of the queen's chamber. The tiled floor was mellow with autumn browns, red and yellows, lions and griffins in heraldic postures. Merielle believed that a closely patterned tapestry depicting the same creatures with the queen's cyphers, crowns, and perhaps the royal arms would tie walls and floor together visually in a way which the hotch-potch of images in the other rooms did not.

The young clerk's quill scratched measurements on to the parchment.

'Can't reach,' Allene panted, on tiptoe. 'Here, lass—' she grabbed Bess by the arm '—I'll hold you up while you measure from the top of that border.'

'Get a stool,' said Merielle.

'Still won't be able to reach. We need someone taller.'

The door opened just wide enough for Sir Rhyan to enter. 'Will I do?' he said, taking the knotted string from Bess and holding a pose with his hand at the top of the wall.

Merielle grinned, groaning. 'I thought you were taking the falcons out with Sir Adam.'

'I am. I came to find you. He wants you to come, too. Can you not do this tomorrow?'

'You go, lass,' Allene said. 'Bess and me'll finish this off for you.' She crossed to the tall leaded window, the lower half of which had been made to open outwards to overlook the queen's private garden, still brilliant with daffodils and crocuses and dripping with white apple-blossom.

At once, the high-pitched squeal of a child's excitement pierced the stillness of the chamber, following by the enticing call of a woman, a whoop of glee, gurgling laughter and another squeal, sounds vivid enough for each of the listeners to picture the scene with instant clarity.

Merielle froze, joined Allene at the window, and peered down into the well-trimmed lawn and the turf-seat on to which a child attempted to scramble, watching in unconcealed envy how the young woman

scooped the merry child up into her arms, leaving the
wickerwork gate swinging freely as if there had been
a chase. The child was wobbly and pink with exertion,
black-haired and wriggling fiercely to be released for
another chase, and Merielle was caught in a longing so
physically intense that she barely felt Allene's arm on
her shoulder, drawing her back into the room. 'Who is
it?' she whispered.

Allene repeated the question to the clerk. 'If it's one
of the laundry-maids, she should not be allowed in the
queen's garden.'

Edmund looked up from his notes. 'Nay, mistress,
that's not laundry. That'll be young Roger with his
nurse. They're allowed to roam where they want,
within reason. There's always two or three men not far
away.'

'Roger who?' Merielle said, frowning. 'Does he
have parents?'

Politely, Edmund stood, glad of the excuse to watch
the pretty young nurse while he explained, smiling as
the toddler scampered off again. 'I should think he
does, mistress. He's the Prince Edward's latest bastard,
known as Roger of Clarendon, for want of a better
name. Don't know who his mother is. Someone at
court, I suppose, but he's lived here since he was born.'

'Which was?' Allene said.

Edmund looked up at the starry ceiling. 'Er…almost
two years now, I suppose. About midsummer. A fine
sturdy little chap. Can't understand a mother wanting
to leave him, not watch him grow up every day.'

'Nor I,' said Sir Rhyan. 'Most women would be
more than content to bear the prince's brat, I would
have thought. There's no finer man.'

'A bastard is a bastard,' Merielle snapped under her

breath, gathering up the notes that Edmund had left on the stool. Her heart was beating loudly, and she could feel the heat creeping up her neck towards her cheeks. Roger of Clarendon was about the same age as the child she might have borne if she had not decided otherwise.

'A royal bastard is no disgrace,' Sir Rhyan said, holding the door open for her. 'That one will certainly want for nothing except his mother. Now, mistress. Shall we go down?'

If she had needed any confirmation of her worst fears, Sir Rhyan's opinion of royal bastards and their parents provided it, and the next three hours on the hill overlooking New Salisbury and the distant mound of Old Sarum were clouded by a sickening dread that not even the thrill of the falcons could alleviate. To her credit, Merielle allowed neither Sir Rhyan nor Sir Adam to know of her sufferings; she could not have explained to either of them why she had been affected by the heartrending sight of a child that could, but for her own actions, have been hers.

In one sense, she was relieved that she had not so far given her assent to a permanent partnership with Sir Rhyan. It was as if she had been waiting for a proof which his protestations, however comforting, had not contained. It was as well to know now, before the pain became too much to bear, her only comfort being that this was what she had known all along.

The hawking-party returned through the gatehouse like a multi-colored ribbon that threaded into yet another influx of arrivals whose sumpter-mules, pack-horses and waggons were being filtered through to the kitchen courtyard. Through the trees that screened the palace from the park, white tents were being erected like rows of pointed meringues on a pie, the throng of men around her so thick that she had no difficulty in avoiding her host's observation and making her way to the kitchen garden. She might, if she was lucky, detect some sign of the nurse and her tiny charge. She might also find someone who could explain the purpose of so many cartloads of provisions being brought in, the stacks of silver-plate, the boxes of figs, dates and raisins, candles and cauldrons, furniture, lanterns and goose-feather pillows.

From the safety of the door to the water-garden, Merielle watched the to-ing and fro-ing and then turned away, closing the heavy door to cut off the noise. Seeing her shadow, the fish in the largest stew-pond darted towards her, expecting to be fed, even touching her fingertips, shattering her reflection into circular bands before diving under the waterfall to gulp at the bubbles of air.

Did they stock up like this at all the royal palaces? Gervase of Caen had often told her of the quantities needed by the households, the sides of pork and lamb, the tons of wine and cheeses, the butter and eggs, but surely that was only for when the king was in residence, and everyone knew that the king was at Windsor.

A face appeared, silently, beside hers in the restored reflection, looking over her shoulder and smiling. 'Expecting me?' he whispered.

'Gervase! I don't believe it.'

'Well, then...' he laughed, holding her against him '...believe that I'm a water-elf and kiss me before I disappear again.'

To have stepped away would have meant a fall into

the pond and it was only after a lengthy kiss, which held little of its former piquancy, that his grip on her relaxed and she sidled away from danger. 'For a water-elf, that was almost human,' she said, taking his hand away from her bottom. 'What on earth are you doing here, Gervase?'

'I saw you leave through the door and I followed you.'

'No, not here. I mean here at Clarendon.'

'Oh,' he said, waving a hand, 'only the usual supplies, that's all. I had no idea you were here, sweetheart, until I caught sight of Sir Adam's livery, and I asked. What a coincidence.' He was as golden as ever, tanned by the day's sun and wind, immaculately dressed in pale green and gold with pale violet lining his hood, the same colour echoed on one leg of his tight hose and on the dagged edges of his gupon which, as usual, barely covered his tightly muscled backside. 'Have you missed me?'

Merielle sidestepped his question. 'It was Sir Adam's idea. The place needs some work doing on it and he wants me to do some sets of tapestries. It was too good a chance to miss, Gervase, though I was not too keen on coming. I shall go home in a day or two, I think.'

He took her hand, smiling and drawing her along the pathway into the seclusion of an arbour where the trellis was already covered by pale new leaves. Seated on the long wooden bench, she held his hand to stop it from slipping down between her thighs.

'So, your cup of motherhood is filled already, then?'

She frowned, not understanding. 'What?'

'The child. Where is it? I didn't think you'd have

wanted to leave it so soon. Why…what is it, sweetheart? What's wrong?'

Holding back the tears, she told him what had happened and did nothing to stop him when he took her
in his arms. 'I'm so sorry, love,' he said. 'I didn't
know. You must have had a rough time of it with that
churl by your side all the way. I realised you must have
gone earlier to escape him, but I could have found out
exactly when he was leaving, if you'd told me, and
then you might have been free of him. Has he been a
nuisance? I'll kill him, if he has.'

Realising that she would never have a better chance
of telling him how things stood between herself and
Sir Rhyan, she nevertheless held back without knowing
why, except that its gradually shifting foundations were
giving her cause for concern. Perhaps she had better
wait awhile.

'We quarrelled a lot at first, but then we came to an
agreement, otherwise it would have been impossible.
But I shall let him take his lands back, Gervase, when
I return home. I've sent stewards up to Yorkshire to
make a report, so I shall not go all the way up there
myself.'

'To Yorkshire? Heavens above, no, I should think
not. Why not stay here for a while? Sir Adam's been
good to you?'

She noticed with some relief that he made no reference to her previously strenuous efforts to keep the
property out of Sir Rhyan's hands, or of his own part
in those proceedings. 'Oh, yes. Sir Adam's been no
problem, but the situation has changed, you understand,
and I shall not be staying in Winchester, after all.
Where do you go when you've seen to the delivery of
the supplies?'

'I shall have to stay for a day or two, just to see to things,' he added, quickly. 'Enough time to be near you and hold your hand, if you want me to. Where's your room?'

'Too many people about. Allene and Bess sleep with me.'

In spite of Sir Rhyan's dim view of Gervase of Caen, his appearance restored a note of normality to events that had speeded up beyond her control, though she had tried from the very beginning to manage them. She wished that the two men could have seen eye to eye; that would have made things easier still for her. As it was, their mutual distrust was such that heaven only knew what revelations might be sparked off if she did not do her best to keep them apart. She knew that Gervase had other lovers and that he tempered the truth to make her feel special, but he had done his best to help her when she most needed it, and for that she could not wish him harm.

The ones who could be relied on to understand her dilemma were Allene and Bess, who had seen her reaction to the royal bastard and to Sir Rhyan's thoughtless remark.

'What does it matter, pet?' Allene said, gently, sitting on the velvet-covered bed by Merielle's side. 'He would never have said such a stupid thing if he'd known what happened. They talk generally, you know. Their own womenfolk are always exceptions, whatever the rules, but he's never going to find out, is he? We're the only ones who know what you went through, and Bonard, and he'd never speak of it, you know that.'

'Yes, love. I know that,' Merielle whispered. 'But it's not just what happened with the king that I'm so ashamed of, it's the *result*, Allene.' She pounded at the coverlet with her fist, making a valley. 'He'd never understand that I could not bear the king's child then, of all times, when I was so newly widowed and grieving over my lost one. It's Sir Rhyan's good opinion of me I stand to lose, Allene, and that would be a terrible thing after all this time for, if I became his wife, I would be obliged to tell him. It's hardly any use learning to trust a man, is it, if I dare not trust him with the very thing I hold against him? What kind of a foundation would that be for a marriage?'

Bess came to kneel at her mistress's feet, taking her fist and restoring it to her knee. 'If what you say is true, mistress, I'm going to have to tell Padraig of all the lads I've known before him, am I?' She shook her pretty head. 'I know I've not been in your position, but keeping a secret from a man you love which you know will hurt him is more of a kindness than a lack of trust. You'd only tell him if you were trying to put him off, wouldn't you? Or easing your own conscience? There are some things…' she stroked Merielle's hand '…that a man has no right to know unless the woman chooses to tell him. He must learn to trust her, too, you know.'

Allene stared at the young maid. 'My God, lass. That's the most I've ever heard you say at one go. Where d'ye get all that from?'

Bess smiled, ignoring the jibe. 'Have ye told Sir Rhyan that ye'll marry him, mistress?'

'No, Bess. I haven't.'

'Then there's no rush, is there? Why not leave things to sort themselves out? They usually do. When you don't know what to do, wait.'

'She's right,' said Allene, with a new respect. 'He's a fine man, is Sir Rhyan, but that doesn't give him rights over your mind as well as your body. Let time sort it out.'

Their advice found a niche in her heart if only because there was, at that moment, little else she could have done. Anticipating which way things might develop was not going to make them happen the sooner.

Returning to the queen's chamber to check on the colours she might use, she found Master Wykeham there with his clerk doing some similar checks of his own on the state of the walls and ceilings. 'Not good enough,' he said to Merielle. 'All this paintwork on an unsuitable fabric. What a waste. We'll have it fixed before you hang anything on here, and then we'll have some battens fixed across the top to hold them up. You put loops on your tapestries, I suppose?' His bright eyes took in her nod of agreement, but his tongue hardly paused. 'You'll have seen the preparations?' He threw the window open, indicating with a nod of his head the white rash of tents in the field through the trees.

'Yes, I saw them. Are we to have games? A tournament?'

He laughed. 'You could say that, mistress. That lot's to accommodate the extra men of the king's party. There's never enough room for them indoors. They'll be thankful the weather's fine.'

Merielle felt the hair rising along her arms. 'The king?'

The inflection in her voice made Master Wykeham turn. 'Didn't you know? Didn't Sir Adam tell you? The king's party is due to arrive some time tomorrow. That's why the supplies arrived today. That's why we're here. His grace likes the hunting here at Clarendon.'

Merielle swayed. 'And the queen?'

'Oh, no. Not this time. You'll have to keep him amused instead, won't you, eh?'

His laugh was meant to divert her obvious shock, but it rose into her gullet and washed over her in a hot wave of nausea. 'Then I have no time to lose, Master Wykeham, have I? Please excuse me,' she said.

Chapter Twelve

With the unquestioning loyalty of Daniel and Pedro, Merielle's two young grooms, their departure from Clarendon Palace was achieved with far more panache than any of them had thought possible. Disguised as servants in livery 'borrowed' from the royal wardrobe, the five of them passed unnoticed through the gatehouse in a multitude of servants, waggons and packhorses coming and going until dusk. Away from Clarendon, Daniel led them off the Winchester road, south-east towards Romsey where his sister and her husband lived, adding a few miles to their journey, but safety from detection and darkness.

They could have asked for shelter at Romsey Abbey, but too many questions would have been asked, and that was the last thing Merielle wanted. Daniel's sister, heavily pregnant with her first child, and shyly delighted to assist her brother's employer, would have given up her best pallet of straw had not Merielle insisted on sharing with her maids. The expectant mother did all she could, with her affable husband, to start them off again at first light to reach Winchester by midmorning, and would accept no payment for food. She and Daniel had not seen each other since a year last harvest, and this was payment enough, she said.

They were a subdued group, the two grooms looking out for overt interest from other travellers and the three women, now changed into plain travelling clothes, looking inwards to shed some light on the ever-darkening duplicity of men. That Master Gervase of Caen and Sir Adam Bedesbury had both known of the king's expected arrival at Clarendon was as incontrovertible as the fact that, when they could both have told her, they had not. Why not? Had Sir Rhyan known, too? And Master John? It was difficult to believe otherwise.

They approached Winchester from the south to avoid the king's party, and Sir Adam's house on the Romsey road, calling at the Sustren Spital on their way to the King's Gate to tell Dame Edith of their return. She would have offered them hospitality but for the two men and the number of horses, but she approved of Merielle's intention to beg Abbess Margaret to house them before they went on to Canterbury.

At St Mary's Abbey, Merielle almost wept with relief at the lovely abbess's enthusiastic welcome. 'Of course you must stay, my dear. We have no guest-house, but my lodgings are large enough and the boys can have the stable-loft and take my two nags to the blacksmith while they're here. Come, you look tired and a little dejected, too. Things did not turn out as you hoped at Clarendon? Ah, well.'

The abbess's extensive lodging was situated behind the eastern side of the cloister with direct access into the church at one end. Merielle, Allene and Bess were shown into a large upper chamber with a view over the fish-ponds, thatched houses nestling inside the city wall, the busy East Gate, and St Giles' Hill rising up beyond the river.

The room was by no means as spartan as Bess had thought it would be. 'Heavens,' she breathed, 'this is luxury indeed. Look here.' She pushed a fist into the white woollen coverlet and watched it disappear almost to her wrist. 'I thought they slept on wooden boards.'

Allene pulled out two truckle-beds from beneath the creamy canopied bed where Merielle was to sleep. They were narrow, but soft and clean. 'Don't get too excited, lass.' She winked at Merielle. 'Tend to the unpacking. My word, it's not what you'd expect, though, is it?' She was looking up at the ceiling where the heavy wooden beams were carved with the grimacing heads of humans and creatures, including an explicit female fertility figure who was either inviting copulation or about to give birth. 'Very proper,' Allene muttered in her most sober voice. 'Don't you look up there, young Bess.'

They were diverted from life's raw realities when a small white shaggy dog squeezed through the doorway and took a flying leap on to the bed, no mean feat for such short legs. A young nun squeezed through after it, whispering apologies, dived on to the bed, missed it when it leapt off the other side and watched (flat on her face) as the thing disappeared the way it had come. The nun scrambled off the bed and tugged at the coverlet. 'Watch out for your shoes,' she told them. 'He eats a pair of the abbess's almost every week.'

Her place was taken by two more nuns bearing jugs of hot water and ale, a basin and towels, and biscuits made of ground hazelnuts and honey. 'We shan't be having dinner until two hours after noon,' they whis-

pered, smiling. 'You'll starve before then if you don't
eat.'

Bess was astounded. 'They're wearing coloured
veils,' she said, wide-eyed. 'And jewellery. Rings on
their fingers…did you see? And I'm sure they'd red-
dened their cheeks and lips.'

Allene agreed. 'Best dressed nuns I ever saw,' she
said. 'So much for sleeping on bare boards.'

'We've just had a visit from Bishop Edington.' Abbess Margaret de Molyns rolled her lovely eyes to
heaven and pressed her palms together as if in prayer.
'If only he didn't live so close,' she added, plaintively.
Her expression changed to one of pure mischief, drawing a smile from her guests. The bishop's Palace of
Wolvesey was separated from St Mary's Abbey only
by a wall and a few houses, its shining rooftops and
towers easily visible from the abbess's upper rooms.

'He spends much time in Winchester, does he?' Merielle asked. 'Sir Adam has been in charge of the alterations at Wolvesey and I would have thought that
might have caused the bishop to live in his other palaces.'

'Unfortunately, no, my dear. The king usually stays
there instead of up at the castle, so the bishop's at home
far too often. Meddling old man.'

Merielle tried not to show her surprise, having taken
an abbess's respect for her bishop for granted. 'He disapproves?'

'Oh, he disapproves of everything except his own
immortality.' She smoothed the folds of her black
woollen habit with slender well-manicured hands, lifting the hem to reveal a pretty red silk kirtle beneath.
'This,' she said, thrusting forward one red fur-trimmed

shoe, '*this* is what he carps about. If he'd given us some notice, we'd have left our colours off, but really…' she spread her hands '…I've never been able to understand how wearing attractive clothes affects one's ability to be devout. We're supposed to wear drawers of haircloth and have them laced tightly down to our feet with strapples. And look what *he* wears. Silk embroidered buskins and stockings, years of embroidery on his cope and mitre, dozens of chasubles to choose from. They don't prevent him from being devout, though. Peacocks! It's befitting the dignity of your office if you're a bishop, but wicked vanity if you're an abbess. Ah, well, I've had my say.' She smiled like a sunburst after dark clouds. 'Come. I'll show you round before we eat, shall I? You're refreshed now?'

At any other time, Merielle's curiosity would have leapt at the chance to look round the abbey, but something of her reticence must have communicated itself to the observant abbess who, instead of leading her guest, took her hands.

'No, forgive me,' she said. 'Not a tour. The last thing you need is a tour. Come, you are quite safe here. No one will find you.' Saying no more, she led Merielle along the upper passageway to her own chamber over the kitchen, dairy and pantry. It was large and every bit as comfortable as Merielle's at Canterbury: a large bed was canopied with deep blue, a jug of brilliant daffodils stood on a table by the window and a log fire burned in a corner beneath a stone hood carved with a pattern of lozenges and grotesques as if to remind the occupant of the terrors of hellfire. The little white dog leapt at the abbess as they entered, ready to snuggle into her arms like a child.

'He doesn't approve of this, either,' she said, nodding to the room. She placed Merielle on a tapestry-cushioned bench and poured wine into a silver goblet. 'Now, my dear. You've run away from him. Why?'

Merielle heaved a sigh and began to talk.

She had scarcely begun, however, before another guest was announced and a white-clad figure swept in, her face flushed with concern.

'Dame Edith!' The abbess rose to greet her friend with a sisterly kiss to both cheeks. 'Why, sister…what is it? Come, sit down. You're wet. Is it raining? Here, let me take your cloak.'

Dame Edith's cheeks were damp, her eyes bright with weeping. 'I had to come and tell you,' she said. Leaning towards Merielle, she touched her hand. 'And I'm glad you're here, too, mistress, being from Canterbury.' She blew her nose and stuffed the kerchief deep into the folds of her gown. 'Where is she?' she whispered to the abbess.

'Why, downstairs with the others, I expect. She's safe. Why, dear?'

'I've discovered who this rogue is.' She leaned back with a heavy sigh. 'That's why I'm so upset.'

'But you already know who he is, Edith, dear. You told me it was a man known as Gervase of Caen. Is that who you mean?'

'Yes, but now I know *who* he is. A messenger came from my late husband's people an hour ago with the information.' She caught sight, then, of the shock on Merielle's face and assumed that it was a combination of apprehension and ignorance. 'Mistress Merielle, your pardon. You must wonder what I'm raving about. It's my daughter, you see. Penelope. She stayed behind in Canterbury with Robert's second cousin when I

came to live here in Winchester at the Sustren Spital.
They have a house not far from the cathedral, near
where we used to live. It seemed kinder to leave her
where her roots are, for she's only seventeen-and-a-
bit.' She clapped a hand to her forehead to cool it. 'But
they didn't watch her too well. She's our late love-
child, you see, and so very pretty, and I suppose it was
inevitable that some keen-eyed young man should try
to turn her head.'

'This...Gervase of Caen?'

Another sigh. 'Yes. Much older than her, he is. A
member of the king's household; something to do with
the provisions department, I believe. At least, that's
what she was told.'

'You mean, he's not?'

'Oh, he probably is, but that's a convenient cover
for what else he gets up to, the blackguard. They, her
guardians, discovered him in her bed!' The words grew
to an outraged whisper. 'In their own *house*! Can you
imagine it?'

Merielle could, quite clearly.

'Naturally, they threw him out and then packed her
off here to me, and Abbess Margaret sent two of her
most reliable nuns to escort her back here where she
can be kept safely until she's got over it, poor mite.'

'How long ago was this? Recently?'

'Yes, she arrived, safe and sound, just after Easter,
about the same time as you, I suppose.'

*Two silent nuns and a young woman between them.
Penelope. In disgrace. Yearning for her lover.*

'So what is it you've discovered about this creature?'
Abbess Margaret asked, closing the small leaded window against the penetrating dampness. She poked at

the fire and threw another log on to the spitting flames.
'He's surely not a French spy, is he?'

'You'll be shocked,' Dame Edith said, flatly. 'I was.
Am. Someone, they won't say who, has been doing
some investigating and he's told them that this Gervase
of Caen makes contact with women that the king has
seen, seduces them and then lures them into the king's
company. *Alone.* The king uses them for a night or two
and then they're passed on to someone in the king's
service, whether they like it or not, to have the king's
bairns under someone else's name. And that's the same
king who founded this high-and-mighty Order of the
Garter a few years ago. He even tried to seduce the
Countess of Salisbury, by all accounts, only she had
enough clout to resist him. What d'ye think of that,
then?'

'His best friend's wife? Oh, good grief!'

'It's true. And my little Penelope next, though where
the king could have seen her beats me. My God, Margaret, that was a narrow escape. If I could lay hands
on that nasty little… Are you all right, Mistress Merielle? It's shocked you, too, I see. I'm not surprised at
all.'

Not only shocked, but sickened. Revolted. She had
known something was very wrong, but to have been
set up for the king's pleasure was beyond anything she
could have believed. Thinking back, she supposed that
Gervase's interest in her had begun when he had first
offered help, as a friend of Philippe, to obtain an audience with the king, then kept her under his surveil-
lance until the king had returned from the French wars
and was ready to make use of her again. It was dis-
gusting.

'At Clarendon,' she said, using all her strength to

push the breath out of her lungs, 'there was a little lad named Roger, about two years old, in the care of a nurse. I was told he was Prince Edward's.'

'The prince's bastard. Yes, he is,' said the abbess. 'One of many. But that particular one is the son of a noblewoman who was not allowed to keep him. She's here, Mistress Merielle, in this convent, wearing the habit of a nun for protection, eating her heart out for a sight and a sound of her child. Roger of Clarendon is hers and she's not ashamed of it.'

'Oh!' Merielle hid her face, stricken by the pity of it. 'Tell her that the child is well and happy and growing strong. Oh, what heartache. Could I tell her of the child myself, do you think? But why does she need protection, lady? Is she in some danger because of it?'

'Cast-off royal mistresses are a prize, mistress. They can be sold for high prizes to any randy old fool who'll keep them busy with bairns till they wear out, able to boast that they married a royal mistress. Heaven knows what goes through their tiny minds, but that's a fact. Even William the Bastard's mother was married off, wasn't she? Fine men, no doubt, but the royals marry above themselves, not beneath, unless there's something in it they can't get otherwise. And apparently, *these* royals, father and sons, can get bastards by the cartload every year.'

Dame Edith laid a hand over her friend's arm. 'Shh, dear Margaret. Careful.'

'Treason. Nay, I think not, Edith. 'Tis well known. The lass might have gone to Romsey or Wilton; they're nearer, but she chose to stay with someone she could be sure of.'

'She still loves the prince, then?' Merielle said.

'Aye. She'd never have lain with him otherwise, but

love is not a part of men's reckoning, is it? Well…'
she shrugged '…you know my view on men. But what
of the handsome Sir Rhyan, mistress? Is he any different from the rest, or have you become cynical, too?'

'On the subject of royal bastards,' Merielle replied,
'I fear he may not be as different from the rest as I
would want a husband to be. And that is my misfor-
tune, for I shall either have to live with his censure or
live without him altogether. And I have chosen to do
the latter.'

After the mid-day meal, Merielle told them her own
story, which took them almost as far as vespers and
Dame Edith's departure. By that time, the lady had
regained her usual composure and had come to realise
how fortunate her own Penelope was in escaping a similar ordeal, and how much they owed to the anonymous
person whose investigations had revealed her danger.

Merielle recognised Dame Edith's Penelope at once
as the young woman at the funeral of Mistress Claire
Waterford. At vespers in the dimly lit church, Penelope
was not, even here, as closely watched as her mother
believed her to be, for her two guardian-nuns were both
sound asleep. The informality, laxness and complete
disregard shown by most of the nuns for the ritual of
the service astonished Merielle, Allene and Bess, who
stood at the back in the shadows. The constant chatter,
giggles, changing of places and scuffles with a pet
monkey that belonged to the cellaress, distracted them
entirely from the chaplain's weak droning.

A thimble rolled noisily on to the stone floor,
dropped by a nun mending the torn hem of her gown
by the light of a candle held by her friend. The abbess's

white lap-dog yapped and was released to chase off after a church mouse, terminating the snores of the oldest nun with a terrifying gurgle. The chaplain, a young man with a minimum of training, gabbled through the office in isolation, speeding towards more earthly matters with a single-minded concentration that Merielle was forced to admire. Far from being an object of reverence, or even of female interest, he was entirely ignored.

'And how involved is Sir Adam, d'ye think, in the whole sordid business?' Merielle whispered to Allene during what passed for the Benediction. 'I can't believe he doesn't have something to do with it, too. Do you think that Laurel…?'

'Hush, love. Not here. Too many ears,' said Allene. She and Bess had been told, naturally, of Gervase of Caen's role and neither had shown any surprise. 'He was never kind to Master Bonard, and I wouldn't be surprised if *he* was your unknown sleuth who's done a bit of digging while we've been away.'

'Bonard? You think so?'

'I would not be surprised at all,' she repeated.

The day darkened sooner than usual, sending the three women quickly up to their firelit chamber instead of into the small enclosed garden or into the sheltered cloister. Hanging low over the church spire, the clouds were pierced into a steady clattering downpour. There would be little point in travelling on the morrow.

Supper was taken in the abbess's parlour with the prioress, the Sacristaness and the three fugitives from Clarendon, whose expectations of a sober meal were well off the mark from the very beginning when the roast lamb, beef and rabbit were served up almost in defiance of the bishop's earlier reprimands.

'He tells me that red meat breeds *lusts of the flesh*,' sang the abbess, noisily emphasising the words while heaping the steaming meat slices on to Prioress Maria's trencher of white bread. 'So we're going to send Maria out on the town tonight to see what she comes back with.'

The abbess's personal cook, well-used to the nun's sense of humour, had playfully served up a dish of minced chicken in the shape of a fish, complete with glazed eye and spreading tail.

'Best fish in the stewpond,' they chortled. 'It clucks!'

Duck breasts set in spiced gelatine, saffron-stained quails' eggs and anchovy tartlets were picked at and the remainder sent down to the refectory to augment the nuns' plainer fare, but the wine stayed within their reach, dispelling any fears of lying awake with worry.

Bess, able only to find Allene's bed or the space between the two, was finally hauled into the one she had lusted after, too far gone to appreciate it. They slept late and, missing even the bell for prime, arose with throbbing heads and aching eyeballs that saw two of the young lady who slipped into their chamber in the dull morning light.

Merielle's attempts to focus added an extra throb. 'Mmm?' she said.

Penelope removed the stool from Bess's wandering aim and sat on it near Merielle. 'I've just come from prime,' she said. 'I tried to speak with you yesterday after compline, but I didn't get the chance. Mother tells me you've been to Clarendon. Please…do tell me what it's like.'

A vast emptiness and a terrible sense of loss blanked out everything in Merielle's memory, its intensity adding to her pain. 'Lovely,' she frowned. 'Lovely place. Why?'

'Well, because I may be going there soon. Is it a village? A manor?'

'It's big. You'll like it.' Even in the dim light, Merielle could see the girl's loveliness, dark, large-eyed and slender. Gervase would have relished the contrast between this and her own full curves. Gervase. The memories stirred, their movement making her wince with pain. 'Ah, yes, it's Gervase of Caen, isn't it? He's the one…'

The sweet smile of a secret first love lifted the corner of Penelope's pretty mouth. 'Oh,' she blushed. 'Mother told you. What did she say? That—?'

'Yes,' Merielle stopped her. 'That.'

'Oh, dear. Well, you see, I love him. He knows I'm here. He's going to come for me. He said so.'

'*What?*'

Bess crashed noisily into the linen-chest, righted herself and did exactly the same again. Allene picked her up, steered her towards Merielle's bed and tipped her on to it with an expressive, 'Tch!'

Penelope seemed not to notice. 'It's not difficult to smuggle letters out of here. You only have to pay the gate-man; he knows all the couriers. I had a letter back from Gervase the day before yesterday. He's going to take me away to this place called Clarendon where he's doing some work. You won't tell Mother or the abbess, will you? They don't understand my love for him, they think I'm still a child, but I'm not. I'm a woman.' She tossed her prettily plaited head, adding to Merielle's impatience.

Yes, she wanted to say, with anger, so are we all women. That's why we have to be careful where we bestow our love. Once we let it free, it's the very devil to catch it again; to bind it; re-use it. 'When?' she said, holding back the burst of pain in her head.

'Tonight.' The child smiled again, almost laughing. 'I'm to wait for him just inside the infirmary enclosure after compline. The two old things who sleep with me snore so loud they'd not hear even if I wore clogs on my feet.'

Allene said what was in Merielle's mind. 'Do you have the keys, then?'

'Er, no…not yet. Hadn't thought of that.'

'I'll get one for you.' She quelled Merielle's look of astonishment with a glance. 'There's a little side door in the north wall of the church, isn't there, where the devils are let out.'

'Yes, I know it.'

'I'll get the key and pass it to you at compline. Right?'

Penelope leapt up, hugging Allene. 'Oh, thank you! You're on my side, aren't you?'

'Yes, lass. I'm on your side,' Allene said.

'I'm so happy, mistress,' she said to Merielle. 'It's a wonderful thing to be in love, isn't it?' She kissed her cheek and left the chamber as softly as she had entered.

'No,' Merielle whispered to the door. 'It isn't. And what are *you* up to?'

'Hot and moist in the first degree, that's what you and this young madam are.' Allene nodded at the prostrate figure of Bess. 'In which case, a tisane of barley-broth is called for. Stay there.'

It took few powers of deduction for Merielle to see that the young mother of Roger of Clarendon, the one who dwelt here at St Mary's Abbey, was none other than the abbess's own daughter. Theresa had the same lovely countenance, the same lofty brow and cool, deep-set eyes as her mother, and the same sadness that made Merielle wonder if the abbess's cynicism regarding men was the result of some personal tragedy. She had half-expected that Theresa, garbed in a nun's black habit, would have adopted the same scornful attitude towards men, and was relieved to find no immediate sign of it.

Huddled in thick woollen cloaks, the two young women sat side by side on the stone bench that ran along the four walls of the cloister and the square garth worn by the feet of nuns at recreation. Hockey, to be exact.

The pelting rain bounced and rattled off the sloping roofs and spilled out of the overloaded gutters, hitting the columned sills, the potted plants and the spiders' webs, filling the bird-bath and the puddles at the women's feet. Other nuns sat in whispered conversation, contemplation or sleep.

'I'm so grateful for what you've told me,' Theresa said. 'I can almost hear his squeals of laughter. I can bear it as long as I know that he's happy, but it's at times like this when my arms ache to hold him. You know?'

'Yes, I know, though I've never borne one of my own. I don't know which of us is the more fortunate. Is your fear of being married off very great?'

Theresa looked at her new-found friend sharply before giving a delicate snort of derision. 'That's my lady mother's fear, Merielle, not mine, as it is her fear that keeps me here, I assure you. I do not have a supply of money to bribe the porters, as young Penelope does; if

I had, I'd be off to Clarendon this minute, regardless of the consequences.'

'Your mother said you were not allowed to keep him.'

'They would not allow me to keep him here at the abbey to grow up in the company of nuns, nor would my mother wish it.' Her voice softened, explaining her mother's part and seeming to find a way of excusing it. 'She brought me here ten years ago when I was fifteen at the time she was elected to the abbacy. She was a young nun when she bore me, here at St Mary's, and my first years were spent with my grandparents. She was seduced, you see, by the Abbot of Hyde Abbey here in Winchester, which probably accounts for her attitude to men. Like mother, like daughter, eh?' She smiled, sadly. 'I think she's still in love with him.'

'It was not difficult, then, for the prince to see you here?'

Theresa looked down at her hands, smiling still. 'You've seen what my mother's hospitality is like, I believe. Secretly, she was as flattered as me by the prince's interest. If she had not been, she would have made it impossible for us to be alone together. I was caught on the very first occasion. You look surprised, Merielle. It can happen, you know.'

She mistakes me, Merielle thought: like father, like son. Unconsciously exploring, Merielle's hands pressed against her body. 'I'm more surprised that a nun who has broken her vows could go on to be elected abbess.'

Theresa's smile broke free into a laugh. 'An abbess is elected by the house and approved by the bishop. My mother is popular with both.'

'With Bishop Edington? But she—'

'Fiddlesticks! He comes so often because he can't

keep away. If Mother didn't have her weekly argument
with the good bishop, she'd feel slighted. They love it,
both of them. And you'd be amazed if you knew how
often this kind of thing happens, both before and after
an election. Mother is not the only abbess to have a
child, by any means. The trouble is, she was able to
keep me by her and now finds it impossible to release
me, even though I've taken no vows. She wants me to
follow in her footsteps, but all I want is to become a
mother. I suppose if I'd had a girl, as she did, things
might have been different.'

'And are men *really* proud of acquiring a cast-off
mistress for a wife, as your mother says?'

'That's something else she wants to believe, Merielle, because it fuels her fear of losing me. As for men
being proud about it, well, what else would they pretend when they're obeying the king's command? Far
from having to pay for the privilege, they're given in-
centives: land, property, titles, positions. That is the
usual practice. The royals prefer their bastards to be
born in wedlock, anybody's wedlock, but they don't
insist on it. As for *choosing* such a woman, well, I
doubt many men would go that far unless she was stunningly beautiful and wealthy, like you. Then they
might, but I doubt very much whether any man would
be happy to have his wife used for that purpose: the
Earl of Salisbury would not have been amused, I'm
sure. No, it's usually the women themselves who are
proud to be chosen, especially if their husbands are
dull.'

'And you?'

'He would never marry me off against my will, I
know it. I adore Prince Edward, but he's in love with

his cousin Joan.' Her eyes filled with tears, brimming on her lower lids and glistening like pools of rain.

'He would not prevent you from visiting your son, would he?'

'No, on the contrary, he always wanted me to be the one to care for Roger. It was my mother who insisted, but I thought my duty to her was stronger than my mother-love. But it isn't,' she whispered. The tears overflowed and splashed on to her hands, and rainwater spouted in perfect arcs from the mouths of stone heads at the four corners of the guttering.

Chapter Thirteen

'Gone, sir,' the captain said, briskly. 'Horses, panniers, the two lads, the lot. I've spoken to the porter at the gate, but he says—'

'Yes!' Sir Rhyan said, crashing the door to Merielle's empty chamber. 'He says that with all the coming and going, he didn't see who was passing. Well, he bloody well should have. That's his job, the fool!'

'Yes, sir. But they'll not have gone far, surely. Who saw her last?'

'Go and find out. Keep asking. Report directly to me. Find Sir Adam and see if he knows anything. Hurry, man!'

The last instruction was lost, for the man was already clattering down the spiral stairwell, the top of his head instantly replaced by Sir Adam's, followed by a voice that called up from the level of Sir Adam's heels. 'She was with me in the king's chamber only an hour or so ago. What's to do, Sir Rhyan? Lost her, have you?'

'Eh?' Sir Adam looked down. 'With you? Why didn't you say so?'

'I just have.' Master Wykeham smiled benignly, emerging from the stairwell like a jack-in-a-box. 'We were discussing the walls, hanging devices, the king's visit tomorrow.' He peered out of the narrow lancet window. 'Can't see the tents from this side.'

'What?' said Sir Rhyan. 'You told me, uncle, that those tents were for workmen, builders. You said…'

Sir Adam glared at Wykeham with undisguised animosity. 'I was not sure…I thought…I was going to tell you later, as a surprise.'

'What's to do?' Wykeham was suddenly serious. 'Surely you don't think Mistress St Martin left because of what I said? Doesn't she like the idea of meeting his grace?'

'No, she doesn't, sir. A lady's privilege. Sir Adam, a word with you in private, if you would be so kind.'

Delivered in that tone, the invitation held little choice but, even so, Sir Adam took the offensive. 'What have *you* said to scare her off, nephew?' he hissed, trapped by the narrow passageway and Sir Rhyan's bulk. 'This arrangement was of my own making and I would have told Mistress St Martin in my own time. You know nothing…'

'I know a damned sight more than you think, uncle. And if *she* had known of the king's intention to visit Clarendon, she would never have agreed to come, and you know it, too, which is why you kept quiet. What other delights have you arranged for her? As a surprise. Another large bed?'

'Don't take that tone with me, sir. If she's returned to Canterbury, it's because she's still upset about the child. Nothing to do with the king's visit. We must find her quickly. Heads will roll for this,' he muttered, turning away.

But Sir Rhyan hooked a hand around his uncle's arm, yanking him back against the wall. 'Find her!' he snarled into his uncle's face. 'Yes, find her for the king, or *your* head will roll. That's it, isn't it?' Savagely, he pushed the astounded man away. 'Don't take me for a fool, old man. I'm neither blind, deaf nor dumb, so find me some answers, while you're about it.'

Furiously, Sir Adam brushed a hand down his sleeve and strode away, his florid jowls quivering, with Sir Rhyan behind him. Round the corner at the bottom of the stairwell, the full force of the sunset flooded through the arched doorway, casting into black silhouette the trio who approached from the direction of the kitchens.

Sir Rhyan's captain stood weightily behind. 'This young man here was seen to follow Mistress St Martin into the water-garden, sir. Says he's a friend of hers. Name of Gervase of…where was it?'

'Caen!' the young man snapped. 'What's all the fuss about, for heaven's sake?' He looked beyond Sir Adam's shoulder at Sir Rhyan and, immediately assessing the seriousness of the situation, saw no option but to bluff it out. He bowed to Sir Adam and waited. 'Sir?'

'Master Gervase of Caen, you are…?'

'Employed in the king's household, sir, to oversee the supplies of food to the king's table while he's in progress to—'

'Yes, yes, all right.' Sir Adam waved a hand impatiently. 'You know Mistress St Martin, do you? You spoke to her this afternoon?'

'Indeed I did, sir. Mistress St Martin and I know each other well.' He glanced at Sir Rhyan. 'Did she not tell you?'

'Got better things to do, I should think. Where is she?'

Gervase of Caen's surprise was genuine, his eyes darting from one face to the next before a slight frown appeared. For a moment, he said nothing as the seriousness dawned on him.

The pause was too long for Sir Rhyan. His hand shot out to grab at the spotless white shirt below Gervase's chin, hauling him round to face him. 'Where is she?' he repeated. 'And how long have *you* known of the king's visit to Clarendon? Well before our last meeting in Canterbury, I'm sure.'

'You two have met?' Sir Adam asked.

'We've met,' said Sir Rhyan, keeping hold. 'His grace's little pie-frill knows more than he's letting on, does he not?' He shook the fistful of shirt.

'No, sir!' Master Gervase pulled himself free. 'This is outrageous! I spoke to Mistress St Martin, with her consent, in the water-garden to tell her what I'm doing here. *Sir.*' He glared at Sir Rhyan. 'And she said she was relieved to see me and that she would shortly be returning to Canterbury. There. Is that what you wanted to know? And what is all this about? Has she disappeared? If so, then it's probably your boorish behaviour that's sent her off. *Sir.*' He appealed to Sir Adam. 'I am honoured to meet you, Sir Adam. Of course I will do all I can to help.'

'You'll do more than that, whelp!' Sir Rhyan advanced again.

Now truly ruffled, Gervase protected himself in his usual manner. 'Then I should perhaps tell you, Sir Rhyan, that Mistress St Martin assured me that she'd be freeing the lands to you that you went to such great lengths to rend from her at the time of her husband's death. I presume that's why you pursued her so relentlessly? Or do I mistake the matter?'

Sir Adam rounded on his nephew. 'Lands? What is all this about, sir? Is it true what this man says? Tell me, if you please.'

'Go ahead, Sir Rhyan.' Gervase backed away into the stalwart captain, retrieved himself and measured his escaping distance. 'Tell Sir Adam how you waited until the lady was at her most vulnerable before you began a lawsuit to retrieve lands wasted by the sickness ten years ago. No wonder the lady's had enough of you. So have I.' He turned away, hoping that in the fracas, his departure would not be missed. But the burly captain grabbed him by the scruff of the neck, even without looking, and brought him back.

'Is this true, nephew?'

'Without the fancy embroidery, sir, yes, it is. I sued Mistress St Martin for breaking a contract her father made with mine. It concerned lands. I did not wait for any particular time. I would have to be a seer to do that. Nor did I know of her husband's death, or pursue her. I pursued the case through the correct channels.'

'Just to regain a bit of land? Are you serious? You sued her for that?'

'No, sir. I sued her because she married Philippe of Canterbury without my consent. It's written into the contract.'

'Good God, nephew. Now I've heard it all.'

'No, you haven't, sir.'

'What else, then? Don't tell me—'

Gervase of Caen intervened. 'No, I don't suppose he will tell you, Sir Adam, how he accepted money from the king himself to leave her alone. Yes, sir—' he traded upon Sir Adam's gasp of incredulity '—Mistress St Martin was obliged to seek the king's help to combat your nephew's claim. He was sent a fee of forty marks

to leave her alone. Can you believe it? Forty marks
kept him quiet.'

'Forty marks, my bloody foot! You think I'd be kept
off for forty bloody marks?' Sir Rhyan snarled. 'Four
hundred, man! Four hundred marks and a command to
back off. What else could I do but obey? So what do
you know about it, Pie-Frill? How do you come to
reach a figure of forty marks? Were you there?'

Gervase of Caen smirked, relishing the new direction
his line had taken. 'No, sir. I was not present at the
interview. Nor was anyone else, not even Mistress St
Martin's two ladies. His grace saw her alone. They
were alone for some time. For four hundred marks his
grace must have enjoyed—'

With the captain at his back, Master Gervase could
not fall at Sir Rhyan's first crippling blow, but was
forced to suffer two more to his ribs before his support
was withdrawn. He slumped on to the dusty courtyard,
clutching at his ribs, his fair hair awry.

'Was that to shut him up before he indicts you further, nephew?'

'It was to protect a lady's honour, sir, something
about which you appear to know less than you ought.
Your own recent proposal to the lady was a disgrace
both to yourself and to her. I proposed marriage.'

'You young dog! You have ingratiated yourself,
abused your position—'

'Save your breath, honourable uncle. Mistress St
Martin has not accepted me. And if her flight from here
is anything to go by, it doesn't look as though she will.
She must be heartily sick of the whole damn lot of us
to have gone without a word.'

'I shall find it very difficult to forgive you for this.
Interfering in affairs which do not concern you is be-

neath contempt. I gave you hospitality, every kindness, and this is how I am repaid. To take from beneath my nose a woman for whom I have—'

'Plans for the king's use, uncle? Like you had for her sister?'

Sir Adam blenched, but was spared having to reply by the appearance of Master John Kenton, who having heard the last part of the conflict, stepped between them with all the foolhardiness of a pikeman in a bullring. He placed a light hand across his friend's broad shoulders. 'Come, Sir Rhyan. I believe there may be something you should know.'

'Too damned right, my friend. There's a lot I should know. Get on with your scheming, uncle, and dredge up some cock-and-bull story to serve to his grace about why his quarry has escaped yet again. You'll both have to hunt the deer instead, unless you can find another woman as lovely as Mistress St Martin before he arrives.'

'You speak ill of his grace, nephew. Beware!' was Sir Adam's parting shot.

'He's able to defend himself. Mistress St Martin is not.'

Master John pressed again. 'Come on, sir.'

'I have to go after her, John. Something happened that I have to know about. It affects everything. Dafydd!' He called to his captain. 'Take that *thing* out of the way…' he nodded to the groaning heap of Gervase '…then saddle up. We're going.'

'With respect, sir,' the captain said, 'the light will be gone in another half-hour, and Mistress St Martin will have to lay up for the night. We can be at Winchester before her if we start at daybreak, and we can ride off-track to avoid the king's party. She'll take a detour as well.'

'You're right. Daybreak, then. First cock-crow, Dafydd. Now, John, what is it you know that I don't? It must be important or you'd not open your mouth, would you?'

There were few places at the best of times free from overhearing ears or overseeing eyes, but Master John had discovered one on a sun-trapped bench where young apricot branches were tied to the wall behind them. There, in the last of the evening light and accompanied by the dance of midge-swarms, Master John told his shocking story to Sir Rhyan who sat with his head back, watching the light disappear into a purple cloud.

'I was there, sir, so I know how it was,' he began.

'He said they were alone.'

'They were, almost. It was this time of day. September. I'd been all that afternoon in the king's chamber at the Archbishop's palace, painting scenes on the wainscot. I'd had to prepare my own paints and clean my own brushes because Padraig was off with a head cold and I dared not take him into the king's presence. I did them in a little closet to the side of the chamber so as not to make too much of a smell. Linseed, you know. Quite pungent. I'd gone into the closet to find some more oil when I heard the king come back into the room. He'd been to the garderobe, I think. Almost straight after that, I heard someone else come in from the clerks' room at the other side, and when I peeped through the crack in the door, I saw the chap you've just floored.'

'Gervase of Caen? He said he was not there.'

'He wasn't at the interview. They spoke for a moment in low voices: I couldn't hear anything except, "Don't come in till I call you," and then this lad went off. Well, I wasn't supposed to see or hear anything. As far as the king was concerned, I was invisible. Not there. So I was just about to clatter and make a din when the lad came back with Mistress St Martin. Of course, I didn't know who she was until later, but all I thought of was keeping quiet until she'd gone. I covered up my workbench with an old fur to stop the paints from drying out, put out the candle flame, pushed the door to as far as I could and just sat it out in the darkness. I found the ladder and crept up a few rungs and sat at the top, waiting.'

Sir Rhyan nodded, and Master John could see the muscles of his jaw tense and relax again. 'Go on,' he whispered.

'I thought the king had suddenly remembered about me when he pushed the door open, but he had Mistress St Martin by the hand and, as soon as he'd pulled her inside, I realised what was happening. I heard her protest—'

'Protest? What…?'

'He shut the door. It was pitch dark: I saw nothing, but I heard it all. She didn't stand a chance against him, a young lass against—'

'Argh!' Sir Rhyan leapt to his feet, grasped the apricot boughs and shook them. 'Stop, John! For pity's sake!' Straight-armed, he dropped his head between them, pushing as Merielle had done, fighting off the attack and gasping for breath. 'He took her by force? Just like that?'

'Yes. She obviously had no idea what he'd intended. She pleaded with him, then went quiet, except for—'

'Shut up!'

Master John became invisible again until he was re-deemed.

'Then what? Didn't she tell him she'd just lost a pregnancy?'

'Not a word. Not unless she'd told him before. I thought he'd never finish. Well...' he collected his thoughts '...he just pulled her out of the door and closed it, and I must admit I was so numbed I don't quite know what I did except stay there, shivering. I heard voices, heard the door open and close, then when servants went in, banging about and chattering, I real-ised his grace must have gone.'

Sir Rhyan's protests came from between his out-stretched arms. 'John, why in God's name did you not *stop* it? Why did you just sit there and let it happen? I shall never be as close to killing anyone as I am to you this moment, and yet I know you are not to blame. No one dares interrupt the king at such a time if he wants to keep his life.' His voice broke, quietly throbbing with rage and shame. He panted, then kicked out at the bench. 'Raped! You should have told me before, John!'

Master John hung his head. 'It was the worst night-mare, sir. I'll never forget it.'

Like a lash of a whip, Sir Rhyan leapt upon his friend, flattening him against the wall. '*You'll* never forget? What about *her*? Is it any wonder she's bolted at the thought of seeing him again? You knew bloody well that must be the reason why she didn't want to stay in his palaces, sleep in his beds, do up his stinking walls, yet you said nothing of it, did you? You watched me bring her to this damned place where his things are all around, reminding her. How could you not speak of it to me? How *could* you?' He released him. 'Ah, forgive me, John. I'd not harm you, truly. You are not to blame. It was me. My fault.'

'You can kill me, if you wish. I'm ashamed of doing nothing to help her, but he's the king and I think I could hardly believe my ears. I'm not proud of any of our sex: we're a sad lot in our dealings with women.'

'Weak,' Sir Rhyan said, sitting down heavily on the bench. 'The mightiest warrior goes berserk when he sees a woman like Mistress St Martin. Who's to blame him?'

'I do,' said Master John. 'I blame him. I saw only a glimpse of her and she was stunning, even then, but that doesn't give even a king the right to molest a gentle, sensitive, lovely creature like that. I can blame him, but I can do nothing to prevent him.'

'So how d'ye think I feel, who drove her to seek the king's aid in the first place? Eh?' His blue eyes sparked fire in the last of the sunset. 'If it had not been for my own madness, she'd not have had to go there that day.'

'A lawsuit is hardly madness, is it?'

'It was nothing to do with the bloody land, John. No fool would believe that of me. I have more land on one manor than all of hers put together.' He swung an arm out wide, tipping his powerful head back to look at the first pale stars, then letting out a gusting sigh that sobbed with anguish. 'A blinding jealousy, John, that's eaten at my guts all these years, though it does me no credit to admit it. I went to fight in France thinking I could conquer it, but it made no difference.

'I saw her when I was a lad. I was with my father and elder brother when the contract was made and she was a cheeky young lass. And later, I saw her when she married that bumbling wealthy old fool from Lincoln, and I was mortally sick at the thought of him

having her. She was miles away when he died and I
didn't get to hear of it, what with all the sickness striking everyone again, and the next I heard she was going
down to Canterbury and I knew I'd lost her for good.

'But there was the contract, and I knew she'd broken
it, so I was determined to make her remember me, even
if for all the wrong reasons. That was the madness of
it. Sheer madness. Because I could not have her myself,
I wanted to anger her, to curb her independence in
some way. Only my timing was wrong and my law-
yer's letter arrived just after the news of her husband's
death and the loss of the babe she was expecting, which
I knew nothing of until some time later. So now I have
that on my conscience, too. Then my uncle married her
sister, by some quirk of fate, and I got the chance to
see her again. But by that time she hated me, and with
good reason, I see now.

'But I thought I was winning, John. I thought I'd
begun to make her trust me, though there was always
something in the way, something she couldn't tell me
about. We've all failed her. The king. Sir Adam. Her
pathetic Philippe. Me. You. But me, most of all.'

'I heard that she was ill afterwards. I made enquiries.'

'Well, she would be, wouldn't she?'

They sat in silence as the sun slipped away into the
black-purple cloud-bank, a horn sounded for supper,
and the darkness invited anonymous whispers.

'Tell me, John. Was she…did she weep?'

In the deep shadows, Master John's shame was hidden as the brightening stars blurred in his eyes. 'No.
She had courage. I was the one who wept.'

Taking a slight detour to avoid any sight of the
king's advance party, they set off at first light to ride

eastwards to Winchester and towards Canterbury. Whether she would stop at Winchester or keep going they had no notion, but she would have to stop before Sunday and it was Friday now.

It was hardly a conversational journey and Sir Rhyan spared neither his men nor their mounts, though they were not unused to his natural velocity. Master John accepted all discomforts as his overdue penance. At the one short stop, for the horses' sake, he refreshed his memory about Sir Rhyan's meeting with Mistress St Martin at the wedding of his uncle.

'I should never have gone,' Sir Rhyan told him. 'She was more beautiful than ever. We didn't speak.'

'But you found favour with her sister, Lady Bedesbury, so I take it you've found out about her?'

'Quite a lot, yes, but spare me the details till later, John, when I can stomach them. I suppose you were invisible there, too, were you?'

Master John prepared to mount, jerking one dark eyebrow into his fringe. 'My God, sir. I'd not be alive to tell the tale otherwise, would I?'

As the captain had predicted, they covered the twenty-five miles in less than half the time of their previous journey without once sighting Mistress St Martin's small group with packhorses which, Sir Rhyan said, was strange, for she also would have wanted to avoid the main highway. He sent two men off to Romsey Abbey to ask there, but they reached him at Sir Adam's house with nothing to report.

Stopping only long enough to eat whilst standing, they rode along the southern city wall towards King's Gate. And it began to rain.

'The Sustren Spital, John. She was friendly with

Dame Edith there. That'll be where she's gone, if not
straight on to Canterbury.'

Without knowing it, they were as close as they had
ever been to catching Merielle up. Dame Edith, however, had gone to St Mary's Abbey, and the young
sister knew nothing of Merielle's earlier visit, nor did
she feel disposed to stand in the rain when she had
patients to attend to.

Master John wheeled his horse. 'Then perhaps *we*
should try there, sir. I doubt she'll have gone through
Winchester without stopping somewhere.'

'Wait, John; I don't want to intrude. If she's there,
I'll not disturb her but wait for her to come out. All I
want is to know that she's safe.'

'Then it's best if she doesn't know we're here, isn't
it? The horses will be in the stables, surely. We can
find out that much.'

The route across the muddy cathedral precinct was
crowded with wet and steaming horses, pilgrims, sight-
seers, pedlars and pickpockets, friars, merchants with
their wagons, minstrels and those citizens going about
their daily business, parting like the Red Sea before Sir
Rhyan's imposing company.

On the other side, the captain slipped through the
heavy gate of St Mary's Abbey that led directly into
the infirmary where the gatekeeper's dwelling and the stables stood side by side. With a generous
bribe, he discovered the best of news. 'They're there,
sir. Mistress St Martin's chestnut, the four others and
two pack-mules. Travelling light for a lady?'

'And the two lads? They didn't see you, I hope?'

'Gone off to the blacksmith down Colebrookestreet.'

'Keep a relay of men here to watch, Dafydd. I want
to know who enters and who leaves, at once.'

'Where will you be, sir? Hyde Abbey?'

'No, I think not. That's up beyond the north wall. We'll find accommodation nearer than that at the Cathedral Priory.'

'St Swithun's? It's Friday, you know, sir. You'll get nothing but fish 'n' pilgrims.'

'I know, Dafydd. But it's not my belly that concerns me.'

The guestmaster, Brother Andrew of Bedford, groaned inwardly at the sight of Sir Rhyan's large party, although his good-natured welcome hid the concern he felt at the drain on the monastery's resources caused by the hordes of guests he was duty-bound to accommodate. Each and every guest, rich and poor alike, was to be treated as if he were Christ Himself. Yet the parable of the loaves and fishes began to wear thin from Easter-tide onwards, and without St Swithun's bones, Hyde Abbey escaped the brunt of it. He was therefore much relieved at Sir Rhyan's assurance that all their guesthouse expenses, including men, horses and Master John, would be met by him. He was also surprised to discover—though his guests were less so—that the best chamber being reserved for a later guest would not now be required. He hoped they would enjoy the view of the monks' garden and the King's Gate.

Usually so sure of himself, so full of the confidence bestowed by noble birth and wealth, Sir Rhyan was finding it difficult not to flounder beneath the weight of guilt that had descended upon him with such force last evening. His immediate and frightening anger with Master John had been no more than a re-direction of his anger with himself. So much they both understood.

But no such reaction would compensate him for the loss he would suffer if Merielle should find it impossible to forgive him, utterly and completely. And why should she? She was proud, and rightly so. She had dignity and sensitivity, both of which had suffered by men's overbearing usage. She had attempted to unravel the mystery of her sister's child, but obviously she had not succeeded, otherwise she would have realised her own part in it. How much had she discovered? How much more would *he* discover?

Having been requested to save it, Master John did not re-open the subject of Lady Bedesbury, for he could see how his revelation had shaken his friend badly. Far from regretting it, he knew that if the relationship were to stand any chance of success, the trust Sir Rhyan was hoping for would not materialise until the last obstacle was removed. He also knew that those closest to Mistress St Martin would no more have divulged their secrets than attempt to fly. According to Sir Rhyan, her ex-manager and close friend had crossed verbal swords with him already, a not uncommon clash of northern brusqueness and southern punctiliousness, John assumed.

He left Sir Rhyan to his thoughts, stretched out on the clean and comfortable bed in the upper storey of the guesthouse, and went down the winding stairwell to where the guestmaster, far from redirecting another applicant towards the stable-loft, was greeting this one with smiles of delight.

The newest guest was of moderate height and distinguished only by a bright red scarf tied lopsided over one eye, obviously the result of an accident, John thought, for the man had not the appearance of a soldier. Sandy hair stuck to his forehead and neck in rain-soaked points beneath his shining leather hat, and his clothes, though muddied, were well-cut and bright, the simple garb of a professional man, though there was something of the scholar about him that appealed to Master John. He bowed, hoping for an introduction.

Brother Andrew obliged. 'Ah, here's Master John. Allow me to introduce a very old friend of mine, sir. Master Bonard of Lincoln.'

'Of Lincoln, sir? You've come a fair distance.'

'Of Canterbury,' Bonard said, shaking himself like a wet hound. 'Your servant, sir.' He bowed and his hat fell off, sending a shower of water over Brother Andrew's already soaking feet.

The guestmaster bellowed with laughter. 'Are you trying to tell me something, my friend? It's I who should be washing yours, I believe.'

This time, there was no provocative remark from Sir Rhyan about Master Bonard's touching devotion to Merielle, not even about the red scarf that had been restored to its former status. Indeed, it was this that indicated the reason for his frantic journey to Winchester.

But Master Bonard was on his guard, nevertheless. 'I intend to visit Sir Adam,' he told Sir Rhyan, with a certain aloofness, 'but I prefer to stay with those I can trust rather than with one I am unsure of.'

'Unsure?' Sir Rhyan probed.

'Correction, sir. I *am* sure of him. I'm sure he's not the best person to have the care of Mistress St Martin. I took the liberty of expressing that opinion to her, but my reservations went unheeded. And now...'

'Yes, I understand perfectly. So it is to repeat your warning that you have come to Winchester?'

'I have said enough, sir. Too much. Sir Adam is your uncle, is he not?'

The three men had sat together over their mid-day meal in the guesthouse refectory with at least twenty-five others whose general hubbub made it possible to speak without the least chance of being understood. Lipreading or sign language being too unrefined for their purposes, they bravely ignored the stares of the curious at the red scarf and retired to a quiet corner of the prior's private cloister to which old and favoured friends were admitted.

In the shelter of the moss-covered roof, white pigeons strutted, the larger males lording it over the others. There was no doubt about it, thought Master John, Master Bonard was on the defensive and Sir Rhyan was doing his best to smooth his feathers.

'Sir Adam being my uncle, Master Bonard, need not deter you from speaking out. I left him yesterday after an acrimonious farewell.'

'That does not necessarily put him in the wrong, Sir Rhyan.'

Touché, thought John.

'In this case it does, since our argument concerned the safety of Mistress St Martin at Clarendon Palace. Or rather, *I* was concerned; my uncle was less so.'

This affected Bonard instantly. 'Mer…Mistress St Martin is at Clarendon? With Sir Adam? What's she doing there? It's the king's place. God in heaven, sir—' he leapt to his feet '—you *left* them there?'

It took both of them to sit him down again with assurances that she was safe and only a few hundred yards away from where they sat.

'Then do not detain me, Sir Rhyan, if you please. I must warn her. If you have her safety at heart, allow

me to go to her now. I've come to take her back home.'
He could not resist the audience, however. 'You no
doubt remember meeting that young scoundrel, Gervase of Caen? Well, I've been doing some investigating
on my own, and you'd be surprised at the pot of worms
I've discovered.'

'I doubt it,' Sir Rhyan remarked. 'But I'd be most
interested to hear what you can tell me, even so.'

Master John's sidelong glance attempted to locate
signs of sarcasm in Sir Rhyan's demeanour, but there
were none, not even when Master Bonard lifted his red
scarf, rubbed his eye and replaced the blindfold before
he began.

Chapter Fourteen

Mistress Allene had not misjudged Master Bonard's ability as a sleuth. None of them, however, had appreciated the depth of his despair at being left in Canterbury while Merielle had gone off, without a proper escort, to stay with a man who could not have had her best interests at heart. It was only when Master Bonard went in person to St Augustine's Abbey in Canterbury to plead with the abbot to send a couple of monks off in their wake, that he learned how Sir Rhyan's party were already performing that function. And though he knew she would not like it, he also knew instinctively that Sir Rhyan would protect her from harm. The fact that the two were now so close and yet so far said little for the two weeks of each other's company, so apparently he had made scant headway. Which, considering the extent of his offence, was hardly surprising, especially as Bonard knew she would never have confronted him with it. A pity, he thought.

What he told Sir Rhyan and Master John about the devious exploits of Gervase of Caen was more or less the same as what Dame Edith had told Merielle and the abbess only an hour or so earlier which, although coming from the same stable, had none of the scholarly embellishments of the horse's mouth, so to speak. As an ex-colleague of Dame Edith's late husband, Robert of Whitstable, and a friend of their neighbourly second cousin, Bonard remembered the late appearance of Penelope, now a spoilt sixteen-year-old. Or was it seventeen?

'I don't quite remember,' he said, stifling a yawn. 'Time flies. But I could not get round there fast enough to tell them about the danger the silly child was in. Well, apart from the obvious one, that is.'

'But to find out about Gervase of Caen, you actually went back to the archbishop's palace, pretending friendship with him, to talk to the clerks there?'

'Yes,' said Bonard, crisply, crossing his ankles and laying his hands neatly on his lap. 'I took the lot of them across to his favourite ale-house and got them to chatter. A few pints and it all came out soon enough. Boastful, they were, and a little envious of his double act. Treacherous little swine.'

'They were all aware of it, then, this procuring of women for the king? Did his grace assault them all, or were they mostly willing?'

The hands flew apart and the ankles uncrossed. Bonard sat bolt upright.

Sir Rhyan tempered his plain-speaking. 'My northern outspokenness again, Master Bonard. I beg your pardon, but I am aware of what happened when Mistress St Martin went to plead her case against me. I accept the blame totally and I believe that when I've had chance to ask her forgiveness, she will look more kindly upon my offer of marriage. Indeed, I believe she cares for me, but cannot bring herself to tell me in what way I was involved. She is too shamed, naturally.'

'And you, sir?'

'Shamed. Mortified. Disgusted,' he whispered. 'And I adore her.'

Unaccountably, untypically, Bonard experienced the warm flush of power, of having in his possession something that would stun this great handsome creature whose declaration took the words from his own mouth, words he would never be allowed to utter. Yet the venom disappeared before he could blink, and the thunderbolt he could have delivered melted at his innate kindness. And even now he balked, not knowing how best to remove his rival's last stumbling-block with gentleness.

It was left to Master John to help him out. 'Shamed, aye. Mistress St Martin had not her sister's safety in marriage, did she, sir, being recently widowed?' Master John said. 'She became ill after seeing the king, Master Bonard, so I was led to understand. Could that have been…?'

Bonard looked away, talking quietly to the curious pigeons. 'She wanted a child so desperately. Still does, I believe. But not *that* one. Not one forced upon her, in widowhood, of all things. No one can blame her.'

The enormity of it, even delivered so gently, had all the effects of the thunderbolt, stunning Sir Rhyan and making him gasp at the pain. Her pain. His head sank lower into his hands, his massive shoulders hunched.

'My God,' he whispered, his face washed pale. 'I cannot ask her to be my wife after this, can I? Do you know what I said to her the other day when she saw the prince's child? My God, how *could* I have said it?'

'What was it you said, sir?'

'I said that most women would be proud to bear a royal bastard. How crass. How arrogant. How can any

man ever know what a woman would be proud to do?'
He thrust a fist against his mouth, quaking.

By mutual assent, his two companions stood some
distance away nearer the heavy patter of the cooling
downpour.

'How did you know?' Bonard whispered.

'Guessed, mostly. She must be a fertile creature if
that Philippe of Canterbury could score one. Not exactly siring material, was he?'

'You knew him? Ah, of course, you did work for us,
didn't you? We never met because that was not my
department. I've been struggling to remember where
I've seen your name. In the ledgers, of course. King's
painter, designer, general—'

'No, not general. Particular. I do not spread my tal-
ents as far as some do.'

'I beg your pardon.'

'Not at all. You knew Philippe of Canterbury well,
Master Bonard. Am I correct in thinking that the king
sent me to design for the St Martin workshop as a
bribe?'

Bonard lifted the red scarf to study something on the
other side of the cloister, then replaced it carefully over
the eye. 'Bluntly put, but yes, you are correct and you
do, after all, have a perfect right to know. According
to Master Gervase's somewhat envious clerical friends,
the king first saw Mistress St Martin when she lived in
Lincoln. And, on talking over the matter with Dame
Edith of Whitstable's relatives, the ones who were such
poor guardians of young Penelope, I discovered something that I had not previously been aware of, that when
Mistress St Martin's first husband died, it was then that
Master Gervase placed the order for the new set of

tapestries for the archbishop's palace, an order that came from the king himself, which—'

'Which I designed, and which Master Philippe was delighted to accept. So how did he suddenly become interested in marriage to the lovely widow in Lincoln, may I ask?'

'Need I tell you, my friend? By the same Gervase of Caen, apparently, who suggested to him that there would be other prestigious commissions for him if he succeeded in marrying her. Naturally, the relatives were as astonished as I was, because of his total lack of interest in marriage until then. However, he persisted, and won.'

'And were there other orders for tapestries, as promised?'

'No, but by then, the king had other—French— things on his mind.'

'And by the time he returned home, Philippe of Canterbury had left a widow behind. The king chooses his men most carefully, does he not?'

Bonard studied him closely, like a one-eyed owl. 'Sir Adam?'

'Yes. Mistress St Martin must have told the king of her lovely sister. The king's greed will get him into trouble one of these days.'

'Then I hope we shall both be well clear, my friend. You know that side of the story better than I. Was Sir Adam's young bride…was her relationship with his grace…affectionate?'

'I know who she was in love with, Master Bonard.'

Bonard followed the gaze that rested on the black bowed head, the clasped hands, the great arms resting on thighs. He sighed. 'Yes, of course. And what of her babe? You think Mistress St Martin will be staying to look after it, do you?'

Master John shook his head. 'Come up to my chamber, Master Bonard, and take a beaker of wine. We still have some talking to do, it seems, and our friend here will need all our support.'

It was a thoughtful Merielle, still wrapped in a heavy cloak, who watched the departure of Theresa, the abbess's tearful and courageous daughter. Hearing her story had had a therapeutic effect which put Merielle's own problems in a different light. The bell for the midday service of sext called a flurry of chattering nuns from the other side of the rain-washed cloister, their garishly fluttering veils making a bizarre contrast in the otherwise sombre scene.

Merielle smiled. They were young, and obviously without vocation, without learning and unable to study, placed here for family reasons with little or no choice in the matter, and needed by Abbess Margaret to keep the abbey viable. How different from her own situation. She was wealthy, educated, independent, and loved.

Yes, loved. How could she doubt it? He had never said as much, but had he not made it obvious by his care of her, his deep and tender affection, his desire to earn her trust, to father her bairns, to marry her?

A movement in the opposite corner of the walk-way caught her eye. The cloaked figure of a man. A heartbeat thudded into her throat, then dissolved. The figure had not his stature, walk or bearing, and he never wore a hat. But she knew someone who did.

'Bonard...ah, my Bonard! You've come to take me home, dear friend. How I've missed you.'

Laughing, he removed his leather-brimmed hat and

held out his arms for her almost flying leap, bracing himself.

'I thought you were a pilgrim,' she cried, hugging him and kissing his damp cheek.

'You're not the only one, mistress. Had it not been for my superior horse and lack of badges, they'd have had me swapping tales from all the shrines in Europe.' He grinned from ear to ear.

She could not help but notice the red scarf while suffering a pang of guilt that she had taken his vow so lightly. Whatever he lacked in stature, courage and romanticism were still his.

They sat together, holding hands, leaving Master Bonard in no doubt that she was pleased to see him, that she was unharmed, but needed his advice more than ever before. She told him all that had taken place—almost all—and admitted that his reservations about Sir Adam had been correct, though she still had not discovered the exact truth about Laurel. Which put his information ahead of hers in that respect.

'So you see, dear Bonard, he's not found me, though I cannot believe it would have been too difficult for him to do so, with all his men and experience. When do we set off for…why are you smiling?'

'Because, mistress, Sir Rhyan and Master John arrived here in Winchester yesterday, hard on your heels. There was scarce an hour in it, I believe.'

'*What?*'

'True. They were there at St Swithun's when I arrived and it was they who told me you were safely here at St. Mary's.'

'They knew that?'

'Of course. But Sir Rhyan would not disturb you. He waits for you to emerge, when you're ready.'

Without a smile, Merielle's slow blink swung her eyes to a shaft of light that sieved the rain. 'Then what?' she whispered. 'What happened to the bold knight? Lost his nerve?'

'Not his nerve. No, his innocence. He has discovered, you see, what happened...' he paused as Merielle's head swung sharply back to him '...with the king, which he now sees as entirely his fault.' He squeezed her hands, hoping for her eyes to soften. 'And he hesitates only because he cannot see how you can ever forgive him.'

'Oh, Bonard.' Her eyes filled. 'You told him.'

'Not all of it. I did not ask him how he knew, nor should you, but I know that the pain you felt is very real to him. All of it.'

'He knows that, too? What happened afterwards? Oh, no!'

'But that was the real barrier, was it not, mistress? How can you go forward with that between you, not knowing his mind on the matter?'

'I thought I did.'

'That was before. Things have changed. Allow him to explain. Trust him.'

'I dare not. It was my secret. I never wanted him to know.'

'And you are allowing it to fester like an open wound. Let it heal now. You are too young to hang on to it. Let him care for you, love you.'

'I'm not sure—'

'He does. He told me so.'

She knew how it cost him dearly to say it, Bonard, the one who had supported her through every distress, adoring her, ready to die for her, if need be. 'You are too good,' she said, placing her chin upon his damp shoulder. 'What would I do without you, my friend? But what shall I say to him?'

He smiled and put her away, gently. 'That, mistress, will be the least of your problems, I should think.'

Bonard was right about that, too, for words would have been superfluous. Sir Rhyan strode along the cloister walk with cloak flying, his strides covering the ground twice as fast as Bonard's, his grace that of a large cat.

Merielle's heart pounded to the same rhythm as when he had first walked into her home at Canterbury, catching at her lungs, her carefully prepared words of greeting having no chance to materialise before she was swept hard into him, enclosed, engulfed and set alight. As with their first kiss at Leeds Castle, their longing was ignited like a heathland blaze, but this time fuelled by such precious gems as 'Sweetheart…don't leave me…never run away from me again…'anted you…waited…never stop loving me…', which before had been buried too deep to find. Sentences fell apart and were snatched away into kisses that rained over faces, ready to re-assemble when breath ran out.

'Promise me…'

'What?'

'That you'll never leave me again. Promise?'

'I promise…yes…I promise. Bonard says you've been here since yesterday.'

His mouth slid beneath her chin, pushing it back to expose the soft pulse of her throat. 'I've had men watching both gates,' he said. 'Another day without you and I'd have burst in here to carry you off.'

'You still want me, Rhyan, after what you've discovered?' There was no immediate opportunity for him to reply verbally, but she got the gist, and was satisfied. 'But I didn't want you to know, my love.'

Being no sylph, it was the first time she had sat on a man's knee since childhood, but with him, she felt cherished and beloved. He wrapped them both round in his great cloak so that, to the line-up of pigeons on the columned sill, they resembled a two-headed body.

'My darling,' he said, 'you could neither tell me of it nor could you have kept it from me. I know. I understand. I am appalled at the burden you've had to carry, but now I want you to let me carry it with you, as I offered to before. I shall not withdraw my offer now I've found out how heavy it is, sweetheart. What I said the other day about royal bastards was the most insensitive thing anyone could have said. Please forgive me, my love. It's not what I meant, truly.'

'Then what?'

'The person I had in mind was your sister.'

'Laurel? Royal bastards? Rhyan…oh, no!'

He held her tightly in his arms, rocking her. 'The king offered Sir Adam advancement if he would marry your sister, knowing that he was a confirmed bachelor, like your Philippe had been, the idea being that such men would not care if the king took over certain of their duties.'

'But, Rhyan, it was I who told the king about Laurel.'

'That's neither here nor there, love, he'd have found out about her through you, one way or another. But strangely, it turned out that neither Sir Adam nor Philippe was as obliging as he'd hoped they would be, because Philippe got you pregnant, which he was not supposed to have done, then he died, which he was not supposed to have done either, and the king turned his attention to Laurel. Similarly, my uncle formed an emotional attachment to Laurel that no one had anticipated, least of all the king, and when little Joanie was born, Sir Adam was jealous of her.'

'He was not exactly the flattered stepfather, then?'

'Not at all. From the sound of things, he was extremely cut-up when your sister died, although he had kept to his side of the bargain to allow the king access to her. Both Master John and Brian Waterford told me of that.'

'And when Laurel died, the king switched his attention back to me? He wanted Sir Adam's cooperation once more?'

'The king's attention was never off you, my sweet. Your nasty little friend Gervase saw to that. He was paid to keep you in his sights.'

She turned her face into his chest, shivering, despite the warmth of his arms.

'Sir Adam felt bound to co-operate, or he'd have lost what he'd gained, all of it, and that was a serious threat. But all he could offer you, once little Joanie was lost, was a place as his mistress as well as the huge commissions for the workshop. With the babe, that was quite a package: without her, not enough. Although he couldn't offer you marriage, he still wanted to own you. You and your sister were the only ones he's ever shown the slightest interest in, and I truly believe he would have been proud to have you at his side.'

'Proud to keep what he'd earned, you mean.'

'That, too.'

'But little Joanie: how did that happen? Was it an accident?'

'In one sense, I believe it was. Sir Adam's steward, Brian Waterford, had been a party to the king's comings and goings at the house. He'd been a friend to Laurel and even advised her what to do, occasionally, and when little Joanie arrived, Brian's wife believed *him* to be the father.'

'She didn't know about the king, then?'

'No one knew except the steward, my uncle and Master John, the painter who was invisible yet who saw everything. Even so, Sir Adam was afraid that when that woman was in hospital, rambling and delirious, she might say enough to set you wondering. So he got her husband to take her some of the wine that had made *him* ill, just to keep her quiet till you'd gone.'

'Which killed her.'

'Which hastened her death, no doubt, though she'd not long to go, had she, sweetheart?'

'Did Sir Adam not want the child, Rhyan? Is that why he didn't have her properly tended when Laurel died?'

'I believe he didn't want a constant reminder of the pact he'd made with the king, betraying the woman he'd come to love. He had no direct hand in little Joanie's death, I'm sure, but he's indirectly responsible for all that's happened, and he knows it. Being childless, and believing the infant to be her husband's, Claire Waterford was only too glad to have charge of her, but she was desperately ill and had no experience. Sir Adam accepted his steward's recommendation of his wife because he wanted to keep him sweet, in case he told the world how his master was being cuckolded by the king. He can see now the effects of his greed and ambition!'

'Even to the extent of betraying *me*, as well as Laurel. Will the king punish him now, do you think?'

'For failing to get you to the palace at Guildford,

then to Clarendon, then for losing you to me, he'll
probably ignore him completely, which is the same
thing. But my heart is not bleeding for him, sweetheart.'

'Even though you're his heir and stand to lose by
it?'

'I stand to lose nothing that matters. I have won
you.' And in the confined space of a large cloak, he
did his best to demonstrate how much it meant to him.

Not far removed from Merielle's immediate concern
was Theresa's sadness at being kept from her child.
What she needed, Merielle said, was a champion to
plead her case with her mother, the abbess, and who
better suited to the task than the impressive Sir Rhyan,
whose aura of male authority easily overcame the abbess's fake vacillation.

She dithered quite—but not quite—convincingly. 'A
young woman alone at Clarendon Palace? The king
there, too? Ah…'

'Not alone in any sense of the word, lady, I assure
you. And the king is accompanied on this occasion by
Prince Edward himself. You would not deny either of
them this meeting after so long, surely? And the child,
your grandson? He should begin to know who his
mother is, don't you agree?'

Abbess Margaret nodded, biting her lip.

'And I will detail four of my best men to accompany
her to Clarendon. They can be there before nightfall.
Would that set your mind at rest?'

It did, as he had known it would, as he had also
anticipated the tears of joy from the young mother herself.

Tears of a different kind flowed from another young

woman, already labeled as a spoilt brat by more than Master Bonard. Sir Rhyan practiced his chivalry on her also by passing on a message alleged to have come from Master Gervase of Caen at Clarendon to the effect that he regretted, due to a hunting accident, that he would not be able to meet her at their appointed time that evening. This, delivered in front of the forewarned abbess, had the predicted effect of putting to an end any hopes of a continued liaison between the injured hunter and his willing victim, though it blighted any chance of Sir Rhyan becoming a hero in her eyes.

At supper with Master John, Master Bonard, Merielle and the abbess, he laughed it off with typical heartlessness. 'I'll recover,' he said, 'and she'll learn not to be so easily duped.'

'Unfair,' said Merielle. 'I was easily duped by him, too, remember. If it had not been for a certain person—' she placed her hand over Bonard's '—I might also have been weeping instead of laughing. I owe you my life, my dear friend.'

Sir Rhyan leaned towards her. 'Then perhaps now is the time to perform a duty which may do much for Master Bonard's view of the world.'

Merielle went to stand behind him, untied the knot that held the red scarf in place, removed it with dignified ceremony and bent to plant a kiss on both his pink cheeks. 'Thank you,' she whispered. 'And now, do you think I might hear the rest of the poem, in Latin?'

But whereas saving his mistress's life was one thing, being required to recite an intimate evocation of lust before witnesses was quite another and he declined, red-faced, saying that he knew someone who could probably remember it better than he. Or so that person had once claimed.

Sadly for Master John and the abbess, they never got to hear it at all. But Merielle did, later, and laughingly told her lover that it was quite shameless.

'Want to try it, then?' he said, trying not to laugh.

'All that protesting? Too energetic.'

'So we'll leave that bit out, then, shall we?'

Epilogue

In the still haze of an early summer dawn, a loose-haired woman crept barefooted through a side-door into the garden, stepping with care over the silver trail of snails on the stone pathway. Clutching at a tendril of her black hair as if for support was a pink fist that took it towards a mouth with a whimper of impatience.

'Wait, little one,' she whispered, laughing. 'Wait. How greedy you Lombards are. How insatiable.'

At the far end of the green and secret arbour, Merielle settled herself on to the upturned wheelbarrow and there, hidden from the upper windows of the house, pulled down her night-shift under the shawl, baring herself to the infant's impulsive search. Its little petalled mouth tugged at her, choking briefly on the first few mouthfuls that overflowed down his chin, then looking up at her in mutual amusement at his lack of finesse before closing his eyes in rapture.

A curlew called from across the moor, haunting, plaintive, a sound she had heard so often as a child in Yorkshire before it had had any meaning for her. Now, it meant home, with Rhyan, and their firstborn probably conceived in a bed of bluebells, as she was sometimes reminded. She watched the little cheeks bunch and felt the soft weight of him upon her lap, his black hair covering his head like a sleek bonnet, and she remembered that time just over a year ago when despair had taken her to its very depths.

She heard her husband's stealthy tread and saw the movement through the trellis before he appeared at the entrance to the arbour and she smiled in readiness for his reproach.

'I suppose there must be a perfectly obvious answer somewhere, woman, but may I know what in heaven's name you're doing out here at this time of the morning?'

'He was yowling,' Merielle whispered, kissing his nose as he squatted beside them. 'I didn't want to wake you.'

'That's only half the story, isn't it, my lass?'

Her sidelong glance through the thick fringe of lashes could not conceal the laughter in her velvet eyes, softened by fulfilment.

'I'll wait.'

The suckling stopped, restarted and stopped again, as the baby succumbed to the sleep that had needed human contact as much as milk to induce it. Rhyan took the infant into the crook of one great arm, cocooned him securely in the blanket and laid him down tenderly upon a pile of straw that lay nearby, ready to bed the strawberries.

He took Merielle's elbows and eased her upright, oblivious to the milk that leaked on to his chest. 'Now, my lovely Venus, I'm not too sure about the reliability of wheelbarrows and I don't think we have bluebells here, but we have honeysuckle. Will that do for the next one, d'ye think? A little lass this time, perhaps?'

Merielle closed her eyes, lacing her arms around his neck and feeling the flood of love surging again, ready to drown her once more. 'Honeysuckle? Mmm…I like the sound of that well enough, knight, I thank you.'

* * * * *

MILLS & BOON®

Makes
any time
special

Enjoy a romantic novel from
Mills & Boon®

Presents...™ *Enchanted*™ TEMPTATION®

Historical Romance™ ✚ **MEDICAL ROMANCE**®

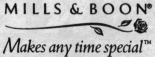

2 FREE
books and a surprise gift!

We would like to take this opportunity to thank you for reading this Mills & Boon® book by offering you the chance to take TWO more specially selected titles from the Historical Romance™ series absolutely FREE! We're also making this offer to introduce you to the benefits of the Reader Service™—

★ FREE home delivery
★ FREE gifts and competitions
★ FREE monthly Newsletter
★ Exclusive Reader Service discounts
★ Books available before they're in the shops

Accepting these FREE books and gift places you under no obligation to buy, you may cancel at any time, even after receiving your free shipment. Simply complete your details below and return the entire page to the address below. *You don't even need a stamp!*

YES! Please send me 2 free Historical Romance books and a surprise gift. I understand that unless you hear from me, I will receive 4 superb new titles every month for just £2.99 each, postage and packing free. I am under no obligation to purchase any books and may cancel my subscription at any time. The free books and gift will be mine to keep in any case.

H0EA

Ms/Mrs/Miss/Mr ....Initials.....................................
                                                        BLOCK CAPITALS PLEASE
Surname ....
Address ....
....
....Postcode....................................

Send this whole page to:
UK: FREEPOST CN81, Croydon, CR9 3WZ
EIRE: PO Box 4546, Kilcock, County Kildare (stamp required)

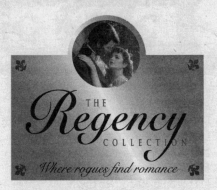

THE
Regency
COLLECTION
Where rogues find romance

**Look out for the tenth volume in this limited
collection of Regency Romances from
Mills & Boon® in February 2000.**

Featuring:

Eleanor
by Sylvia Andrew

and

Miss Weston's Masquerade
by Francesca Shaw

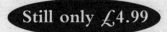

Still only £4.99

MILLS & BOON®

Makes any time special™